SHIFT OUT OF LUCK

KILHAVEN POLICE 3

BROCK BLOODWORTH

H. CLAIRE TAYLOR

CONTENTS

Chapter 1 — 1
Chapter 2 — 9
Chapter 3 — 19
Chapter 4 — 30
Chapter 5 — 51
Chapter 6 — 59
Chapter 7 — 68
Chapter 8 — 75
Chapter 9 — 89
Chapter 10 — 101
Chapter 11 — 119
Chapter 12 — 131
Chapter 13 — 139
Chapter 14 — 153
Chapter 15 — 164
Chapter 16 — 179
Chapter 17 — 193
Chapter 18 — 200
Chapter 19 — 210
Chapter 20 — 226
Chapter 21 — 243
Chapter 22 — 252
Chapter 23 — 266

The Kilhaven Police Blotter — 283
Deep Shift — 285
Also by H. Claire Taylor — 287
About the Authors — 289

"Don't let him into a crate!" came Corporal Bruce Bannockburn's voice through the radio on Officer Norman Green's shoulder. The night air was thick and hot, and the rookie sucked in the lungful he needed to keep sprinting.

Officer Green had no intention of letting this son of a bitch magician get into any goddamn crate. He was only human, but if there was one thing humans, or any prey for that matter, got plenty of practice with, it was running at top speed. All he had to do was keep the suspect within his sight. That was rule number one when in a foot pursuit with a magician: keep eyes on them at all times. To be fair, that was an important rule of police work no matter what type of creature you were dealing with. Still, when it came to magicians, you didn't have to worry about them pulling a weapon so much as vanishing entirely. Into thin air, as it were.

The suspect, IDed as Kyle Todd, aka Trombolo the Tremendous, wore a black satin cape that fluttered behind him as he took a hard left and slipped around the corner of a rusty steel crate.

"Shit," Green muttered, pumping his arms and legs faster, feeling the handle of his Taser jab ruthlessly into the side of his thigh with each step.

On the whole, he hated foot pursuits. And Kilhaven's largest shipping yard wasn't exactly an ideal location for keeping eyes on anyone. But at least it was relatively well lit.

He expected the magician to have already disappeared by the time he rounded the corner, so he was pleasantly surprised to find that wasn't the case.

"Got eyes on him again," he called into his radio.

This was *not* the kind of magician Green remembered from his childhood in the predominantly human town of Bowers. *Those* magicians were simply illusionists that gave the *impression* of magic.

Weren't they?

Since moving to Kilhaven and joining the Force, he wasn't so sure. Because in this metropolis, where smog was a normal weather condition and unidentified pools of liquid in the streets and gutters outlasted even the most severe drought, the term "magician" meant something else entirely.

Namely, a pain in the ass of every law enforcement officer.

Corporal Bannockburn's voice came through again. "Location, 9-07?"

That was a damn good question. At the corner of Crate and Another Fucking Crate.

"Turned left after a yellow one, then turned right a few—"

"Never mind. Just keep on him."

As far as he'd glimpsed, this guy was unarmed. But you never could tell what these assholes had up their sleeve, literally. He'd heard horror stories at the substation of magicians pulling fully loaded Uzis from behind ears and even one tale about a cornered magician transforming himself into a giant pipe bomb with a flourish of his cape.

From Green's own limited experience, though, the magic was usually much pettier—making stolen items disappear so that not even the most thorough pat-down or cavity search could find them, or simply jumping into an open box or closet to escape custody.

That was the most present danger here. If any of the shipping crates weren't properly secured, and if this caped dipshit decided to use his brain instead of his annoyingly agile and toned legs, they might be short a suspect.

Regardless, Green was gaining on him.

It'd started with a simple trespassing call.

Of course, calls were never reliably simple. He was starting to understand that.

But even the corporal, who Green had been riding double with for the last month as a precaution, thought this would be straightforward.

Then they'd glimpsed the man's black cape through the shipyard office's window, and both knew this was not going to go smoothly.

And it would be complicated further, no doubt, by Green's condition.

But so far, *that* hadn't come into play, and maybe it wouldn't. There were entire calls where it was a non-issue.

"Stop! Police!" Green called when he was within ten feet of the man. He pulled his Taser, but his gun wasn't far from his mind if it came to that. And he hoped it didn't. "On your knees, hands on your head!"

The magician pulled up when he realized what Green already had: he was cornered. Tall red and yellow and blue metal rose up on all sides.

He turned slowly toward the officer, his hands raised, but only slightly. His elbows were bent at ninety-degree angles, which was just as likely his natural instinct of wanting to cover the vitals at a moment's notice as it was the first indicator that he was going to try something stupid.

Green listened for the heavy boot falls of his corporal but heard nothing now. "On your knees!"

"I can't." The suspect spoke calmly, though he was clearly as winded as Green felt.

"Why not?"

"My pants are too full."

Green glanced down at the man's slim, black slacks. They didn't look full of anything but legs. He sniffed the air. They didn't *smell* full of anything either. Not the usual, at least. "What do you mean, your pants are too full?"

"I'll show you," said the magician. "But it will require lowering my hands."

"Then forget it," said Green. "Corporal! I have him over here." The echoes ricocheted off the crates, throwing his voice. But still, he heard no approaching footsteps.

"On your knees! This is the last time I ask." He closed in on the suspect, keeping his Taser drawn. God only knew what might happen if he had to tase a magician. Would the suspect go up like flash paper? Shoot spring-loaded snakes from every orifice?

"I already told you," the suspect said impatiently. "My *pants* are too *full*."

"Corporal!"

Still no reply.

And then he felt it. It was like the rumble of an earthquake deep in the ocean floor. A wave would follow, building quickly, gathering strength until it turned into a devastating tsunami.

A devastating tsunami of piss-poor luck.

Goddamn leprechauns.

He needed to wrap this up before it went south.

"Just stay where you are, hands in the air. No, higher than that."

The suspect complied with this order, and Green scrambled over, gripping the Taser firmly until he was behind the man.

It was when he grabbed the magician's wrists and yanked them back for cuffs that he heard the first squeak.

It came from the man's pants.

"What…"

"I *told* you," said the suspect exasperatedly. "My pants are full!"

The tidal wave of his curse headed straight toward shore, and Green's mental sirens blared their warning, even as he dropped to his knees to pat down the suspect.

Not yet. Just wait one goddamn second before hitting me. Please, please, please…

Green lifted the right hem of the man's pants to check for ankle weapons—

—and felt something soft and furry.

"What in the—"

"What did I say?" the magician said smugly. "My pants are full… of BUNNIES!"

The wave of shit luck struck just as the fluffy white bunnies began pouring out of the man's pant legs.

Green jumped up, and as he did, he tripped right over one of the idiot animals. It squeaked as he tumbled backward. Impossibly, the bunnies kept flowing from the suspect's pants. Dozens of them.

"Stop!" Green landed on his ass. He cringed as a jolt ran through his tailbone and up his spine. "Ow! Make it stop!" But there was little chance the man would listen to him.

The magician slipped the cuffs easily and took off. Green grabbed his Taser and fired while the suspect was in range.

The cartridge failed to deploy.

"Of course." He stared down at the impotent weapon. Drawing his gun at this point would be a huge breach of conduct. But more importantly, it was probably best if he didn't handle a gun at all while he was in the deepest throes of the leprechaun curse.

Bunnies still trickled out of the magician's pants leg right as he sprinted past Green and out of the dead-end, kicking the defenseless animals aside to clear a path as he did. With one last quick shake of his leg to free a white fluff ball that wouldn't budge, the suspect turned a corner and disappeared from sight.

Green struggled to get his feet under him without crushing any of the animals surrounding him.

Finally, the echo of heavy footsteps met his ears.

Bannockburn appeared under one especially bright security light, and Green called out to him. "Keep going! He went that way."

But instead, the corporal pulled up short, and his face, contorted with exhaustion, slackened. He slapped a hand to his forehead. "For the love of... He got away, didn't he?"

Green made it to his feet and dusted off some of the white hair already sticking to his uniform. "Was it the bunnies that gave it away?"

Bannockburn looked around, no doubt assessing whether the pursuit was officially a lost cause. He seemed to decide that it was, and his ready posture relaxed. "Oh, are there bunnies? I didn't even notice."

Green tiptoed through them, debating whether to break up a pair that was already humping before deciding, hey, what were a few more bunnies?

"Guess we should call animal control," Green said once he'd made it through the thickest of the drifts.

"No point. If they even make it here within forty-eight hours, which we both know is unlikely, they'll find some reason why the situation is dangerous. We'll be stuck dealing with this mess anyway." He sighed and bent down, tucking a bunny under each arm. "The suspect has no doubt vanished already. Might as well start loading these things into the trunk."

Green grabbed two for himself. "But how are we supposed to fit all of these— Ow!" He cursed and dropped the bunny that had just bit the inside of the wrist. He made to kick it—not hard, but just enough for retribution—but his planting foot went right out from under him.

He went down hard, his full weight landing on the bunny he'd only intended to kick. He could feel the crunch beneath him, and he shut his eyes against the remorse. "Shit."

Bannockburn cringed at the mess as he helped Green back to his feet. He nodded at the smooshed white pancake. "Now that's just bad luck, but I guess you already knew that."

Green felt something wet seeping into his pants where he'd fallen. "Bunny juice" was as close as he'd let himself come to thinking about it.

"As to your question," said the werewolf, "no, we can't possibly fit all of these things into a single trunk, even without the one you just murdered with your ass. We'll have to call for backup."

Green felt his face grow hot.

At least Officer Heather Valance was still on vacation and wouldn't be around to witness the snow-white evidence of his inability to make an arrest.

"I tell you," the corporal said after summoning backup over the radio, "I'm starting to think *I* was the one cursed with bad luck. And it happened the minute Sergeant Montoya assigned me to babysitting duty."

Bannockburn grunted, gazing at the white herd that moved like popcorn over an open fire. Many more bunnies were humping now. "I think we have a net in the trunk. I'll go get it. You stay here and try not to commit any more animal cruelty. Got it?"

Green glanced down at the smashed bunny. Some of its friends approached and sniffed it with a detached psychopathic interest. He thought they might start nibbling soon. "Yes, sir."

CHAPTER TWO

Green yawned and refilled his thermal mug with coffee. It was his third before he even left the substation for what would no doubt be a long night shift.

Bad luck, as it turned out, was downright exhausting.

He'd come in early to finish his report on the vanishing magician, and now all he wanted to do was find somewhere to take a power nap. He wouldn't find it in the sterile break room, though.

It was a Friday, which made it day two of their unfortunate Thursday-Sunday rotation. He would've given his left nut to work a Tuesday night shift right now instead of the kick-off to a wild weekend. Not that there wasn't ample crime in Fang sector *any* night of the week, but it tended not to result in the record-setting clusterfucks when the employed portion of the population was staying home to sleep for work the next day.

It was also the first of the month, which made it the worst kind of Friday. Paychecks were rolling out, and many of the businesses in Fang paid out in under-the-table cash.

Which culminated in something Green had begun to think of as Night of the Living ATMs.

He wasn't a religious man by any means, but it couldn't be good for the soul to carry around so much cash.

More pressingly, though, it wasn't good for survival.

Wads of cash led to heavy drinking.

Drunk men with wads of cash led to aggression in strip joints.

And drunk men who'd just made a big goddamn show of their money in strip clubs led to fruitful armed robberies at 3 a.m.

And that was where Green would have to step in.

"How's it going?" Officer Aliyah Brooks grinned at him as she crossed the cramped break room. With her thick hair pulled back in her usual voluminous ponytail, irresistibly smooth, dark skin, and a sweet southern accent that had tricked many a criminal into wrongfully assuming she'd be lenient, Brooks caught his attention any time she entered a room. He liked to think it was her buoying optimism, or perhaps nihilism (the two often blurred in this line of work) that made him struggle to keep his eyes off her.

More likely, though, it was the memory of how close he'd come to hooking up with her before completely blowing it. Some men might take that as a failure, and normally he would, too. But instead it saw it this way: If he could fumble his way to that close call once, he could fumble his way back there again. And this time he'd see it coming and be prepared with something smooth to say.

"Feeling lucky tonight?" she said.

Green raised his eyebrows. "Huh?"

"It's Friday! You ready to get in some trouble?"

He frowned at his hot mug. "Always."

"You know," she said, scooting him to the side with a nudge of her hip so she could get at the coffeemaker herself, "I once heard of an officer who was cursed with bad luck like you have for five straight years."

"Did he stay on patrol during that?"

"Oh yeah. Apparently, he just treated it like IBS. You'd be surprised how many officers end up with that from all the gas station food."

"I doubt it."

"Yeah, true. Anyway, this guy, the cursed one, I think he might've gotten some sort of prescription from a hag to help lessen the symptoms. Maybe you could do that."

"I'd rather just have a judge hurry up and issue the order for the leprechaun to reverse it."

It was easy to ignore the length of time that passed between when he arrested someone and when he was summoned to court for it. But now that every passing day was a threat to his life and those around him, he was keenly aware of how much criminal justice reform was needed to get things moving through the system.

It seemed like it should be clear cut, easy. The leprechaun that had cursed both Valance and him following the shillelagh-heavy raid was locked up. They'd caught footage of the little turd casting it on multiple dash cams and body mics on scene. There was no question of who did it or if he did it. All that needed to happen was for a Shankwright County Judge to hear the charges, inspect the evidence, and order that the luck be reversed.

Everyone he'd talked to around the sub had assured him that the judge would rule in his favor. So what was the hold up? Were the county courts really this overloaded? And could a case like his, which threatened public safety, if he were quite honest, not be nudged ahead in line?

But on the few occasions that he bugged his sergeant and the prosecutor about it, they'd sworn their hands were tied, and things would move at the pace they moved at.

If Officer Heather Valance weren't off using all of her vacation days, he might've asked her to poke around, ask some questions. Not even the legal team was immune to her laser-like death stare, the fact that she could back it up with action, and the reality that she was just crazy enough to do it.

He didn't so much *miss* his former field training officer as he missed what the werewolf could get done in a mud-slow bureaucracy when she wanted to.

"We'd better get in there," Brooks said, tossing the stir stick in the garbage. "Don't want to start the night with Sarge all pissed off."

"True. I like this upbeat version of him."

"Don't get too attached to it. Valance will come back from vacation soon enough, then the fun's over."

When they entered the meeting room for show up, only a few others on the Fang 900s were already there.

Jeremy Lawrence and Patrick Harmon chatted at the front of the room by the projection screen. Jeffrey Wong, a Fang day-shift officer who'd been taking advantage of the scant numbers on the 900s by picking up more OT than was technically safe, slumped in a chair in the center row, half asleep already.

Green grabbed a seat in the front so he could stretch out his legs, and Brooks began chatting up Harmon and Lawrence.

When Sergeant Montoya entered the room, Green knew

immediately that something was wrong. The were-bison's brow hung low over his dark eyes, and the corners of his mouth pinched toward the center. He was practically stomping, causing the projector to rattle on the table as he neared it. He dropped the stack of papers in his arms onto the table and grunted.

Something was definitely up, but Green wasn't stupid enough to ask. That kind of empathy never went unpunished at work. Neither did that kind of curiosity.

He didn't have to wonder long, though, as a roar of deep laughter burst in from the hallway.

Green turned lazily in his chair to see Corporal Bannockburn enter, looking more mirthful than he had in a month.

He held open the door for the next in line behind him, and she strolled through with a kind of careless swagger that didn't add up for her.

It was Valance. She was back from her vacation.

And by God, if the woman wasn't smiling. And tan.

Shit, she looks good tan. His body conspired against him. Lusting after Valance, even momentarily, was a sure sign he needed to see a shrink. It ran counter to every bit of his survival instinct.

The rest of the shift immediately greeted her excitedly, minus Montoya, who simply grunted louder than before, and Wong, who was fast asleep.

Green sat up straighter, but he didn't get out of his chair, just smiled and nodded at her with a quick wave of his hand when she looked his way.

She didn't look his way for long.

Even this new, rested version of Valance didn't find him particularly interesting. Noted.

"All right, all right…" barked Montoya a few minutes later. "I'm sure we all want to know how Officer Valance's semester abroad went, but don't forget it's a Friday night in Fang, and you need to stay focused."

"Missed you, too, Sarge," Valance said, resuming her usual position with Bannockburn against the back wall.

He scowled at her briefly before pounding a fist on the projector to get it to turn back on.

As they ran through the announcements and BOLOs, Green struggled not to glance over his shoulder every time Valance and Bannockburn snickered at the back of the room. They seemed to be *especially* happy to see each other.

And what about Valance's bad luck? Did it not affect her anymore? Had she found a way to beat it?

Green could feel his own starting to build at that very moment. But he'd learned to just stayed where he was, not do anything risky if he could help it, and wait for it to pass. So, he crossed his arms and remained seated and unmoving as the sergeant listed off all the rapists and murderers to keep an eye peeled for throughout the night.

Montoya turned off the projector and flipped on the overheads. "Valance?"

"Yes?" she said in a voice sweet like antifreeze.

"Assuming your relaxing vacation wiped from your mind all that liability paperwork you had to sign to return to duty, I'll remind you that along with the waivers, you read and understood the verbiage about your restrictions should you elect to return to patrol rather than work desk duty until the judge—"

"Yeah, I remember. I think about the *verbiage* all the time. Repeated it to myself on vacation when I felt homesick. Love me some robust verbiage."

Montoya's annoyance shaped itself as a grunt. "You're doubling up with Brooks."

"Oh, come on!" Brooks shouted. "Haven't I been a good officer? Didn't I just arrest two pedophiles last week? Why punish me by sticking us in the same vehicle?" She turned to Valance quickly and said, "No offense."

"None taken. I wouldn't want to be with me either."

But Montoya shook his head firmly. "Sorry, Brooks. But you know the new policy since... Well, since *the incident* in Ecto sector last month. Women double up with women."

"Okay, sure," Brooks said. "Then why not stick her with Marrow?" She nodded to the short officer next to her.

Officer Tara Marrow glared at her. "Screw you."

"You have five years' experience on Marrow, Brooks. It just makes sense that I would assign a liability like Valance to the female officer with the most experience."

"To be fair," said the ever-handsome Jeremy Lawrence, "Valance has been a liability to the department since *way* before she got cursed, and you never made her double up then."

"*Thank* you," Brooks said.

"He's not wrong," said Valance, who seemed to be thoroughly enjoying herself.

All eyes were on Montoya as his tanned face turned red around the nose.

Green tried not to laugh. Montoya could make everyone's life hell, and he often did, so this little game was one they played as a warm-up before their shift. Of course, the game hadn't happened while Valance was away.

"She's riding with Brooks," Montoya forced through gritted teeth. "That's final."

Brooks shrugged. "Fine. Risk the life of the only black

officer on the shift. I'm sure the elves at the *Kilhaven Tribune* will totally miss that detail when Valance gets me killed."

"Um," said Green, "I'm sitting right here."

Brooks raised an eyebrow. "You're light-skinned. No one cares."

"No one cares anyway," said Lawrence. "Shit, Brooks, you're starting to sound like a human with all this skin-color talk." He nodded at Green. "No offense."

"None taken." There was a little taken, but not more than the usual for the things that came out of Lawrence's mouth.

Montoya bowed his head and pinched the bridge of his nose. "I swear that anyone who has not vacated this room in the next ten seconds will be assigned to homeless outreach for the next month."

Despite the fact that this wave of the curse hadn't yet passed, he jumped up from his seat and joined the rest of the shift as they made for the door. "Wong!" He paused just long enough to punch the dozing officer in the shoulder to wake him. "Time to go."

In the car lot, Bannockburn and Valance chatted animatedly by the trunk of Bannockburn's vehicle while Brooks loaded up the trunk of the car next to theirs.

Green wasn't sure what he'd expected to happen when Valance returned, but it wasn't this. The laughter, the uninhibited grinning, the (sexy) tan, and the relaxed posture left him wondering if they had an impostor on their hands.

He thought back to when they'd first learned Valance was going on vacation after the bloody drug raid. Bannockburn had warned him that her departure was an ill omen for anyone in the department who didn't want to get fired or killed. He'd called it a crusade, hadn't he? He'd said she'd be on a crusade.

After what they'd discovered—the missing girl turned vampire, the leprechaun drug cartel covering for vampires—had she really just taken off for some R&R? Not that the woman didn't need it. If anything, her scalp deserved a vacation from the tight ponytail she wore day in and day out on the job.

"Ah," she said when she saw him. "Officer Green." She moved forward to meet him in the middle as he approached. "Just the person I was—"

A squirrel chose that moment to run right in front of her. She stumbled, failing to avoid it completely. Green, distracted by the whole thing and still riding the tail end of this hour's bad luck, tripped over his own boots in such a way that recovery was impossible. They launched toward each other, and before either could do a thing about it, their foreheads collided with a sound like warring coconuts.

He stuck out his arms to break his fall, and his right hand found something soft.

It was the side of Valance's breast not covered by her Kevlar.

A garbled string of cursing flowed freely from her mouth as they managed to continue to twist and flail against each other for an impossibly long time.

He felt like crying, even as he fumbled around for four-letter words that eluded him. The only one that came to mind was *boob*, and thankfully he didn't sputter it like a horny teen feeling up a girl for the first time.

They both ended on the ground, Valance on her side, and Green on his hands and knees.

He pinched his eyes shut tight against the immediate

pounding in his head. Maybe when he opened them, he'd find it was all a bad dream.

A deep, smooth voice from behind him: "If you wanted to be bottom, Rookie, you just had to ask."

Green scrambled to his feet. Lawrence was smirking as he approached. "I don't usually swing that way, but you're just so desperate. Almost feels like my duty to help out."

Bannockburn had already helped Valance to her feet, and she, too, was blinking hard and rubbing at her forehead. "I'm fine," she snapped. "Stop touching me. The rookie did enough of that to last me a week." She stuck a hand under her armpit to massage the assaulted area.

"I'm so sorry," Green said frantically. "I swear I didn't mean to grab you—"

"I sure as hell hope not," Valance said, eyeing him appraisingly. "If that's how you think women prefer it, you should forget about the gentler sex entirely and take Lawrence up on his offer."

They loaded up, Green riding shotgun with Bannockburn as usual, and he checked his forehead in the visor mirror. A little bit of swelling, but no discoloration. Not yet, at least.

Then, through the fog of his humiliation, the clouds parted to make way for a strange, comforting realization.

Valance hadn't found a way to overcome the curse. She was just as fallible as he was until this was all over.

At least he wasn't alone.

Granted, an extra dose of the curse could quite easily get them all killed, but there were worse things than dying.

He was fairly sure that grabbing an unintentional handful of Heather Valance's side-boob was among them. Especially when it was the most action he'd gotten in months.

CHAPTER THREE

Everything about this call, from the very start, dripped with bad luck.

It was bad luck that a drunk driver had killed a family of four in a head-on collision on Highway 7.

It was bad luck that the driver had survived essentially uninjured.

It was bad luck that the driver was a were-bear and could shift and take off on foot at incredible speeds, even while intoxicated.

And it was bad luck that it all happened in Fang sector.

But none of that was Green's or Valance's bad luck. It belonged, instead, to the universe—bad luck that the whole thing was created in the first place and worse luck that it contained within it the ideal conditions for loving, sentient life to spring into being, only to wreak devastation upon itself in creatively horrific ways such as this.

"Stay in the car!" Bannockburn barked at Green as the were-bear galloped through the low-income housing a block off the frontage road. The dark fur made the beast invisible in the stretches where the streetlights didn't touch.

"Nope. I'm coming with you," Green said.

"You're gonna screw it all up!"

"If a wave is going to hit, I'll screw it up regardless of if I'm in the car or not."

He couldn't tell if Bannockburn agreed with him because the corporal took off at a sprint without saying another word.

That was fine. Green took it as permission from a commanding officer.

He locked the car and rushed after the corporal, who shouted into his radio, requesting permission from Sergeant Montoya to shift.

"Oh, come on!" Bannockburn growled after Montoya denied the request.

Determined to be neither the last to catch up with the suspect nor the reason the suspect got away, Green forced his mind to stay present in yet another unpleasant, though exhilarating, foot pursuit. At least were-bears couldn't pull bunnies from their ass.

The corporal put on the brakes and glided to a halt at a cross street, and Green caught up with him. Both were dishonorably out of breath. "See where he went?"

Bannockburn shook his head. "I think he might've dodged between buildings."

Echoing steps managed to break through the cacophony of Green's racing pulse and gasping lungs, and he turned to see two other officers sprinting up the side street.

"Don't tell me you lost him," Officer Brooks said as she slowed.

Either Brooks and Valance hadn't run as far to get there,

or they were in much better shape. Green went with the former.

"He disappeared behind a parked vehicle, and I didn't see where he came out. You lost him too, genius," Bannockburn spat. "Okay, we should double back. If he assumes he shook us, he might pause to take a break. After all, the suspect is highly intoxicated."

"Look for bear vomit, then?" Green asked.

The corporal nodded. "Or human vomit. He could have changed back by now."

That prospect was an unwelcome one, and Green tried not to cringe. While wrangling a bear was no school-yard game, if the suspect had shifted back to a human form, that meant he was naked (or mostly naked; sometimes the socks managed to stay on during the shifts), and it was never a great night when one had to wrestle a naked person, especially a murderer covered in his own vomit.

But, then again, that seemed on-brand for the first Friday of the month in Fang.

"Valance, Green, you double back the way we came. Brooks and I will head the other direction. Be sure to check the trees, too."

Officer Green considered asking if he'd been paired with Valance to isolate all the potential bad luck, but he already knew that was the case, so he didn't bother. He'd save his breath for another possible foot pursuit.

"Keep your eyes high, I'll look low," Valance ordered, and then they were off at a light jog.

Only after they'd covered all the ground that he and the corporal had already run did Green succumb to the reality that he was indeed out of shape. It couldn't have been more than 200 yards.

"Anything?" Valance asked when they approached the cruiser.

"Nothing."

She grunted. "Great. At least they can't try to pin it on us. We just straight up lost the guy."

Green was about to respond, but then— "Nope. There he is."

Valance whipped her head around just in time to see the were-bear pop over the top of a privacy fence between properties.

She radioed to Brooks and Bannockburn immediately from her shoulder mic.

They bent low and hurried with silent steps toward the yard where the suspect was last seen. But they'd hardly made it ten yards before she hissed, "For fuck's sake!"

"What's— Oh, no."

He felt it too. But how did it know? How did the goddamn curse know the exact worst moment to hit?

Although, he supposed there were very few *good* moments for it to hit when one was a cop. And to be fair, this was the first fit of his night. If anything, that could be considered lucky.

But no, that reframing felt too forced.

"Wait," he said. "Are we in sync?"

"Seems so," she whispered, "but it doesn't matter. I have an idea."

Somehow that was more terrifying than if she'd said, "I don't know what I'm doing."

"Okay," was all he could muster.

She adjusted the volume on her radio just before Bannockburn gave his location on the opposite side of the fence. "Got eyes on him," he said.

"Don't do anything yet, Corp."

Green wasn't all that surprised that Bannockburn did what his ranking inferior told him to. Not when the ranking inferior was Valance. Unlike official leadership in the department, she held a kind of rank that could only be claimed, not bestowed.

She put her face up to a crack in the fence, then stepped aside and waved Green over to do the same. The were-bear stood on a concrete slab that was likely considered a patio for the low-income multiplex. The suspect was hunching slightly, and it took a moment for Green to figure out what he was doing.

Instead of groaning, he simply bit his lip and turned to Valance, mouthing, "pooping."

She nodded.

"When he's done, I need you to lift me over the fence."

The tension of the curse was like a knot in Green's stomach now. Still, he knew better than to question her, even if he did want to ask if she'd lost her mind or had forgotten how to police while she was on vacation.

He nodded.

"Whatever happens, stay out of it, understood?"

He nodded again.

Into her radio, she issued instructions for Bannockburn and Brooks. They didn't protest, but *surely* they considered the possibility that she'd gone completely mad.

Suddenly, she was hissing, "Now, Rookie, now!" and Green scrambled to go down on one knee before her, clasping his fingers together in a stirrup for her to mount and clear the fence.

It was a six-footer, and since Green was just shy of that, he had to crouch low to view her plan unfold through a chip in one of the boards. The wave of bad luck made him dizzy, and he fell forward, catching himself on the fence and driving a thick splinter deep into his palm. He winced but didn't take his eye off of Valance as she snuck up on the hairy suspect, who was now sniffing an upside-down paper plate in the dirt of the yard.

There was just no way her plan, whatever it was, would work. Luck wouldn't allow it, would it?

As it turned out, no, luck wouldn't allow it.

Someone inside flipped on the porch light just as Valance was feet from the bear. That caused the suspect to whirl around. Valance drew her gun. "Police! On your back!"

Bannockburn came over the radio. "Do you need—"

"Hold your position," she yelled.

The bear stared into the light, and from this distance, Green could still make out the were's glassy, dazed expression. The drunk animal swayed almost imperceptibly. Would he make another run for it?

Valance holstered her weapon.

What the hell is she doing?

Green adjusted his stance to get a better view through the fence. But his foot planted on an awkwardly shaped rock, and he rolled his ankle hard beneath all his weight. "Ung!"

That was what did it. The were-bear jerked his head toward the source of the noise for only a moment before charging straight at Valance.

It took everything Green had not to run to her rescue, but he knew such an action wouldn't be doing anyone any favors.

Valance sidestepped the charge and might've even missed the bear's fierce swipe—it was hard to tell from

Green's angle—then suddenly, she was on top of the thing, her arms clinging around its neck. Was she trying to choke out a bear? He'd once heard a couple of officers in the men's locker room joke that she could strangle a bear with her thighs, but he'd dismissed the notion as particularly uncreative joking.

The black bear didn't seem to be lacking air as he galloped in a tight circle before making straight for the fence. Could he clear it with Valance on his back?

The answer was both yes and no.

Yes, under normal circumstances, the were-bear could have easily cleared the obstacle with a rider.

But these weren't normal circumstances. Because this particular rider was cursed to shit, and, as it turned out, she'd managed to transfer some of that curse to the suspect.

When the suspect's front paws met the top of the boards, they found two incredibly *loose* boards that someone ought to have attended to.

The wood planks flipped out from under him, causing him to tumble backward. Valance rolled off just in time to keep from getting crushed, and while the air was knocked out of him by the fall, Bannockburn and Brooks cleared the fence and managed to subdue him.

Carefully, Green stood and climbed over. Miraculously, he managed to tear a hole only in the left knee of his pants in the process.

The suspect was naked on the ground now, moaning and playing the innocent card as lights flicked on in the building. Two residents wandered onto the concrete slab to investigate the commotion.

Bannockburn, being chivalrous, Green supposed,

manhandled the naked killer while Brooks approached the understandably concerned residents.

"Need a hand up?" Green asked.

Valance was lying flat on her back, arms and legs outstretched like she was going to make a dirt angel. "Yes, but not from you."

"I can't believe that worked," Green said.

"Neither can I," she admitted. "But I've seen weirder—Ow!" She jerked and slapped at something on her neck. "Jesus—ah! God—damn!" She continued swatting as she scrambled to her feet. The ground where her head had been was flowing outward from a single point. Green aimed his flashlight at it to confirm. "Oh crap," he muttered before tossing the light onto the ground to free up both hands for brushing the fire ants off her neck and back. Mercifully, her hair, pulled into its tight bun, was covered with enough gel to create a veritable helmet impenetrable to the fire ants. Green wondered for the first time if there wasn't a considerable tactical advantage to her hairstyle of choice.

Leave it to Valance to turn beauty into defensive tactics, he thought as he continued brushing off the ants.

———

Green leaned against the hood of Bannockburn's cruiser while Valance applied ample after-bite from the first aid kit.

"It'll go through soon," Valance said, providing no further context.

"What will?"

"The court order. For the curse."

"Oh, right."

She tucked the stick of ointment down the front of her

shirt, shifting her shoulders forward to free up space under her vest. Green averted his eyes.

"Until then, Rookie, we just need to lay low."

"And by laying low, you mean… riding a bear?"

"*Were*-bear. A drunk and clumsy one. I would never ride a natural bear, whether it was drunk *or* sober."

"Always good to know your limits," Green said offhandedly, wondering when Brooks and Bannockburn would wrap up the call, and hoping his vehicle didn't get stuck carting the piece of shit to jail—he could do without brushing up against his horrific ex, Nurse Becky Hellstrom, at county.

"You got any snacks in the car?" she said. "I'm starving."

When he returned with a nut bar for them to split, she took the whole thing and said, "Thanks," before taking a big bite.

That was just as well, he supposed. The cluster of angry, swollen ant bites on her neck and jaw swept the legs right out from under his appetite.

"Where'd you go on vacation?"

"The beach."

"Oh." Not what he was expecting. "Which beach did—"

"And the jungle."

"That so?"

"Yep."

He paused, the question burning. He knew Valance wanted him to ask it, and for that reason, he considered resisting. "What beach and jungle did you go to?"

"Technically, neither have a name. As far as our government knows, they're unpopulated."

Dammit. This wasn't boding well. "Should I even ask which continent?"

"If you want."

"Which continent?"

"South America."

He didn't have to ask where precisely. He already knew.

Valance had used her vacation time to revisit the killing fields where she'd been stationed during the war. Maybe it was obvious why. For one, it was a psychotic way to spend free time. Perhaps it also made sense for someone to go back and make amends, to try to soothe the cognitive dissonance between protecting people now and killing indiscriminately then. But there was nothing in her tone, or in anything he'd ever learned about her, that would make him believe that had been her purpose.

"What part of South America?"

"Can't say."

"You go back to reconnect with friends?"

She chuckled. "Something like that."

"You know what?" He snatched the remaining quarter of the nut bar from her hand. "I don't want to know. What happens in South America can stay in South America."

When she chuckled this time, it held no amusement. "If only that were the case, Rookie."

"Sometime soon, we need to talk about what happened in the swamp." Gruesome images of the staking of Caitlin Holloway hadn't left his mind since the event. They'd only gained purchase in his subconscious since the raid on the warehouse, though he couldn't explain why.

"How about we wait until we're not standing right in front of a dashcam?" she suggested.

"What are we going to do about it?"

She popped the cap on the ointment stick and arched an eyebrow at him. "Nothing."

"You don't have a plan all laid out?"

She shrugged. "Nope. No plan. I'm not worried about it. It wasn't a big deal, Rookie."

"Wasn't a big—!" He pulled up short. She was right that this wasn't the time for it.

But how could she say it wasn't a big deal? They'd murdered a baby vampire together. That was *absolutely* a big deal.

He glared at her, unable to hide his disgust, but she didn't seem to notice. This new, low-key version of her was a real fucking nightmare.

"Shit!" She slapped at her inner thigh. "I'll be damned, they get around. You hold it down here. I need to sneak away and get these pants off."

He opened his mouth to respond with a half-hearted jab, but she beat him to it. "And no, I don't need help."

CHAPTER FOUR

Their shift had just started, and it was shaping up to be a startlingly slow night in Fang. That was the only obvious explanation for why Bannockburn assigned them to a call out at Olympus Mall two hours before it closed.

But once Green read the call text, not even boredom could explain his corporal's decision. "Uh… why?"

"Corporal O'Brien did us a favor by sending her officers to Fang when we were hammered with that shoot/stab call last week. I told her I'd pick up some of the less urgent in stuff in Demon with you when I got a chance."

"Fair enough," Green said as they pulled up to the east entrance and parked in the fire zone, "but this is Demon we're talking about. *Nothing* urgent happens here. Could we at least have picked a different type of call?"

"What,"—Bannockburn killed the engine and undid his seatbelt—"you scared of a horny necromancer?"

Green wasn't scared, per se, but rather cautious. Necromancers were a rare enough presence in Kilhaven that they hadn't even gotten their own slide in the academy presentations; they'd shared one with zombies.

So all he really knew of them was hearsay, and none of it was particularly appealing. They injected their consciousness into the dead, hence the zombie pairing. Then they made the dead do their bidding. They were also reported to have sex with the dead, which lined up in a strange way with the text for this call:

Necro disturbance - Olymp mall, Build-a-Human - spc humping dolls, won't leave.

Maybe this necromancer wasn't ready for the commitment of having full-time zombies at his disposal, and so he was working up to it this way.

All Green knew was that he wanted to get this over with and get back into Fang.

Two calls had been placed to 911 separately—one from the store employee, one from a bystander—and as they approached the open storefront of the Build-a-Human location inside the mall, a man in a teal polo shirt and khakis was waiting eagerly for them by the entrance.

Green formed a plan in his mind. Get the scoop from the employee, buddy up with the necro as if humping stuffed humans was totally understandable, cuff the necro if need be, and get the hell out of the mall. One, two, three, four.

Something about this call gave him the heebie-jeebies, but he couldn't put his finger on it. Then again, it could be *everything* about this call, starting with going to a giant indoor mall for the first time since he was fifteen. He certainly hadn't been in one since becoming a cop. Now all he saw when he took in his surroundings were balconies with a clear shot down at him, hiding places behind kiosks, and a whole hell of a lot of collateral damage carrying too many plastic retail bags on their arms as they power-walked ignorantly by, drunk on cheap consumerism.

Bannockburn was the first to address the employee. "You call in about the necromancer?"

"Yes, sir."

"Corporal Bannockburn, and this is Officer Green. Any reason to believe the man is armed?"

"No, sir. None at all. I didn't frisk him, though. Should I have?"

"No." The corporal cleared his throat, and Green just managed to keep his professional demeanor as well. "You're sure he's a necromancer?"

The overeager witness nodded. "Oh, yeah. He said it a bunch of times when he was humping one of the dolls with red hair. I think he prefers gingers. But even if he hadn't said it, I would've guessed. You get to know the type, yeah? My cousin dated a necro for a while after she died, so I've been around one at weddings, family reunions, stuff like that. It's something about the eyes. You can just tell."

There was, admittedly, a lot to unpack with that, but because none of it related directly to the present situation, Green merely shared a quick glance with the corporal, who then thanked the man and asked him to hang around to give an official statement in a moment. The request was met with enthusiastic agreement.

They got eyes on the necro easily enough—the man wasn't exactly bashful about his pursuits. He had a life-size, or more specifically, a child-size, stuffed human with bright red hair pinned against the wall under a *Build Your Own Outfit* sign. The doll, however, had no outfit on while the necro humped him furiously.

Bannockburn nudged Green forward. "Don't let him finish."

"Excuse me, sir," Green announced, approaching cautiously.

The necromancer slowed his thrusts until he was able to pull himself away. "Greetings, officers." His mousy brown hair hung down in thick, greasy strands to his shoulders, and when he whipped it back with a flick of his wrist, a putrid smell like rotting cabbage wafted from him.

"We got a complaint about you molesting the dolls," Bannockburn said. "We'd like to hear your side of the story, though."

The necro looked Bannockburn up and down and sniffed the air. "I have a severe allergic to werewolves. Do you mind?"

The corporal looked at Green, who nodded.

Bannockburn grunted, then took in the surroundings of the open front half of the store where colorful clothes and signs hung brightly lit around. "I'll go take the caller's statement," he said before he walked off.

Green pulled out his notepad from his breast pocket. "Name, sir?"

"Maxwell Jones."

"Nice to meet you, Maxwell. I'm Norman Green."

"That's a nice name. Respectable."

Green would never describe it that way, but he didn't mind the adulation. One couldn't afford to mind it when one almost never received genuine compliments. "And you're a necromancer, correct?"

"Indeed." The doll hung limply by Maxwell's side. "And you're a human."

"I am."

"I prefer humans. But I bet you feel out of place on the Force."

"Less and less each day. You mind walking me through what happened here?"

Maxwell appeared almost cheery then, as suspects often did when they knew someone was going to have to sit and listen to their bullshit justifications for doing something undeniably idiotic and just plain wrong. "I was walking through the mall—I needed to get one of my girlfriends a new bra to help keep her remaining breast from falling off— and I passed the Build-a-Human and thought, I bet the girls wouldn't mind if I had a fuckpuppet to call my own. They get a little sick of my sex drive, you know? I have too much of it for them. I'm insatiable. So, I walked in here and saw a couple of the display models—the big ones—and thought I would give one a test drive."

He said it all like it was a perfectly normal thing to do, so Green played along. "Of course. You'd have to give it a test drive to know. I bet those things aren't cheap."

"Not at all! That's what started this. I asked the young man working here how much it was, and he said five hundred. Five hundred! For a sock puppet!"

"That *is* pricy."

"I told him I didn't have it, and he told me I had to leave."

"Mm-hmm. And then what?"

Maxwell shrugged. "Well, it was just prejudice, clearly. He wanted me out because I'm a necromancer. That was obvious enough. You can't just kick someone out because they can't afford the highest-priced thing in the store." He lifted his chin in a startlingly unwarranted gesture of dignity. "So, I said I might buy something else."

"And when did you begin mimicking sexual intercourse with the doll?"

"Oh, that was pretty much right away."

The blunt honestly was refreshing, and Green decided to reward it by not remarking. "Were there other people in the store at the time?"

"No, no. I never would have behaved that way around, say, children. Sex is an adult delight. The store was empty."

Green looked around. There were a few rows of tall shelves in the back half of the store that ran perpendicular to the entrance. He couldn't see anyone who might be back there, but considering what had been transpiring at the front of the store, it made sense everyone who might have been obscured behind the shelves would have fled. "That's responsible of you."

Maxwell nodded humbly.

"Officer Green?" Bannockburn called to him from where he stood interviewing the employee. Except now, the employee looked somewhat cowed, and Bannockburn was strangely still and unexpressive.

"Just one second," Green said to the suspect. "Hang tight, and I'll be right back."

The necromancer nodded amiably.

"And don't start humping that thing again."

"Of course not, Officer."

As soon as Green approached his corporal and stopped, he was waved closer. He leaned in.

"This guy"—Bannockburn nodded to the man in the polo shirt—"is not the Build-a-Human employee who called in."

"What?" Green looked at the witness, baffled.

"This is the second caller. He works at the pretzel store over there."

"Where the hell is the other one, then?"

"That's the question."

Green looked back toward Maxwell just in time to see him dodge behind one of the shelves in the back. Green took a quick step toward him, but Bannockburn grabbed his arm. "Slow there. You have a rapport with him. Don't blow it."

The corporal ordered the pretzel man to step back, and then the officers closed in.

Green called from just outside the entrance, "Maxwell?"

"I have a knife!"

Both officers cursed quietly.

"Maxwell, what happened? I thought we were good."

"Don't bring the werewolf in here, or I'll have to kill him."

"Kill who?" Green called.

"David."

They exchanged a look. "Does David work here?"

"Not once I kill him. I'll slit his throat and add him to my brothel."

Bannockburn brought his radio to his mouth and began calling in backup.

It was one of these calls then, wasn't it? Dammit.

"You don't need to do that, Maxwell. We can get you whatever it is you need." Green turned to his corporal. "Should I clear out?"

"What?" His eyes grew large. "Oh Christ, you're not about to have one of your spells, are you?"

"No. At least I can't feel anything yet."

"Then you stay. He seems to like you, and I need you to

stick around until backup can arrive. Keep him talking, and whatever you do, don't give him an ultimatum. Just keep feeding him hope that he can walk out of here."

Passersby slowed at the sight of the two officers huddled at the entrance to the toy store, but no one stopped. A mother and her two sons made straight for the door, and Bannockburn jumped out, grabbed the woman, and redirected her. "Jesus," he muttered, returning to his position.

Corporal O'Brien, a tall blonde with forearms to reckon with, arrived shortly with two of her Demon 800 officers. "You still owe me," was her greeting to Bannockburn. She instructed her men to post up on the other side of the entrance, behind the concrete column at the edge.

"Yeah, I know. It just escalated."

"You said he's claiming he has a knife?"

Bannockburn nodded.

"Have you seen it?" she asked.

"No, and I doubt we will unless we can get someone back there with him."

"What about TU?"

"No way. You can't bring the telekinetics around this many people, and clearing out the place would be a nightmare."

"True enough. What's the plan, then? Call in the sergeants, let them stick their necks out on this one?"

"We'll call the sergeants, but I'm not letting them take this over. It'll be a complete mess. You know Montoya and Gemini can't stand each other."

"Then we'll just call Gemini. It's his sector, anyway."

Green stepped forward. "Sorry, but I had a pretty good

rapport with him. I'd be willing to go in there and see if I can talk him out."

O'Brien squinted at him. "What's your name?"

"Norman Green."

"Oh, hell, you're the human."

"Yes, ma'am."

She looked at Bannockburn. "You think he could do it?"

"So long as his luck holds. What's your plan, Rookie?"

"I just need to get a look and make sure there's even a knife. We haven't heard signs of life from the employee, either. I'll get a look, and if I can distract him, someone can come around from the other side and tase him."

"Uh-uh," said Corporal O'Brien. "Can't tase necros. Doesn't take them down. Only charges them up, and you don't want to see that."

"Someone still needs to get eyes on the situation, right? I think I have the best chance."

"What's going on out there?" came Maxwell's voice. "You plotting against me?"

"Not at all," Green replied. "I thought you wanted some space. I'm giving you some space."

"Oh. Thanks."

The corporals exchanged a look.

"Yeah, okay," O'Brien said on a heavy sigh. "They seem to speak the same language."

After a quick brief wherein the corporals blasted him with one directive after another—maintain space, no sense of urgency, no obvious lies, tell him what he wants to hear, confirm proof of life and weapon, and get out of there until the hostage negotiators arrive—they gave him their blessing and took their positions.

"Hey, Maxwell, you doing all right? Can I get you anything?" He crept into the store again.

The only response he got was a steady but rapid drumming sound coming from the back of the store. He had a good guess what activity was causing it. *Please let it only be the doll.*

The store took on a much more sinister appearance now as Green moved slowly through.

"Maxwell, can you say something?"

A long sign above the checkout counter on Green's left depicted the various stages of building one's human.

Step one—Select your human's preferred shell from over 100 shades of skin and 50 shades of hair color!

Step two—Decide on eye color, and your attendant will sew them onto the human shell!

Step three—Add in voice box! You can add in all kinds of personalities, or even record your own words to be recited each time you squeeze the human's hand!

Step four—Stuff your human!

The image for that particular step depicted a naked human with latte skin, not unlike Green's, with a hose jammed into a small slit in the doll's backside.

There had to have been *someone* on the design team who thought there were better places to pump fluff, right?

And then there was step five, sew your human's ass shut.

The steps went on with clothing and accessories, but Green turned his attention instead to the rhythmic thrumming at the back of the store, somewhere behind the shelves, past the rows of colorful butt-stuffing machines.

"Maxwell." This time more assertively.

The thumping stopped.

"It's Norman."

"What do you want?"

"Just wanted to continue our conversation, but you took off."

"I have a hostage."

"You mentioned that. Is he okay?"

"He's alive if that's what you mean."

"How can I know that? I don't hear him."

"He's gagged."

"Gagged people can still make a sound." Another step closer. "How do I know he's alive?"

A thud, then a muffled groan. "There. You heard him, right?"

"I heard *someone*. How am I supposed to know it was him?"

"Trust me, it was him."

"I want to trust you, Maxwell. You've been completely honest with me so far, and I appreciate that. But understand, my supervisors aren't going to be happy with me if I don't see for myself and then let them know. That make sense?"

Silence, then. "You're just going to shoot me."

"No, no. I don't want to shoot you. No desire. Listen, this is just the process, just how we do things. We make sure the hostage is okay, then once we confirm that, we start getting you what you want. It would be pretty dumb of us not to make sure you're holding up your end of the bargain first, wouldn't it?"

"You'll give me what I want so long as he's alive?"

"Of course. That's how the deal works." A horrifying thought crept into Green's mind. How would he even know if David was still alive or simply being animated by the necro?

He was only five yards from the first row of shelves when Maxwell spoke again. "Okay. But I want you to keep your hands up. Reach for your gun, and I slit his throat."

"Fair enough."

He had been honest about not wanting to shoot anyone. And no one with a gun said, "I have a knife." They said, "I have a gun." The claim was a show of power, and no one in a situation where they needed to show that kind of power would claim they had less than they actually had.

So he kept his arms in the air. "I'm coming around the corner. Don't want it to be a surprise for you."

Green rounded the corner and caught his first look at the tubby clerk, his ankles and wrists bound together with purple ribbons, lying on his belly with a doll skin shoved in his mouth as a gag. Bulging from his acne-covered teenage face, his eyes were large, pupils dilated. There was something zombielike in his expression, but Green suspected it was only fear. "Mm-mm-ummm," he said.

All around them in the aisle, the empty doll shells hung limp, sorted by skin color and hair type. And in the center, perhaps ten feet from where Green now stood, was Maxwell, pinning his favorite doll to the wall with his hips. He really couldn't control himself, could he?

"Max."

The necromancer whirled toward Green in a way that made his trigger finger twitchy. "Don't call me that!"

"Sorry, sorry. I get it, man. I hate when people call me Norm."

"You've seen him alive. You can leave now, right?"

"I need to speak with him, ask him if he's all right. Can

you remove the gag for me? Then we can start getting you what you want."

Complying, the necromancer grabbed one of the doll's legs that stuck out from between the hostage's lips and pulled. The rest of the doll came free, and Green tried not to gawk at how much material the poor kid had been sucking on.

David whimpered.

"There. You heard him. He's fine."

"Now, slow down. David, are you okay?"

"No, I'm not fucking okay!"

You're welcome for the rescue. Brat.

"Are you injured?"

"I'm fucking hogtied. Are you stupid?"

"Okay," Green said to Maxwell. "I believe you. He's fine."

The necromancer shoved the limp doll skin back into David's mouth, and Green didn't object. He wasn't big about the blade of the knife suddenly being so close to the kid's throat, but he wouldn't nitpick. He kept his hands in the air. "Now, let's talk. You and me. What's this all about? What can I help you with?"

And now Maxwell appeared perplexed for the first time. "I guess... I guess I just want this doll."

"You're not leaving without it, are you?"

"No way."

Green nodded, trying not to let it show on his face how unbelievably stupid this whole deadly scenario was. "That's understandable. It's five hundred, you say?"

"Yeah, and I don't have that."

"That's fine. I have it. They pay us pretty well for this job." Again, he refrained from laughing. Buying a raincoat for a homeless man was always in his budget; an overpriced fuckpillow for a horny necro was not. "How about this? I pay for the doll, you untie David, then you walk out of here a paying customer. Totally legit."

"What about all the pigs waiting outside?"

"I'll tell them to leave."

"And they'll listen to you?"

"If I'm dropping half a grand on your sex doll, they fucking well better."

Maxwell laughed, and Green noticed his knife hand lower. "You tell them to back off, and when they do, I'll untie David."

"David, does that deal sound okay to you? I pay for the doll, and you get untied and can go home?"

Of course it did, and he nodded so adamantly, he banged his chin on the floor and groaned.

Great. Where did he go from here? How did he relay the message without taking his eyes off the suspect? He had to act it out, go through the motions.

"Corporal," he called.

A pause, then, "Yes?"

"We've reached a fair deal. I'm going to buy Maxwell this doll, and then he's going to walk out of here and go straight home. No harm, no foul." Not how the law worked, but hopefully, Bannockburn would catch on. "Can you make that happen?"

"I'll have to get the chief's approval on this first."

Like hell you will. Green tried to imagine Spinner signing off on something this stupid. But he played along anyway. He turned to Maxwell. "Can you wait for the chief's approval?"

"The chief of police?"

"Yeah, he's a good man. Honorable. Sticks to his word." Green had no reason to believe that was actually true.

Maxwell swallowed hard. "Yeah, fair enough."

Green hollered back his confirmation to Bannockburn.

But he returned his attention to the necromancer, movement farther back caught his eye. Lawrence peeked out on the other side of the shelves. When the hell did *he* get here?

Don't do it. God, please don't do it.

But how to convey it without drawing Maxwell's attention that direction? And how did Green suddenly know the right thing to do? Who the hell did he think he was? How in the hell had he even made it this far?

"You got your girlfriends waiting at home, Maxwell?" Green asked, determined to keep the man's attention so Lawrence didn't ruin everything.

"I do."

"They're sure going to be glad to see you back, huh?"

"I doubt it. They don't feel much of anything."

"I was dating this woman for a while," Green began. "I thought she was something else, you know? Turns out, she was just another woman who wanted to suck me dry and ruin my life. Women."

A small smile cracked the corner of the necromancer's lips. "Can't live with them, can't live without them... unless they're not living. That's what I always say."

Green chuckled while also thinking, *I swear to god, Bannockburn, if you don't hurry this shit up...*

As if the corporal could read his thoughts, he called, "Chief says it's a good deal. We're clearing out now."

"Great," Green called back, hoping the desperation wasn't audible. "Tell me when you're ready." He turned to

Maxwell. "Here's how we could do this, and let me know if it works for you: Once they've officially cleared out, you'll take the doll and go, and I'll stay here with David to untie him and make sure he's okay."

"How do I know they're really gone?" Maxwell asked. It was a fair enough question, considering they absolutely wouldn't be.

Green needed something big to secure the suspect's trust.

Thankfully, he had a pawn he could sacrifice.

"Because the chief said so. And because I want this to go well. Officer Lawrence." Jeremy Lawrence wouldn't like this one bit. Neither would anyone in the department because it meant Green was burning his only immediate backup.

At first, there was silence. Lawrence didn't want to play it this way. Too bad.

"Officer Lawrence. Can you step out with your hands up, so Maxwell doesn't have to worry about you?"

The necromancer's eyes went big as saucers, and he whirled around, following Green's line of sight.

Lawrence stepped out, hands up as instructed. "It's just protocol," he explained. "But I guess we're done with that now."

The sudden appearance of a second officer clearly stirred up Maxwell, who pivoted in his crouch, looking from one cop to the other, the knifepoint only an inch from David's neck.

"Hey," Green said smoothly, "no worries, Maxwell. He's surrendering. He's not going to do anything."

Lawrence remained still, with his hands in the air, looking as if *he* might be the more likely man to maim Green right about now.

"Clear out, Jeremy. You know the deal."

Officer Lawrence would make him pay for ordering him around, but *man,* there was nothing like a necromancer with a knife to clarify priorities.

Lawrence was smart enough to make a lot of noise as he left. The handsome shifter wasn't exactly a genius, but he understood tactics well enough.

The knife gained distance slowly from the skin of David's neck. A few minutes later, Bannockburn hollered, "Okay, everyone's cleared out but me, and I'm leaving now."

"Promise?" called Green.

"Promise."

"How can I be sure?"

A moment of pause then, "You initiated Twilight Delta protocol, Officer. You know the department respects that."

Green didn't act right away. He was only fifty percent sure Twilight Delta protocol was completely made up. It was, in fact, the name of a trailer park in sector. What were the odds?

Finally, he sighed and looked at Maxwell. "He's got a point. The department is legally obligated to clear out for negotiations like this if requested by an officer."

"Are you shitting me?" Maxwell said.

"Nope. It's a federal law, actually. Case of *Bowers vs. Hellstrom* established it."

"Huh." The necromancer paused. "So I just... walk out of here?"

"I'd prefer you leave the knife, but yes."

"How do I know you're not going to tackle me as soon as I put the knife down?"

"You can put it down once you pass me if you want. Just set it on the counter before you leave. Part of the deal, though. If you want to walk straight out of here and get home to your brothel, you have to leave the knife."

Maxwell exhaled deeply, his cheeks puffing as he did. "Yeah, all right. I guess I can do that." He straightened from his low position by the hostage, and Green said, "Don't forget your doll." He nodded to the floor where it lay limp, defenseless. He almost felt sorry for it.

Maxwell paused and then broke into genuine laughter. "Right. I can't believe I almost forgot it."

"If I'm paying for it, you'd better take it with you."

The suspect grabbed it and wiggled it in the air demonstratively. Green nodded, stepping to the side, giving this horny lunatic a wide berth to pass. Once Maxwell did, Green gave the front of the store a hard look. Thankfully, he couldn't see any of the officers, wherever they were hiding. Two pale, white, glassy-eyed women sat on a bench by some fake plants in the large walkway between stores. They seemed calm enough. Maybe the cops really *had* cleared out.

Shit. They wouldn't do that, would they?

"Maxwell," Green hollered once the man was next to the counter. "You can just leave the knife there, please."

He set it flat on the counter and said, "You have a good one, Norman."

And just before he left the store—

Green should have noticed it earlier.

While the necromancer was setting down the knife, the two women on the bench got up stiffly. They approached the concrete pillars on either side of the glass storefront, behind which Green was almost certain hid his backup.

The women weren't just pale, they were *dead*.

Bannockburn and Lawrence stepped forward, guns

aimed at the necromancer. But they didn't get an order out before the corpses leaped and tackled them to the ground.

"Watch out!" Green called out, too late.

Maxwell took off at a sprint, and Green gave chase.

He left Build-a-Human just in time to see Corporal O'Brien bracing over the apprehended necromancer. She had a knee in his back and snapped the cuffs on in a heartbeat. Other officers emerged from their hiding places behind large ferns, escalators, and kiosks.

The zombie women were easily subdued once Maxwell was incapacitated. No decapitation required.

Bannockburn pushed himself to stand and went to offer Lawrence help up, but the officer was in no mood. Instead, he did it himself, cursing and checking his lip for blood, his ego no doubt still smarting from Green's outing of him inside the store.

David. Someone needed to attend to the hostage. But Green knew it couldn't be him, because, at that moment, a tide rose inside him. It wasn't the curse, it was something even more humiliating.

Sheer, uncontrollable panic. The sensation he'd been repressing during his encounter in the store. It tasted like bile and vinegar in the back of his mouth.

"David," he blurted, hoping one of the available officers would understand and take over. O'Brien was the one to hear him and issue the command to two of her men who were doing a whole lot of nothing by the adjacent piercing pagoda.

"Hey." Bannockburn approached Green where he stood just outside the entrance staring vaguely at the pretzel shop across the way. "Great work in there, Rook—"

"Not now," Green whispered, trying to make his eyes focus through the thickening haze enveloping him.

The uncontrollable shaking started in his hands.

"Yeah, I understand," Bannockburn said. "We asked a lot of you, but you outperformed—"

"*Not now*," Green rasped, then he made for a bench by a small, coin-filled fountain twenty yards off and collapsed on it as the shaking in his legs caused his knees to buckle.

In under thirty seconds, his whole body was shivering so persistently that he worried the nuclear forces holding his particles together might dissolve completely.

Officer Tara Marrow, who must have been late to the scene, took a seat on the bench beside him. He hardly noticed. "You gonna make it?"

The concerned voice of a woman nearly broke him. But Green had promised himself on the first day of academy that he would never cry on the job.

He needed to get away. The tears pounding at his ducts, and he was pretty sure they were about to kick down the door if he didn't answer their demands.

"I'm fine."

"Hey," she said, "look at me."

He met her eyes reluctantly, and her steadiness gave him somewhere to plant himself.

She leaned forward. "This is normal. This is just the body's reaction. It has to shake it out, and sometimes it has to cry it out, too. But you will *not* cry in front of these people, you hear me? That being said, it's a natural function. It's like shitting after you eat. Now, do you need me to make up an excuse for us to get you somewhere you can cry?"

Green's nose was starting to run. He nodded.

"There's a family-accessible bathroom two stores down that way. Single stall. Take your time, I'll cover for you. Shouldn't be hard with the clown show out here. Cold water and hand dryer on your face afterward. Then get a jalapeño pretzel or something else spicy as hell to eat after. Use that as your cover."

"How do you—"

"Eight years on this job, never once cried. Ate a *lot* of spicy food at odd times, though."

Green had always been cool toward Marrow—they'd never really clicked, and she preferred to keep herself out of trouble where she could—but he was sure as hell grateful for her then.

What if it'd been Valance on this call instead?

He shuddered.

Less than a minute later, he ran the sink and let the biological response overwhelm him.

CHAPTER FIVE_

An entire large deep-dish pizza, twenty leisurely minutes on the toilet, and six solid hours of uninterrupted sleep was all Green needed to feel much better going into work the following evening. His encounter with Maxwell Jones no longer seemed more real than an especially vivid dream. And considering most of his vivid dreams were simply a replay of the time he shot a fellow human, this one was almost a welcome departure.

The dreamlike nature of the previous day rubbed off like soap scum once he'd downed his first cup of coffee, however. All the many ways things could have taken a turn for the worse paraded past his mind's eye in a stark series of images as he dressed, ate his microwavable sausage biscuit, and drove to the sub.

Two people were already in the break room when he arrived. One was a corporal from the Fang 300s, who was likely just on his lunch break for the day, and the other was Officer Valance.

He'd hardly made it three steps across the ancient

spongy carpet of the break room before she nodded at him and said, "You really did it this time."

"Huh?"

"Mom and Dad are fighting, and I heard your name come up."

"Mom and—"

She was leaning against the counter next to the coffeemaker—sitting was never her thing—and had her legs kicked out, one shiny boot crossed over the other. "You didn't hear when you came in? Sarge is chewing out Corp like I've never heard."

The other corporal in the room shot her a quick glance but clearly wasn't interested enough to stick around and risk getting involved in office gossip, and so he left.

Green unscrewed the top on his thermos and grabbed the half-empty coffee pot, coming within an uncomfortable foot of Valance's penetrating gaze by necessity. "Fine," Green heard himself say. "Maybe he *should* be chewed out."

Valance chuckled. "For what, making you a hero?" She reached behind her and pulled out a copy of the paper. After setting down her coffee, she opened it and said, "There it is. You made the paper."

She held up the article just long enough for him to read the headline. *Kilhaven Police Use Human Officer as Live Bait.*

His lips parted in dumb confusion. "What..."

She hurriedly folded it up again and tossed it onto the small, rickety table. It landed with a slap. "I'll spare you the trouble of reading it. You get mentioned by name exactly once, and you are described as *lucky,* so clearly whatever elf wrote that didn't do his homework. At all. Meanwhile, human rights activists are demanding a full investigation into the department to see if situations where humans are used as 'live bait' are tacitly encouraged among leadership."

Green cringed. "I wasn't used as live bait. I agreed to go in. Sure, one of the corporals probably should've said no, but I offered. I wasn't bait."

Valance laughed and grabbed her coffee mug again. "You keep telling yourself that. But everyone is live bait to a necromancer. It's not like dead *humans* are their only turn-on. Well, maybe for some of them, but others will take a dead *anything*. Hell, I once had to fight off a small army of necromanced squirrels to get at one of those assholes."

He was mostly sure she wasn't joking.

"Sucks that your big day is now embroiled in political controversy. Otherwise, I bet this story could get you quite a bit of ass in whatever flamboyant bar you frequent."

He stirred the half-and-half into his drink. "I wouldn't do that."

She shrugged and pushed off the counter. "Then you're an idiot. You gotta use the best parts of this job to trick people into thinking you're a hero. It helps combat everything else about being a cop that systematically drives people away. And I think talking down a necro with a hostage is a pretty good start."

Brooks entered just as Valance was gathering her stuff to leave.

"Man of the hour," Brooks said.

Valance rolled her eyes. "Gonna be one hell of a show-up, Rookie. I'd better hurry and get a good seat."

"I heard what happened," Brooks continued, scooting in close to Green to fill her thermos from the coffeemaker. The contents ran out almost immediately. "Balls." She freed her hands and began preparing another batch to brew.

"Are you going to tell me I was used as live bait, too?" Green asked.

Without looking up from her work, she scoffed. "You mean more than we all are all the time? You know what you do for a living, right?"

"Yeah, yeah…"

"Jeremy said you talked the guy down like a real pro. He said he kept thinking you'd said or done the wrong thing, but it just kept working."

"*Lawrence* said that?"

She nodded and closed the top of the appliance before flicking the switch to On.

"Huh. I thought Lawrence was pissed at me for outing his position and sending him away."

"Oh, he is. I reckon he'll get you back eventually. But, hey, you managed that whole thing without a wave of bad luck hitting you. Maybe you're recovering." She shot him a half grin and didn't move away, and the proximity wasn't lost on Green.

As much as he would have liked to be the type of guy who could pull off some slick line about getting lucky, he knew he didn't have the linguistic abilities for that; and besides, it was sexual harassment.

Although, if her body language and their past interactions were any indications, she wouldn't mind.

"Afraid the curse is still quite active. It just comes in waves. Didn't hit until much later this morning while I was lying in bed, so I was fine."

She nodded and sighed, seeming to break from her temporary cloud of adoration. "Well, that's good, I guess. I'd hate to see you get taken out in a Build-a-Human." She slapped him on the shoulder. "I reckon Valance is probably right. We're in for one hell of a show-up. I'll meet you over there as soon as this thing's done brewing. Don't want to miss the fireworks."

Green knew that was his cue to scram and, not wanting to press his luck in a situation where he was seen as a bit of a hero for once, he was more than happy to oblige.

When he entered the meeting room, it felt like someone had pressed the mute button on the entire space.

Montoya stood at the front of the room, staring fixedly at a stack of papers in his hands, his jaw visibly clenching over and over again like he was biting glass. Against the back wall, Bannockburn and Valance leaned with arms crossed.

Neither said anything and for once, Bannockburn looked more murderous than Valance, whose face held an unmistakable hint of amusement.

Officer Marrow nodded to him when he entered, and he nodded back.

He spotted Jeremy in the front row, so he forewent his usual spot as of late and looked for a more advantageous position.

He *wanted* to be in another room, but since that wasn't an option, he took a seat in the third and final row that was closest to the door. As he pulled out his chair, the rubber on the bottom of one of the legs made an awkward squeal against the concrete floor, cutting through the thick silence.

It was as if everyone had been waiting for an excuse to make noise, because, in the instant that followed, Brooks entered, announcing, "Fresh coffee if anyone wants it," Bannockburn coughed up something phlegmy, and Montoya smacked the top of the projector to turn it on. "Lights, Brooks," barked the were-bison.

Then he launched into it. "As I'm sure you already know, the Fang 900s made the news last night."

No one said a thing.

Making the news was almost never a victory.

"*Apparently*, I can't keep my guys in check," he continued, and it occurred to Green that Montoya must have had a thorough ass-chewing from the commander prior to passing it on to Corporal. "Maybe that's the case. But let me tell you, this is the *last* time I put my career on the line to keep any of you from getting suspended. If this department wasn't chronically short on officers, and no shift more so than ours, I'm positive at least one of you would be at home drinking away your sorrows this morning rather than in my warm and charitable presence.

"But the past is the past, as I'm so often told. Nothing to do but walk through it and explain the myriad ways yesterday's call at the Build-a-Human was a complete bungle, as if orchestrated specifically to draw the ire of human rights activists..."

As Montoya broke down the call and all the various dangerous decisions, he peppered in commendations that Green really could have done without.

"...Of course, despite that terrible error in judgment, Officer Green's quick thinking allowed the situation to be salvaged..."

"...And while I have no idea where Green came up with that idea, it managed to save our asses one more time..."

"...And thank God for Green's decision to..."

Each one felt like an added bounty on his head.

Please make him stop commending me. Please, just make it stop.

The animosity came in waves off Bannockburn. Green regretted selecting a seat so close to the back after all, since it left no physical barriers between him and the corporal.

The worst of this nightmare, however, was when Montoya played the security footage of the encounter, which lasted precisely one-fiftieth as long as Green remembered it.

The whole thing was feeling more and more like a sick joke.

He toyed with the idea of never committing a heroic act again if this was what it felt like the next day.

Montoya finally ended it. "So, in short, if you ever pull something like that again, you're all fired. Even if you weren't on scene. I don't frankly care at this point. I'll probably be fired too, but not before I fire each and every one of you. Any questions?"

Green didn't see Valance's hand go up, but he did see Montoya's expression change from disgruntled to outright disdainful when *he* noticed her. "Officer Valance? You have something to add?" Green whirled around just in time to see her arm lower.

"It's slightly off-topic, but I'd like to get caught up to speed since getting back from my vacation. Where are we on the missing children cases?"

Montoya's features turned to stone. "Which missing children cases? You're going to have to be more specific. You know children go missing every day."

"Caitlin Holloway and Anna Pfaff. The ones from Crown Tree. The ones who came from mixed parents and hadn't yet shown definitive signs of which parent they would take after. Any of this ringing a bell?"

Montoya's face showed no sign of recognition, but Green knew better than to think that meant there was none. "Not sure why you pair those two cases together as if they're related just because they share a few similarities. Careful. You can draw a line between *any* two points, Officer Valance."

What could she have possibly hoped to achieve by asking that? Why now? It wasn't a genuine question, after all. Bannockburn had assuredly filled her in on any updates. Why the show?

But when Montoya said, "We're over time. Everyone get out of here," Green wasn't so curious that he stuck around to try to figure it out.

"Except you, Corporal. I still need to talk to you."

Green winced on behalf of Bannockburn, who had more of a tongue lashing to come, and scrambled out of the room, feeling suddenly claustrophobic.

CHAPTER SIX

To say the atmosphere in the car that evening was tense would be like saying a jackrabbit-shifter on meth seemed a little worked up.

The corporal was in no mood to hear even so much as a peep from the rookie.

Green hoped things would smooth out once they started hopping on calls, but after an hour and a half on a domestic disturbance, Bannockburn was in an even sourer mood.

So, when they arrived at the jail with their male suspect, the prospect of seeing Becky Hellstrom was more than Green could bear, and he faked an oncoming wave of bad luck to stay in the car and type up the report.

Bannockburn rolled his eyes but agreed that Green should stay in the sally port rather than risk some kind of accidental jailbreak that ended in a mass slaughtering.

Unfortunately, Green hadn't anticipated how long the processing would take. By the time Bannockburn returned two hours later, Green thought he might scream if he didn't get in on some real Fang-sector action soon.

As if some forgotten god had heard his wish, Valance came over the radio a few minutes later, requesting assistance from Fang 9-07.

"That's me," said Green. "We'd better go."

"She's only requesting you because she needs a human as some sort of bait. Did you learn nothing at show-up today? Oh wait, I guess you're a hero. Of course you want to go charging in."

"All due respect, but I was only a hero under your command."

"And I'm not making that mistake again."

"You don't even know what she needs help with. Maybe it has nothing to do with me being a human. Maybe it has something to do with those missing girls."

Bannockburn grunted but didn't speak right away. With an expression that would've looked at home on the face of a man passing a small kidney stone, Bannockburn spoke into the radio. "Fang 9-80. I'm on my way with 9-07."

But as soon as the corporal cradled the radio again, he said, "You know she doesn't have your best interest at heart, right?"

"Of course I know that."

"She doesn't feel any personal responsibility to you just because she trained you. If she had to cross a field that she suspected held land mines, she'd have no problem asking you to go ahead of her."

That seemed extreme. "Yeah, I get that."

"Just want to make sure you're clear. It's easy to project things onto Valance, but in the end, she's not like the rest of us."

"You make it sound like she's a psychopath."

"Haven't ruled it out. Just glad she's on our team."

"Is she?"

Bannockburn paused. "Yeah, well, I guess I don't know about that, either."

The fact that the address of the call was that of the First Draculan Church of Kilhaven helped Green's case that this was something they should go check out.

But as soon as they'd parked and gotten a good look at the two men Valance was speaking to, Green realized that Bannockburn had been right. "God dammit."

The two men wore leather jackets with the telltale markings of Eden's Fist, a human supremacist gang that had it out for vampires almost as much as Valance did.

Of course, they also had it out for everything that wasn't human, including werewolves.

"There he is," Valance called. "He just can't stop being a hero, can he?"

Green glared daggers at her as they approached.

Valance and the two men stood in the glow of her headlights. Half of her face was in shadow as she watched her backup approach. Even still, Green could tell she was pissed. How long had she been on scene, enduring the insults of these men? And where was Brooks?

They weren't in cuffs, though, so maybe it hadn't been so bad. Or maybe Valance hadn't seen a safe way to cuff one without getting stabbed by the other. That was just as likely.

"Here's your man," she said to the larger of the two gangbangers. He was white—they both were—and Green hoped his darker skin wouldn't be a problem. It never was until he was dealing with other humans. No one liked to think of themselves at the bottom of the social ladder, so humans simply created lower rungs.

Once he was close enough, one of the men squinted at

his name on his shirt. The man's eyes lit up. "You're the one they sent into Build-a-Human yesterday, aren't you? Yeah! I thought I recognized you."

Green hadn't pegged them for the informed type, but it made an unfortunate kind of sense. If they needed to cultivate and maintain a high level of hate for everyone but humans, reading the paper was a good place to amass the proper fertilizer.

He decided not to answer the question. "What brings you two gentlemen out here tonight?"

The same man answered. "We were just walking home."

He nodded along—why not? It was complete bullshit, but they didn't need to know he knew until he had a better idea of the situation.

"Bad timing," Valance explained. "They were walking through here right after a neighbor reported that two men in leather Eden's Fist jackets were throwing things at the windows of First Draculan."

The whip of a flashlight beam caught Green's attention back toward the church, and Brooks emerged from behind the corner of the building.

"It wasn't us," said the larger man. "I know it looks bad, but you got no proof."

Not the smartest, that one.

The other man was suspiciously silent, but his right hand was placed on his chest, just below a square, metal pin of some—

Shit. The man had a body camera. They were filming this whole interaction. Did Valance know?

What was he thinking? Of course she knew. There was no way he'd notice and she wouldn't.

Why did it make him nervous? They were standing right

in front of Brooks and Valance's car, meaning the scene was already being filmed by the dash cam.

"I got this, Officer Valance," Green said. "Why don't you go take a break and let me talk to these fellas?"

Had he ever said "fellas" in his life?

The two men relaxed as soon as she was away, as he'd suspected they would. After all, they were terrified of her, and not just because she was a particularly terrifying person. No one who joined Eden's Fist wasn't, deep down, terrified of werewolves. And he was pretty sure the fact that she was a woman only enhanced that fear.

And now he was stuck. What he might have normally done was play along with their hatred. Maybe say something like, "Listen, I get it. I've been in that church, and it's is a real horror show." He wouldn't even be lying if he said that. The memory of chasing a naked man on PCP through the halls, passing coffins at every corner, hadn't simply faded away or turned into a great party story. Not yet, at least.

But he couldn't say anything like that to gain their trust because they were filming him. And who knew what they intended to do with that footage.

"All right," he said, his heart racing. "This looks bad for you guys, but if you say you didn't do it, I believe you. After all, if you'd really bashed in those windows, you'd be proud of it, right? You two don't strike me as the type of guys who wouldn't own up to something just because the cops showed up." They nodded, but he caught the uneasiness in it. "Anyway, would you do me a favor and let me just pat you down really quickly so Officer Valance over there can see she was overreacting? Just a quick one, then we'll talk."

When they didn't immediately consent, Green leaned forward and added, "You know what it's like to be a human, right? Puts you on edge all of the time in a city like this. It's nothing personal."

The larger one sighed and lifted his arms in the air with a nod, and Green asked the smaller one with the camera to please step to the side.

He pulled two knives off the first human, but he expected there were additional ones in hard-to-reach places. As long as they stayed hard to reach, that would give Green the edge if the man decided to go for them. And while Bannockburn, Brooks, and Valance chatted leisurely back by the other cruiser, he knew they were still keeping watch.

He held up the knives. "These go right back to you after we finish up. Don't worry. What's your name?"

"Brooks. Keith Brooks."

Normally, Green might have said, "Brooks, eh? That's her name, too." He'd read somewhere that sharing a name with someone formed an instant kinship. But he didn't think that would be so successful between a human supremacist and a shifter.

So instead, he waved the other one over. "And your name, sir?"

"Marcus Brooks."

He got Marcus to hold his arms out and started a pat-down. "Brothers? Cousins?"

"Brothers," said Keith.

Green finished the arms, pulling one knife off of Marcus's wrist, and then stepped in front of him, blocking Keith's view as he patted down the man's chest and, with a deft maneuver, flipped off the body cam and continued the frisk. Of course, that put his back to Keith, but it was a quick risk, and there was no indication violence might erupt. Not with two werewolves and a shifter within view.

Now that that bit was done, and Green had two more knives off of Marcus, he placed it with the rest of the weapons in Valance's car and returned to the two men. "Like I said, you'll get it back. Where do you two work?"

Casual conversation was best until he could communicate what he needed to the other officers.

As the Brooks brothers continued answering questions about themselves, Green nodded along, even laughing a couple of times at their creaturist jokes.

The first unpleasant tingle of the curse nipped at his insides. As subtly as he could, he made eye contact with Bannockburn and nodded him over. He was likely the least objectionable of the officers available, what with him being a man.

Green had heard enough of these two, anyway. "Level with me, would you?" he said after they'd had a good laugh. "You two strike me as strong dudes. You did this vandalism, right?" He held up a hand before they could speak. "It's a minor charge at best. You get a night in jail, and you're likely released in the morning with a fine. And you got a good story to tell the guys." He grinned like they were in this together.

He neglected to mention the increased charges because this was a place of worship and that it was widely acknowledged that crimes of any kind against vampires or vampire institutions never resulted in just a fine and a misdemeanor.

Marcus was the first to speak, but before he did, he nonchalantly reached for his camera as if Green wouldn't notice. He was trying to shut it off before the confession, but flicking the switch would just turn it back on right in time. The wave of bad luck was growing, but not strong yet, and there was still a smidgeon of good luck to be had, it seemed.

"Yeah," said Marcus. "It was us. That place is fucking creepy, and you know those vamps have been stealing human children and turning them, right?"

Green hoped his shock at how close that guess was didn't translate on camera. "They don't do that," he said quickly before pulling his cuffs from his belt and hurriedly wrangling and cuffing Keith. Before Marcus could react, Bannockburn had him by the wrists and took him out of the action.

They dropped both suspects into the back of Brooks and Valance's car, and as soon as Green shut the door, he addressed his corporal over the roof. "I can feel another spell coming on."

"Goddamn… Go sit in the car."

He hurried over to it, where Brooks and Valance were standing around but not speaking.

"You feel it too, Rookie?" Valance said.

"Yep."

"Shit."

Brooks rolled her eyes and groaned. "Corporal, how about you and I double up on the way to jail? Just this once?"

Bannockburn was more than happy to agree.

Valance took the driver's seat, tapping away on the HAM as she filled out her report. The engine humming soothingly, and Green struggled not to fall asleep. He thought he'd eventually grow used to the nocturnal hours, but it hadn't happened yet. So long as he was engaged in a call, he was fine, but in those moments in between, his body often rebelled in an attempt to steal a few winks. Good thing the breaks usually didn't last long in Fang.

"They mentioned something about vampires," he said.

She didn't look away from the screen. "You don't say? They mentioned something about vampires while they were standing in the parking lot of a vampire church and committing a hate crime against vampires?"

"I mean, they said something about vampires stealing human children and turning them."

"I'm sure they did say something about that. Human supremacists have been telling that story to their children at bedtime for generations."

"But don't you think they might have meant with the disappearances?"

"Do me a favor and shut your damn mouth for once. All I want is peace and quiet until this shit passes."

"Sure, but are we—"

"Shh…" She killed the engine, leaving them in still silence.

Green shut his mouth, stared out into the darkness, and rode out yet another wave of shit luck.

CHAPTER SEVEN_

Green slept through most of his weekend, which in this rotation was Monday, Tuesday, and Wednesday. What else was he going to do? He supposed he could go out, but with who? He didn't know anyone except cops and criminals in this town, and both of those were bad news once you got alcohol in them.

By the time Thursday afternoon rolled around, he was antsy to get out of his crummy apartment and get back to work.

He arrived at the sub fifteen minutes early, filled his thermos without seeing anyone from his shift, and headed to the meeting room for show up. The idea of sitting in the room, alone, sipping his coffee sounded inexplicably indulgent.

I've just spent three straight days alone, and I want more alone time?

Maybe he was turning into a misanthrope. He'd have to ask Valance what the signs were since she clearly lived it.

But when he walked into the break room, Sergeant

Montoya was already there, hunched over the small table stacked with papers. The were-bison alternated between grumbling and grinding his teeth so loudly that Green heard it across the room.

An empty spot of the wall at the back caught his eye.

Dare he?

He wasn't particularly in the mood to sit, and being far away from Montoya seemed wise.

But as soon as Valance and Bannockburn entered and she caught sight of him in her usual spot, her top lip curled like she'd smelled something sour, and she glared at him like he might've been born stupid.

"You're too new to the job to have a wall spot," she said, shoving him aside.

"What?"

"Jaded cops only," barked Bannockburn.

What was this, a middle school cafeteria?

"I got here first," said Green, so apparently, yes, it was a middle school cafeteria. "And I thought Valance stopped being jaded after vacation."

"Shine wore off after those Eden Fisters," Valance replied impatiently, shoving him again. But when her eyes landed on Montoya at the front of the room, it clicked. "Ahh. I see. He's pissed today, and you think it's your fault." She shared a quick look with Bannockburn, who shrugged.

"Fine," she said. "But only today."

"Good chance we'll all be fired anyway," Bannockburn muttered before leaning against the wall on Valance's other side.

The sergeant didn't hesitate once the rest of the Fang 900s arrived. He launched right into the rant had very likely been gaining steam inside him all weekend.

"Remember when I said not to screw up again?"

It wasn't me, Green assured himself. *I didn't do anything wrong.*

But instantly, his mind went back to that body cam on Marcus Brooks, and he already knew it had something to do with that.

A few seconds later, once Montoya had cued up the footage, Green's suspicions were confirmed.

"Fuck," mumbled Valance.

"I hope you all had a fantastic weekend," Montoya said. "But no matter how good it was, it didn't stack up to the fiesta human rights activists had around Kilhaven." He pressed play on the projector.

The exchanged between Valance and the Brooks brothers played, with Valance the only one in the frame. It was unremarkable. Everything seemed to be going well, and Green couldn't figure out what the problem was. They insulted her in a few specific ways, and the camera caught a small, murderous smile tug at the corner of her lips, no doubt a reaction to whatever gory fantasy she was indulging in at the moment while keeping stock still and professional. She took their IDs, handed them off to Brooks, who went and ran them. Brooks returned, nodded to Valance that they came back with no criminal activity, and said she was going to go have a look around. Valance continued her chat with the Eden's Fist members and offered to have a human talk to them.

Montoya paused the playback. "See anything wrong?"

The room was silent. Green couldn't for the life of him think of a better way to handle it. Maybe Brooks ought to have stuck around and backed her up? But if their history came back clean...

Maybe they should have frisked the men sooner? But that would have likely escalated things. Only Green himself could have built up the rapport with them to get it done without a fuss. What was he missing?

"Those men aren't named Keith and Marcus Brooks."

"You sure?" asked Officer Brooks. "They look just like me. Could have sworn we were related."

Tara Marrow stifled a laugh.

"Fake IDs," said Montoya.

Brooks replied, "But they checked out on the system, sir. They looked completely legit."

"They were good fakes, then."

"I couldn't tell the difference, either," Valance said, sticking up for her fellow officer. "You can see I gave the IDs a look over—I half expected them to be fake—and still, they seemed legit."

"That's not the point," barked the sergeant. "The point is that it turns out these two men are Loren and Henry Friedell."

The room was silent.

"Doesn't ring a bell?" Montoya asked.

"Wait," said Harmon, "were they the two responsible for dragging that shifter behind their truck for ten miles down a dirt road last year?"

Montoya clenched his jaw, his big, hairy forearms crossed over his chest. He nodded.

"And I suppose they were never caught," Lawrence added unnecessarily.

Montoya slowly and wordlessly shook his head.

"Shit," muttered Brooks.

From beside him, Valance called, "What do the human

rights activists have their panties in a tangle about? They're mad that we arrested two garbage humans?"

"No," Montoya said. "They're upset you called in a rookie human—the same rookie human who handled that necromancer just last week—to deal with two psychopaths on his own."

"For fuck's..." Valance sighed heavily.

"This makes no sense," Brooks said. "Green was safer than all of us with those two! Where the heck are the *shifter* rights activists on this?"

Montoya clenched his fists and jammed them under his armpits as if to restrain them from doing anything stupid. "It doesn't *have to* make sense for the elves at the *Tribune* to grab ahold of it and swing it around like a mace."

"Brooks and I did everything right," Valance said. "And, as you've just informed us, we arrested two men suspected of murder. If we'd stayed next to Green, he never would have earned their trust to get that confession. And when he needed us, we were there. What *should* we have done?"

"Not called Green to the location," Montoya snapped. "For God's sake! He's still cursed! You know that as well as I do, Valance. Until a judge reverses it, *both* of you need to lie low, understood?"

Green nodded quickly.

"Yes, sir," Valance said lazily, and there couldn't be a single person in the room who believed she meant it.

"Need I remind you," Montoya continued, "what I said would happen if this shift screwed up again?"

"You'd fire all of us," Valance called back. "So, are we fired?"

He glared at her. "Do you *want* to be fired?"

"Depends. If it was wrongful, like this would be, I could

sue and spend my days on some tropical beach. So, maybe I do."

Green was sure this slight would be stored in Montoya's mental evidence locker, filed under V, for a long time to come. But instead of responding, he addressed the room. "No calling Valance or Green for backup unless it's absolutely necessary."

"Doesn't that rule out Brooks and Corporal, too?" asked Lawrence.

"Seems so," Montoya grunted, and Green suspected the sarge hadn't considered that element of it.

Once they were dismissed, the usual chatter in the parking lot didn't follow. Green loaded up into his car with Bannockburn without a word.

Sensing that his corporal's mind was still on the meeting as they pulled out of the depot, Green said, "Valance is going to get herself fired."

Bannockburn scoffed. "Yeah, right."

"What do you mean? She was practically asking for it."

"No, she was literally asking for it. But it can't happen."

"Why not?"

Bannockburn snuck a skeptical glance his way. "Have you met the woman? Does she strike you as the type to go down without a fight?"

He had a point.

"Besides," he added, "she knows too much, and command staff knows that." His serious demeanor cracked, and he chuckled. "She wasn't kidding about suing, and she would get it, too. Whatever she asked."

"I can hardly imagine her relaxing on a beach, though," Green said.

"That's because it could never happen. An unemployed

Heather Valance is nothing but a public menace. It's better for everyone if she stays on the Force until it kills her."

"That might not be long at the rate she's going."

Bannockburn snorted. "You might be right, Rookie. Regardless, you'll never see me bet against that irresistible nightmare of a woman. Never."

CHAPTER EIGHT_

Green's lungs burned as he pursued the suspect around the corner of an abandoned bakery that smelled tauntingly of stale bread. Security lights from the neighboring operational warehouses were the only glow Green had to work by in keeping an eye on the sprinting evader. He'd already told the man to stop twice, and he wondered if yelling it a third time was worth the effort.

Bannockburn was just a few yards behind him. While Green didn't have the mental energy to spare for it, he still derived great pleasure from knowing he could outpace his corporal on foot, so long as the werewolf didn't shift, of course. He wouldn't here, though. There was no reason to request it; the suspect who hurdled a small pile of discarded crates and wheezed loudly with every step was a human. And Green was gaining on him.

The man was reportedly armed, but he wasn't stupid enough to reach for it as he ran, and Green was awfully grateful for that.

Please keep your hands where we can see them. Please don't reach for your pants…

"God dammit," Bannockburn puffed out when the suspect cleared a six-foot chain-link fence at the edge of the dingy, dark lot with hardly a pause.

It was a smart move on the suspect's part. The academy really should have included a practical about hopping fences without getting anything from your belt hooked. But with the rate at which he found himself doing it, Green would be a pro in a few short years anyway.

He managed to hurdle it without anything becoming dislodged from his belt, but Bannockburn was a different story. Green heard something clatter to the cement behind him, and the corporal cursed, but Green knew it was best if he continued on.

He narrowly avoided stepping on an empty vodka bottle as he radioed in his location, hoping someone would manage to cut off the suspect from the other direction, although based on how many officers were stuck at the scene of the shooting where this all started, he held little hope of it. Making sense of a scene with five bloody victims took up serious resources.

The inescapable sound of traffic that permeated all of Kilhaven to some extent grew from a trickling stream to a waterfall.

Shit, were they already nearing Highway 7? That had to be at least a mile from where the report of the shooting at an apartment complex had taken place.

Nothing but pure dread fueled his muscles now.

And then he felt the first tingle of something else.

"Fuuh!" he said on an exhale.

The only good bit of luck was that the suspect hadn't

disappeared from sight. Yet. The human seemed to be locked in on Highway 7, which was actually good news for the Kilhaven Police Department. This man was cornering himself. No one in their right mind would try to cross eight lanes at night. And if that was this guy's plan at the moment, he would quickly realize the flaw when he arrived, and his delay might be just enough for Green to pounce on him and wrap this thing up before the full force of the curse settled in.

His radio came to life, and Valance announced that only one of the victims had made it. And did she just refer to "the children" in her list of victims?

Jesus. Humans could be monsters, just like the rest of them.

Killing yet another human wouldn't sit well with his career, but why was he even doing this job if not to uphold justice?

And laws, came an obnoxiously sensible voice. *The two are not always the same.*

Shut up, he told it.

The bad luck bubbled up further from the depths.

No! He would *not* let this stupid fucking leprechaun curse result in this suspect going free. Absolutely not.

The image of Valance riding the were-bear popped into his mind. Could he do something like that? Could he attach his curse to this guy somehow? Maybe make him trip over his own shoelaces before he even reached the frontage road?

He thought he heard a blip of sirens in the distance, but he couldn't be sure with the rush of cars on the horizon drowning it out; it was late, but big-rigs never slept on this thoroughfare.

The LEDs of the highway's light posts poked holes

through the canopy of trees. The unending pursuit now led him through overgrown grass between a long row of buildings—a strip mall on one side, a storage complex on the other. A musty blanket held down by a broken piece of concrete waved in the wind as Green passed it, some relic of a homeless fort, no doubt. If a used hypodermic needle didn't jab straight through the sole of his boot and into his foot, he would call this current wave of bad luck a win.

When he planted on a beer bottle that went right out from under him, he managed to catch himself from falling, but only just.

His time to end this safely was running out.

Highway 7 was a blur of red and white lights ahead, only a hundred yards now. And the suspect was already halfway there.

Green willed his arms to pump faster, his screaming legs to man up, and his lungs to just hold on for a few more seconds. The human would have to pause to reconsider his plan before crossing, and Green would have him then.

Just as expected, the suspect pulled up short at the edge of the frontage road. Then he looked both ways.

Oh no…

"Don't do it!" It wasn't so much a lawful order as a plea.

The suspect looked over his shoulder for the first time, but his face was covered in shadow, obscuring his expression. Would he listen?

Green didn't want to spook the guy, so he slowed.

He knew right away that it was a mistake—his muscles would never get him back up to full speed now.

It was like the game Red Light, Green Light he used to play as a kid. As soon as the suspect returned his attention to the road, Green urged his body to sprint again. This had to be it. He had to tackle the man, or at the very least, tase him.

The suspect looked both ways one more time and then sprinted onto the frontage road.

"No, no, nooo…" Green pleaded, rushing forward. He had to get to the man before he cleared the lesser of the paved dangers and made for the highway proper.

Green cursed right before his boots hit the pavement of the frontage road. Department policy forbade officers from crossing highways in pursuit, which meant this man was well on his way of escaping if another unit didn't pick him up on the other side.

The suspect made it across the empty frontage road easily enough, and a moment later, he was climbing through the gulch toward the highway. The overgrown grass came all the way up to his armpits, and he waded through it with his arms raised above the surface.

Valance had mentioned children. Green was sure of it. Department policy or not, there was no way he was letting this piece of shit get away after murdering children. He'd take a slap on the wrist for pursuing across a highway if it meant making the arrest.

Despite his burning muscles, he urged his legs to go. But before they could, something pulled him back. "Oh no, you don't." Bannockburn gripped each of his wrists like he might cuff him. And the corporal might've had to if Green had just a smidgeon less sense in his head.

"He's getting away," Green said. "That son of a bitch killed children."

"I know. But we'll get him later. I already put word out

to the Claw 700s corporal. His guys will catch him on the other side."

The suspect was across the sea of weeds now and stood at the edge of the highway, timing the onslaught of cars and trucks zooming toward him.

"Let him have his moment of relief that he got away with it," the corporal continued. "It'll make it that much sweeter when we—OhsweetmotherofGod!"

Green let out a similar exclamation, and his gut churned.

The suspect had miscalculated.

Green watched part of the man's body complete its gory arc fifty feet in the air. The whoosh of traffic morphed into a cacophony of brakes squealing, crumpling metal, and horns.

While his brain yelled, *Do something!* Every other system in his body yelled, *Don't move!* And *Run away!*

The eighteen-wheeler responsible for the initial impact kept on driving with only the tiniest of swerves, which was the only ideal part of any of this. If the driver even realized what had happened, and it was entirely possible he did not, it was best for him to pull over somewhere further along rather than on the side of the road.

It was the drivers in the other vehicles, the ones who'd witnessed the collision from behind and dealt with the raining human bits on their windshields, who slammed on their brakes to the detriment of their back bumpers and, likely, the soft tissue in their necks.

Bannockburn cleared his throat before grabbing his shoulder radio. "Suspect down. He tried to cross Highway 7. Suspect is down. We're going to need a lot of units to redirect traffic on the northbound lane of Highway 7, just south of the Williamsburg exit. Multiple vehicle collisions, human remains scattered around. We'll need homicide, medical examiner…"

Thank God Bannockburn had the lead on it. Green stepped back from the frontage road, which would no doubt be complete gridlock into the morning hours as police diverted traffic around the gore, and leaned against an old oak to catch his breath.

As his lungs recovered and the burning in his legs turned to a dull ache, and the curse crested. A bird shit on his shoulder from the branches above, and he used a latex glove from his belt to wipe it off without giving it much consideration.

Did I transfer my bad luck to him?

It was a ridiculous notion, but ridiculous didn't mean impossible; being a cop had taught him as much. And Valance had managed to confer some of hers to the were-bear.

I didn't touch him, though.

Was that a necessary part?

Shit, he knew so little about how this all worked.

And so what if he *had* shifted some of the curse to the suspect? He was pleased to discover that he felt no guilt about it. The man had killed children. Instantaneous death was more than he deserved. If Green had played any part in it, he was happy to be of service.

Then a truly chilling idea ran through his head.

Oh no. Am I turning into Valance?

Nobody on the Fang 900s had managed a wink of sleep. That much was clear at a glance when Green strolled into the sub the following evening. The foot pursuit had come to its grisly conclusion only an hour before the end of their shift, which meant everyone was stuck on scene well past sunrise and into the following morning, until the day shift moseyed over.

Before Green made it ten yards into the building, Brooks waved him down and told him to follow her.

"There's footage," she explained.

Valance, Lawrence, and Harmon were already crammed into a small room off the main hallway. It wasn't much larger than a cleaning supply closet. And if the overwhelming chemical smell burning his nostrils was any indication, that's what it once was. It had since been repurposed to a video playback booth, and Lawrence worked the playback on a tiny monitor, using a knob to rewind. "Yep, it should be right about here."

"Where's this from?" Green asked.

"Gas station."

Lawrence let go of the knob, and the video began. It was grainy—maybe one day, the department would pay for officer body cams, and they wouldn't have to rely on what was little more than stop-motion animation to review cases.

The suspect, who they had learned was named Jeremiah Stilt, stepped onto the right lane of the highway. Somewhere in Green's sleep-deprived mind, he thought, *Maybe he'll make it this time.*

One lane down, three to go. And then there was the southbound traffic.

But, of course, he'd never make it that far.

"Virgin's blood!" shouted Officer Harmon, right in Green's ear.

The others moaned and groaned along. Even Green swore anew as he stuck a finger in his ringing ear.

"Just as bad the second time?" Brooks asked, and he nodded.

Valance said, "I think I saw his head in midair. The trajectory looked about right. I stood watch over that damn thing all night." She scowled disapprovingly, as if any decent person would know to keep his severed head to himself.

"Again?" Lawrence asked, and there was a general consensus that, yes, this was the kind of thing one needed to watch more than once.

Three more times just about sated Green's curiosity, and he decided to back out of the tight space before the visuals and smell of bleach brought up his breakfast all over his shift mates.

The shared trauma worked better than any team-building exercise, and the mood among his fellow officers was almost cheerful as they each filled cups and thermoses of coffee from the break room and filed into the meeting room for show up. Rather than sitting or leaning against the back wall, Green and the others stood in a small circle, cracking jokes and recapping their individual duties from the night before.

But when Sergeant Montoya rolled in, he cut through the chatter with, "Well, you killed another human. Way to go."

Right. There was that.

The officers and Corporal took their usual places.

"Eh," Valance said, preserving her good mood, "he got himself killed. You know what they say: Highway 7's the fast-track to Heaven. Except, you know, not for this guy."

"He mighta died on the northbound side," Brooks said, "but he's southbound for sure."

Lawrence and Marrow snickered beside her.

"I'm glad you all think this is so funny," Montoya snapped. "Because the press is all over our ass about a human fatality."

Valance had a quick answer to that. "What about the four, possibly five shifter fatalities that the piece of crap human put in the books before getting himself killed? The press give two shits about that?"

"Of course they—"

"His girlfriend and her four kids, Sarge. He annihilated an entire family. If the oldest daughter pulls through, the rest of her life will be a nightmare. I didn't get a goddamn second of sleep last night because I was too busy scrubbing a mixture of children's blood and tears off my goddamn boots." She pointed at her toe. "But look, Sarge, I got them all nice and shiny again. Almost like those babies never existed."

Green was afraid to breathe. Montoya didn't look like he was feeling all that much braver. The contempt in Valance's voice formed a toxic condensation that clung to every surface of the space.

Sergeant Montoya inhaled deeply through his round nostrils and nodded a single time. "As much as you won't believe it, I get what you're saying. I was on patrol for most of my career. I've reviewed the events and what minimal security footage is available, and I see no procedural issues. And just between us, I'm not especially sad to see a child murderer taken care of so swiftly. But still, I'm not in control of what the papers put out about the department."

"Ever heard of the serenity prayer?" Brooks asked. "It's a good one."

Montoya's eyes jumped to her only briefly before he

ignored the comment. "Unfortunately, the City Council cares what the public thinks of its police department, and we're beholden to the citizens of Kil—"

"I'm sorry," Valance said, shaking her head as she tossed the paper wrapper from her fast-food breakfast into the trash. "I just can't with this bullshit today."

"Officer Valance," Montoya growled.

She waved him off. "I promised the surviving members of the murdered family I'd check in with them, so I'm gonna go knock that out. Aliyah?"

Officer Brooks looked all too happy to jump up and follow Valance out of the room.

To Green's surprise, Montoya didn't keep after her. Instead, he bowed his head and pinched the bridge of his nose. "Yeah, go on and get out of here. Everyone. You're dismissed. Just get to work." He sounded as tired as everyone else.

Green nodded at Bannockburn across the room.

"Officer Green," Montoya called. "Not you. I need a word first."

Green only just kept from mouthing "help me" to his corporal. Bannockburn arched an eyebrow but didn't seem in the mood to provide backup. "I'll be in the cruiser."

Reminding himself that he was a police officer, not to mention a grown man, Green stood and approached the sergeant. "Yes, sir?"

To his surprise, Montoya appeared almost as weary as he felt. "Well, as you know, we've been having a bit of a PR problem lately with some of the human rights groups around town. So, Chief Spinner has asked command staff to recommend human officers he could chat with to get a better feel of life for your kind in KPD. Make sure you're not being, um, discriminated against or anything like that. I recommended you as a candidate, and as soon as I explained your history in the Force, he was eager to meet with you. You have a meeting with him before your shift tomorrow. Report to the main HQ downtown, and then I'll have Corporal Bannockburn pick you up from there whenever you're finished. Understood?"

Green nodded, hoping the act might shake the jumble of information into place in his skull. "Yes, sir."

Montoya flared his nostrils as his eyes did a quick sweep of Green's face. "Good. I have complete confidence that you'll represent the Fang 900s well to the chief."

Which, of course, meant the opposite, and Green knew it. But he also didn't begrudge Montoya for his concern, especially while the curse was still living its best life inside him.

"Thank you, sir. Am I...? Should I go meet Bannockburn?"

"Huh? Oh, yeah. Yes. Have a good shift. And by that, I mean lay low. Shouldn't be long now until a judge sees your case, and in the meantime— Well, you know the drill."

Green nodded and hurried out to meet Bannockburn in the parking depot.

"Commendation, reprimand, or both?" the corporal asked as Green slipped into the passenger seat.

"Not sure, actually. I have an appointment to talk to Chief Spinner tomorrow before the shift."

Bannockburn's head whipped around. "What for?!"

"I'm supposed to tell him about... being a human police officer?"

Bannockburn snorted and shook his head. "Not likely. He wants something else from you. Maybe that's how he's gonna get it, but he would *never* waste his time asking a human about his feelings. That son of a bitch was one of the biggest opponents to letting humans join up at all, back in the day."

"Really?"

"Oh yeah. He argued that we don't allow officers with no arms, so why would we allow officers who are just as handicapped?"

Green cringed. "Rude."

Bannockburn jabbed at the Human Accessible Monitor, looking for their first call from the queue. "Yeah, well, it's his words, not mine. I've certainly known enough dumb-as-rocks werewolf officers to know it's not the kind of creature you are that matters." He selected a low-urgency stolen vehicle call. "I don't think you should meet with him."

"Why not?"

"Letting the chief know your name is essentially career suicide. Once he knows who you are, you enter the pool of people he'll throw under the bus whenever he needs. Best to go under the radar."

Green swallowed hard. "But I don't have a choice here. Sarge just told me I was going."

Bannockburn shrugged. "Then it's career homicide. Either way, I think you should come up with an excuse not to go."

"Spinner already knows my name, though."

"Fair point. But he might forget it if he doesn't have a face to put with it."

He remembered his sergeant's remark about the chief, that Spinner had become interested after learning Green's career history. "Unlikely. Pretty sure Sarge told him that I shot a human, was the one you sent into Build-a-Human to take down that necro, and was the unlucky witness to Stilt's bloody demise on Highway 7."

Bannockburn chuckled. "Man, you really are one unlucky son of a bitch. Even without the curse."

Green couldn't argue with that.

CHAPTER NINE

When he couldn't sleep and finally concluded that it wasn't because of the early afternoon sun poking in between the curtains at just the right angle to hit him in the face, Green got up and decided to be a bit more proactive. His meeting with the chief was in four hours, so he showered, microwaved a sausage biscuit, ironed his uniform, and still had three and a half hours to go.

So, he went for a run, showered again, and...

Two more hours.

While on the run, he'd noticed a small gap in his knowledge that niggled at him until he thought it might drive him mad: Chief Sevante Spinner was an arachnid. And not the typical kind Green often went after with a broom. Basically a were-spider, as he understood it, but the whole problem was that he didn't really understand it. He'd never met an arachnid. They were rare in this part of the world. Apparently, their native land, wherever that was, had never faced enough of the necessary famine or war to drive its inhabitants across the globe.

Basically, there was a lot Green didn't know about the kind of creature he was about to have a critical conversation with, one that might determine the future of his career.

An hour and a half might be just enough time for him to use the infamous Kilhaven internet to solve some of these questions.

As the page loaded, millimeter by millimeter, he went and brewed some coffee, poured himself a cup, mixed in a little milk and sugar since there was no need to be macho and take it black in his own home, and returned to his desktop computer.

The last inch of the page was still missing, and for a second, he thought it'd stopped loading, then *pop!* There it was all at once. The more he read, the less he wished he knew.

The graphics lagged behind the text, and when the first image loaded three-quarters of the way, he yelped, "Oh, holy shit!" and rolled his chair back from the desk to give himself some space.

Why had he imagined that they changed into a normal-size spider? Even a tarantula would have been better than the horse-size monstrosity in the image. *That* was what he had a meeting with? That big, black, hairy, multi-eyed nightmare?

He clicked out of the window and shut down the computer for good measure. Then, with an hour remaining before he needed to leave, he packed up his gear and went to the donut shop.

———

The chief's office was on the top level of the downtown station in central command. Unlike the faded paint and scuffed floors of the substation where Green usually spent his time, the central command offices looked like a millionaire might walk through any of the office doors at any time. If Valance's cynicism about the way the city worked was right, that could be the case.

The chief's door opened, and he strode out, looking unremarkably human, with the usual number of limbs and everything. While Green had seen plenty of pictures of Spinner in the papers and had even shaken hands with him at graduation, the whole spider thing had warped his memory, and he'd half expected to see a round hunchback of a man come through the door. Fortunately, that wasn't the case at all. Chief Spinner could have been an elf with how tall and lean he was. If the man had ever gained patrol pounds around his middle, they were long gone. He was fully silver-haired and had the kind of pronounced but proportioned nose a sculptor might chisel onto their statue to represent masculine power or some sort of eugenic wet dream.

The chief extended a hand. "Officer Norman Green! So great to meet you!" They shook, and Green tried not to think about Spinner's other seven hands. Or were they all feet? "Come on in! I'm so excited to pick your brain!"

He was certainly charismatic, but it would be suspect if the person in charge weren't, perhaps implying a more sinister means to the top position. Because, obviously, merit didn't belong anywhere in this building with its waxed floors and natural light.

However, the overhead fluorescents inside Spinner's office drowned out the orange glow of dusk coming in through the window. Green surveyed his new surroundings. There was hardly a square foot of blank space on the walls. Framed awards and pictures of Spinner glad-handing the rich and powerful covered almost every inch. The only exception to the theme was mounted directly behind the chief's chair—a giant, painted canvas bearing an abstract red, white, and blue design. A design that looked remarkably like a web.

He motioned for Green to take the chair at the desk and then sat in his on the other side. The artwork framed his square shoulders and peaked out above his silver hair.

Any chance Green had of forgetting he was talking to a giant fucking spider went right out the window.

"It's not often I find myself speaking to such a distinguished rookie." Spinner grinned.

Was "thank you" the right response?

Green remained silent and nodded instead.

"Sergeant Montoya says you were the one who talked down the necromancer at the mall the other day."

"Yes, sir."

"Where did you learn those negotiation skills? They're not teaching those in the academy, as far as I know. Legal decided it was too much of a liability to lead on cadets that they know what they're doing in that regard. But you've got me wondering if we should reexamine that policy."

Green had to think about it. "I don't know, sir. I never learned them in any formal way. I guess if you grow up in enough tense situations, you learn how to talk people down."

"Hmm..." The chief brought his hands together on his desk. "Yes, I suppose there must be some sort of learned survival skills that come with growing up human." He paused, narrowing his eyes on Green, who was so very thankful that Spinner only had two of them at the moment. "That's one of the things I want to talk to you about, Officer Green. The department cares deeply that all of its officers feel equally protected and supported. The ugly truth is that until recently, humans weren't even allowed to apply." He shook his head with fatherly disapproval. "As such, it's come to my attention that despite our best efforts, we might be a little behind the curve on making sure our human officers have what they need to perform their best on the job and stay as safe as possible in the process."

He leaned back in his chair, his elbows on the armrests, his fingers steepled above his lap. "You strike me as a type of man who doesn't back down, Officer Green. What you pulled off at Olympus Mall the other day... I've viewed the security footage. I saw the fear in your eyes and the strength of your spine. I'll never tell my officers not to be scared, but I'll always ask them to face their fears, and you did that. You walked straight into what could have been a swift death for you.

"Now, I know you do this on a daily basis, but rarely are the situations so tense as the one you entered into—and all with only your gun on you! Of course, it never should have happened. The corporals involved have each been reprimanded for their recklessness."

Green's mind flashed to how one of those reprimanded corporals was scheduled to pick him up after this meeting.

"I can't help but think," Spinner continued, "that some of what motivated those commanding officers to send you in so poorly protected was that they don't value your life as much as they do the lives of their paranormal brethren." Green bit his tongue to keep from interrupting and contradicting the chief. "And that worries me. So, I'd like for us to keep in touch. Have regular check-ins, so you can talk frankly about any situations where you felt your life was put in unnecessary danger because you are a human. You know, any moments when you're made the sacrificial lamb in a dangerous situation. Does that sound like something you could do?"

What was he to say? "Yes, sir."

Spinner nodded slowly, pensively, and Green heard the man's teeth clicking together. Then he said, "I'm aware you're on a shift with Officer Heather Valance."

Green's hair stood on end, and his heart, which had only just begun to settle into the new environment, pounded a staccato against his ribs.

He may be only a human, but he wasn't without animal instincts, and they were all telling him to flee.

"Yes, sir. She was my field training officer, as well."

"You and Officer Valance spend much time together?"

"Not if I can help it, sir."

Kindly humor crinkled at the corners of Spinner's eyes. "Just between us, would you say that Officer Valance has a history of showing you disrespect because of your species?"

The smile was gone from the chief's eyes now.

Rather than saying, "Yes, but she hates every species equally, sir," Green recognized and resented the trap being set for him and instead went with, "No, sir. In fact, she went out of her way to help me with scent training, something the department failed to do in both the academy and my time since."

That wasn't the answer Spinner had been looking for. He clicked his teeth again. "That's awfully nice of her. Does she do that for every human?"

"I don't know, sir. I'm the only human on our shift, and I don't pretend to know what Officer Valance does in her spare time."

"Really?" he said. "The two of you don't spend time together outside of work?"

"No, sir."

"But you just mentioned the scent training."

"Right. But that was just for a while, and it stopped a few months ago."

"What caused it to stop?"

Struggling to follow the thread of the conversation, Green chose his words carefully. "I suppose she thought I'd gotten as far as I could with it, being a human and all."

"Did she say that?"

"No, sir. Not that I remember."

"Then I don't understand why you believe that's the case."

"I just assumed."

"And why did you assume that?"

When had this turned into an interrogation, and why had it become one? And what the fuck information was the chief trying to get at? Green weighed his words carefully. "I guess I assumed it because that's the way I felt. I hadn't made any further progress in a while, and I thought I'd hit my limit. Right around that time, she stopped bothering to teach me. I put the two things together."

"Was that before or after the unsanctioned raid on the warehouse that both you and Heather Valance were involved in?"

Green's tongue turned to lead in his mouth. "Before, sir."

Chief Spinner's intense gaze loosened its grip as the

arachnid relaxed his shoulders and smiled warmly. "Don't worry, Officer, I know enough about that to know that you were put in a tight spot. Both you and the female officer—the shifter, what was her name?"

"Officer Brooks."

"Right. Both of you had very little choice but to follow the orders of your commanding officer. And by the way it sounds, you likely feel indebted to Officer Valance for all the help she's given you. I've been around long enough to notice the inevitable dynamic between officers and their former FTOs. The loyalty—or hatred, as the case may be—can last for years afterward. No, I don't blame you for charging in foolishly like that, not when you had so many senior officers barking orders at you. Corporal Bannockburn is, yet again, the one to blame for putting you in danger like that." Spinner paused, and Green could have sworn he saw a small twitch below the chief's left eye. "I don't know what's gotten into him lately, to be honest. He's always been one of our best. Well, I have an idea of what's gotten into him, or rather, *who,* but I won't trouble you with that. You probably know anyway, having the insider view, as you do, to the way Valance works.

"Regardless, the name Bannockburn still means something in this part of the world, and I'm sure he'll find his way again." The synthetic smile that followed wasn't fooling anyone.

The chief exhaled deeply through his nose. "Oh, and I understand you're currently under a leprechaun curse?"

Green's brain reeled from the topical whiplash, and he struggled to catch up. "Yes, sir. A leprechaun cursed me after the..." He wouldn't call it a raid. "After the warehouse raid." *Dammit.*

"That was over a month ago, wasn't it?"

"Yes, sir. Almost two."

Spinner's eyes widened. "And you've worked this whole time while under the influence?"

"Yes, sir. But it comes in waves, and I've learned to recognize when one's coming and take myself out of the action." *For the most part.*

Spinner's brows cinched together, reminding Green of two furry tarantula pinchers. It was likely that everything would remind him of a spider in one way or another until he could get out of this office and suck some fresh—or at least outdoor—air into his lungs.

"How come it's taken so long for a judge to see your case and order a curse reversal?" said Spinner.

Instead of replying that wasn't that just the question of the fucking week, Green said, "I don't know, sir. I've been told it usually takes this long."

Spinner's eyes did a quick sweep of what parts of Green could be seen above the desk, then said, "Yes, I suppose it sometimes does. But one of the perks of being Chief is that you know people. I'll look into it and see if I can't speed things along. Clearly, there's a gap in our criminal justice system that needs to be addressed if it takes this long for two of our officers to be cleared up in such an open-and-shut judgment." He crossed an ankle over his knee, and the bendiness of his thin legs made Green's skin crawl. "I don't want to come across the wrong way. Heather Valance has been on the Force for a long time. I've had plenty of positive encounters with her, and I know that she's one of Kilhaven's finest and most competent officers. We don't always see eye-to-eye on the issues, but I do want it to be known that KPD takes care of its own. The world isn't kind to disgraced officers, and we don't let ours go lightly. When you're out on the street, you have to make hundreds of split-second decisions a day, and it wouldn't be right to fire someone for making a handful of the wrong ones over the course of a long career." He chuckled, his chest convulsing in jerky movements. "If that were our policy, hell, no one would make it to retirement."

Green mustered up a smile. "Good to know, sir."

"I know you feel the pressure on your shoulders as one of the few humans in this department. Every one of your failures is viewed by others as a failure for all humans, and every one of your victories is dismissed as an exception or a lucky break. Well, maybe luck isn't the right word lately. But you know what I mean."

"I do, sir."

"Don't let Heather Valance's high standards stress you out unnecessarily. I think you're doing great, and I want to see you have a long and fruitful career with us. Okay, Officer Green?"

"Yes, sir."

Spinner tapped the fingers of his right hand against his thumb—pinkie, ring, middle, index, pinkie, ring, middle, index—and examined Green closely. "You have any interest in leadership? Once you get the years on patrol under your belt, I mean."

"I hadn't really thought about it, sir."

"I think you should consider it. A man like you could go far. And I like you, Officer Green. I could *help* you go far."

Green heard the unspoken implication: *And I could keep you from ever leaving the Fang 900s.*

"I appreciate that, sir."

"You'll keep it in mind?"

"Of course, sir." In fact, the notion would likely rattle around his skull and elevate his blood pressure for the next forty-eight hours, easy.

"Good, good." For a fleeting moment, the chief looked like he was about to stand and end the meeting. But Green's hopes for freedom were dashed when Spinner's finger tapping increased in rapidity, and then stopped in its tracks. "My wife's been trying to plan a family vacation for us this summer, but she's not sure where we should go. I'm looking for ideas. Where are you from originally?"

"Bowers, sir."

"Where's that?"

"In Texas, sir. About four hundred miles from here."

His eyebrow arched. "Really? Never heard of it. Is it nice?"

"Not at all, sir. It's a horrible place."

"Hm, hm…" The finger tapping resumed. "Where was it that Officer Valance went on her vacation again?"

Green's limbs felt heavy with a rush of adrenaline, and it took everything in him to avoid the programmed impulse to reach for his belt. "Excuse me, sir?"

"Oh, well, it's no secret that Heather's saved up about two full years of vacation time. I figure if she's finally going to go somewhere to get away, it must be a damn fine place. You remember where she said it was?"

"No, sir. I didn't ask her. Didn't seem like my business."

You're lying to the chief of police. What are you doing? Stop this. It's not your job to protect her.

Spinner's soft expression tightened around the mouth, and the finger tapping stopped again. "Surely you heard her mention it in show up or on a slow call together."

Tell him the truth!

Green pressed his lips together in a pout and shook his head. "No, sir. Can't recall anything. She said something the day she got back that made me think she had gone to see some ex of hers, and I didn't want to know anything else after that."

While he was impressed by the ease of his lie, Green saw little bits of the future career he'd hoped to have flash before his eyes then blink out.

"Fair enough." Spinner pushed rapidly to his feet, his rolling chair shooting back behind him and into the wall underneath the large painting. "I suppose I respect your desire to keep your personal life unentangled with hers. Probably for the best, given her track record for destroying men's careers with her recklessness. I just hope for your sake, Green, that you'll know when enough is enough with her. Unless you learn to be a little less trusting of her, it's not a matter of if she drags you into one of her schemes again, just a matter of when."

His eyes flickered to the door, and that was as much of a signal as Green was going to get. Okay then.

"Thank you, sir. I appreciate your concern for the humans under your watch. I won't forget it."

There was little he would forget about this boggling conversation, though much he *hoped* to forget, and even more he wished had never been said.

Just as his hand found the door handle, the strong, clear voice of the chief called after him. "Tell Corporal Bannockburn I send my regards."

"Yes, sir." And then he left before another itsy-bitsy threat could be thrown at his back.

CHAPTER TEN

"Huh," said Corporal Bannockburn as Green dropped into the front seat of the cruiser and shut the door. The werewolf stared at him appraisingly, but Green had had enough of that for the day.

"Just say it, Corp. Please. I'm tired of guessing."

A hint of a smile tugged at the corners of his mouth, and he nodded. "You look tense. But you also look relieved. If you'd snitched, it would be the other way around—relieved until you got in the car with me, then tense."

"I didn't snitch on anyone," Green said, more harshly than was wise when speaking to his commanding officer, even if his commanding officer was unlikely to punish him for it. "Spinner was pumping me for information, though. God, the whole thing was creepy."

Bannockburn put the car into drive and pulled past the front of the station where he'd been waiting to pick up his ward for the night's shift. "You were thinking about all those legs, weren't you?"

An involuntary shiver ran down Green's spine. "Off and on."

"Can I give you some veteran advice?"

"Sure."

"Don't. Don't think about the legs. Think about anything *but* the legs."

"The eyes?"

"Well, no, don't think about those, either." After a pause, the corporal added, "You know, I heard once that men are scared of spiders because the things remind them of vaginas. It's, like, a primal fear or something. Hell, I'm half-convinced the reason Spinner made it to the top is that this department's full of men with mommy issues who were too afraid to challenge him."

Green gazed out the window through the dusk at the various dirty surfaces of downtown. He'd never equated the two things before, spiders and vaginas, and he was in no hurry to start. As if he needed anything else standing in his way of getting laid. "Could we talk about anything else?"

"Sure. How about you tell me what Spinner really wanted with you. None of that BS about human relations. I don't buy it for a second."

Green jabbed at the HAM, logging on for the night. "Yeah, I didn't either. He wanted to know about Valance."

"What about her?"

"Pretty much anything he could get. But I think the main thing was where she spent her vacation."

Bannockburn cursed under his breath. "Of course. You didn't tell him, did you?"

"I didn't snitch."

"I know you don't *think* you snitched, but you might have snitched without meaning to."

"She was in South and Central America, Corporal. The place is still war-torn with infighting. Anyone with half a brain would know she didn't go there to relax."

"And anyone who knows Valance would know she couldn't relax, not even with a gun to her head." He silently considered his words, then added, "Actually, that might be the most relaxed she gets."

"I'm horrified to admit you have a point."

"Murderous calm is still calm, I suppose."

Green switched to the call screen and found one nearby. "Accident on the northbound frontage road of Highway 7, just south of St. Albert's Boulevard. Possibly a DUI."

"And I'm possibly a werewolf." He flipped on his lights and sirens and muscled his way over a lane to speed onto the highway.

Traffic congestion leading up to the spot and the lack of blue lights against the dark canvas of sky indicated they would be first on scene. Green's pulse quickened as it usually did. Before he'd become a cop, rarely had this intense physiological reaction been more than an embarrassing nuisance to be managed. But now he understood how useful it was. His brain needed all the oxygen it could get to make the split-second decisions a scene like this required. And the muscles in his arms would need an extra helping of fresh blood pumping through them if he needed to pull an adult out of a burning vehicle and to safety. Being able to appreciate this function of his body rather than dread it was one of the major unexpected joys of the job.

"Enough with the rubbernecking," Bannockburn growled at the cars ahead of him. "Do lights and sirens mean nothing to you idiots?" He grabbed the handset for the megaphone. "Move onto the shoulder. Get out of the way." He shoved the handset back into its cradle. "One of those days, I wish I could curse at them."

"I'm surprised that's not every day."

Bannockburn shot Green a sideways glance. "You're spending too much time around Valance. It's making you cynical before your time."

The accident wasn't as bad as Green had feared (hoped?), which was the only reason they could cut through traffic to it as quickly as they did—it wasn't a satisfying show for the gawkers.

A pickup truck had come to a stop perpendicular across the right shoulder and two lanes, and the occupants of it had already evacuated and were huddled by the waist-height concrete barrier on the edge of the highway. The vehicle appeared to have been knocked off its course by the sedan that had come to a stop right in the middle of it. The sedan's hood was accordioned, the driver still inside, conscious and clutching the wheel like he stood a chance of maneuvering around truck if he only focused hard enough.

A pretty standard DUI.

Green knocked on the driver's window, and slowly the man turned his head, angling it up to focus on the officer's face. He did a poor job of the last part.

After motioning for the man to lower the window, which he eventually did, Green said, "Sir, would you mind stepping out of the vehicle?" One of the man's eyes lolled down to Green's badge, and the other followed in due course.

"I think I'd rather stay here." The driver's speech was thick and slurred, his tongue weighed down, no doubt, by the same bourbon Green smelled on his breath. "I'm not injured."

"I just have to be sure of that, sir. And it's not safe for you to stay in your vehicle when it's in this condition on the highway. Just standard procedure."

Standard procedure for drunk drivers.

Green led him over to the shoulder, helping him step over the cement barrier and onto a small grassy ditch separating the highway from the frontage road. He made sure the suspect was out of earshot of the woman and two children from the truck, who Bannockburn was interviewing ten or so yards down the gulch.

Green called for backup to help divert traffic before beginning the standard field sobriety tests on the driver. Talk about a formality. The man was already falling over as he reached in his pocket to pull out his ID. Kirnan Chivers, were-bison. Green jotted down name and date of birth in his notepad, sure it would come back with priors, and handed the ID back to its owner. "My sergeant is a were-bison," he said, by way of conversation. Never a bad idea to make nice with a subject before putting them in cuffs.

But to Green's dismay, Kirnan Chivers said, "Sergeant Montoya?"

Shit. "You know him?" There was no getting around arresting this driver for a DUI, no matter what close relationship he might have with the sarge. Now it was just a matter of how much shit he would get for doing it.

"He's my cousin," replied Chivers. But then he quickly added, "Real pompous piece of crap. Haven't spoken to him in years. I was hoping he was dead, actually."

Green relaxed. Maybe this day wouldn't turn out to be entirely bad, after all. Sure, the meeting with Spinner was brutal, but if Green had learned anything recently, it was that luck could change in an instant. "Can I have you close your eyes and hold out your arms, Mr. Chivers?"

It was as the were-bison struggled to remember what letter came before M when incoming blue and red lights signaled the arrival of backup. About time. Nothing contributed to bottlenecking like a live demonstration of sobriety tests.

The doors opened, and Brooks was the first to get out, lifting herself lithely from the driver's seat. Which meant that the other one was...

Green's chest tightened with unexplained anxiety a moment before Valance stepped out from the cab and took in the sights of the call. Her eyes glanced over Green without so much as a hitch. And yet, he couldn't help feeling like the beacon of a lighthouse had just flashed past, leaving him temporarily blind.

"B-C-A," finished Chivers proudly.

Green returned his attention to the man. "Right. You're under arrest." He snapped on the cuffs.

"But I passed!"

"Not even close. Come on."

The ambulance was staged between the back of Chivers' sedan and Green's cruiser by the time he managed to assist the drunk back over the concrete barrier. "We'll get you checked for injuries before I take you downtown." But he was hardly listening to himself because Bannockburn had left his post with the mother and children and was marching straight to where Valance stood by the back of her car, unloading orange cones from the trunk.

"No, no, no," Bannockburn said with each step. "Not you. I don't want you on scene."

Green shoved Chivas to one of the paramedics. "He's not

a flight risk. He can barely walk." And then he hurried over to the confrontation.

"You seeing this?" Valance said to Brooks, setting down the cones as Green got within earshot of their conversation. "This man doesn't think a woman can do this job."

"Don't you start that nonsense," Bannockburn ordered, bravely shaking a finger at her. "It's bad enough I have to haul Green around with me. I can't have both of you on the same scene, you know that."

"Please," she said with a dismissive flick of her wrist. "I've already told you. I can feel when it's coming. Even Green can manage that much."

"I don't see why that's relevant. You feel it coming, and then what? You're still on scene. This is a simple DUI crash, and the last thing we—" The corporal's eyes shot open wide, and Green followed his horrified stare just in time to see the sea-foam green car slam on its brakes. But not in time to avoid the collision, and not in symphony with any true attempt to steer the vehicle away.

It slammed into the front end of the ambulance with a crunch, causing the backside of the emergency vehicle to whip around, missing both paramedics by no more than two inches. But as it was, the EMTs and Mr. Chivers were only left gaping.

Smoke rose from the hood of the sea-foam lump as all four cops sprinted toward the new crash site.

It was difficult to tell the sex of the driver with that much blood on their face. But Valance ripped open the bent door with frightening force, and once the dazed driver was extricated, it was clear they were a she.

It was also clear she was drunker than a shirtless uncle

at a crawfish boil. The empty beer cans littering the floorboards told enough of that tale.

The woman stumbled in Valance's arms, her fancy footwork doing her no favors as her left foot crossed in front of her right every second or third step toward the edge of the highway. Once Bannockburn saw with his own eyes that the driver had good odds, he rushed over to the others to check on them, bringing Brooks with him.

"Hold her for a second," Valance said, turning the bloody woman to face Green and shoving her forward.

He grabbed the woman's shoulders to steady her. "Okay, what are you—" He jumped back just in time to keep the sludgy vomit off his vest, but he couldn't save his shoes.

"There you are," Valance crooned, rubbing the woman's back. "Just get it all out. We'll start there. All done? Oops! Nope, there's some more."

Green stepped back farther, his arms fully extended as he turned his head to keep from getting splashed in the face.

"All good?" Valance asked. "Perfect. I'll take her back, now, Green."

Bannockburn came marching over. "No, you won't. Brooks can handle her, and I just called for more backup who aren't bad luck."

"Bad luck?" Valance said coolly. "We just had a drunk driver veer into an ambulance, and no one was hurt. Some might argue that was good luck."

"Stop trying to spin this, Heather."

"It wasn't us," Valance said. "I told you, we know when it's coming."

"I'm supposed to believe that a drunk driver hit our ambulance at the scene of a drunk driving crash without the influence of supernatural poor luck?"

Instead of answering, Valance remained quiet to let the corporal puzzle it out for himself.

"Yeah, okay, I suppose it's not impossible."

"We still haven't put out the reflective cones."

"Fine," he barked. "Then you two go set those out. Make sure to leave room for an ambulance"—he cast a look at the smoking vehicle—"a fire truck, and a few more patrol cars."

"Yes, sir." She nodded for Green to follow her, but she didn't seem in any kind of rush.

He caught up—he was tired of trailing behind her like a duckling—and she tossed him a glance. "Heard you had a meeting with the chief."

"I did."

"You hang me up to dry?"

"Dammit, Valance. Of course I didn't. Give me some credit."

"Ooh, I didn't know cranky pants were standard issue now."

He swallowed down his petty reply, knowing it would only make him sound like his standard-issue cranky pants were perhaps a few sizes too tight.

She handed him half the stack of cones as the second ambulance broke through the delighted rubberneckers and pulled up next to the first ambulance, aka the scene of the second crash.

"And what was the pretense under which our dearest and most admirable chief pulled you into his office?" she asked.

"He said he wanted to know more about what it was like to be human on the Force."

Valance chuckled. "That's a good one." She nodded toward the front of the growing train of destruction. "You start on that end, and we meet in the middle."

Green walked the length of the site, passing the newly arrived ambulance, where the paramedics scurried around while swapping looks with each other that clearly said, "How in the ever-living shit does something like this happen?"

Brooks was growing visibly exasperated on the shoulder as she attempted to administer the sobriety tests to the bloody, vomitous woman. He admired her attempt to stick with the formalities, so some scumbag lawyer couldn't get his client off on the charge by citing faulty procedure, despite the fact that not just the woman's car, but her *puke* smelled like a bathtub of warm IPA.

The mother and her two children were still huddled in the grass, ignored now that there were more pressing medical matters to attend to. She was on her phone, and Green could imagine her conversation, though he couldn't actually hear it: "You will not believe this, Susan. I know it's late, but can you maybe send Leonard out to pick us up? We need to get out of here before more shit hits the fan." Or something similar.

Perhaps it was instinct, or perhaps he really was becoming cynical before his time, but he gave himself an extra twenty paces beyond the end of the sideways truck before marking the edge of the perimeter with the first of his giant orange cones.

He did the math on cones versus distance, walked out fifteen paces, set down the next, walked five paces, then stopped dead in his tracks.

There it was.

Slowly, he looked up from the asphalt, searching for Valance's eyes across the distance. She was already looking at him, and their eyes met. This one was strong. He could feel it rush toward him, and it was clear she could, too.

"Shit." He said, dropping the cones. "Shit, shit, shit." He jogged over to her. "We gotta get away from the scene."

"Why are you running this way? Go the other way! Split up!"

"But I'm already over here! I can't run by the scene again!"

She cursed, grabbed his wrist, and yanked him toward her.

They never got the chance to run. The oncoming SUV missed him by mere inches on its determined path over one of the orange cones and straight into the second ambulance's side.

"How are they even going so fast?" Green cried, looking at the slow flow of traffic merging from four to two lanes around the scene.

But Valance didn't answer; she was already sprinting over to the latest crash.

He shouldn't follow. In fact, *she* shouldn't even be going. The wave might have crested just then, but it hadn't passed.

Bannockburn appeared from the other direction and beat Valance to the back of the ambulance. This time, the impact *had* caused injuries. Two of the four paramedics were clutching various parts of themselves. Though the bloody woman had been spared as she'd stood out of the way with Brooks, Chivers was now face down on the asphalt, dangerously close to the flow of traffic. Bannockburn beat Valance to the paramedics, who nodded and waved him on. He shouted something at her that sounded a lot like, "Get the hell away from me," as he rushed to attend to the drunk lying prostrate on the highway.

Valance stopped moving and stood in the middle of it all, her back to Green, her hands on her hips. Then, after taking in the scene, her head drooped forward, and she turned and jogged back to him. "Yeah," she said, "I think that one was on us."

"Should we get out of here?"

She narrowed her eyes at him like the curse might've turned his brain to mush. "I think that's pretty obvious."

"Are we even safe to drive?" She walked past him to the car she'd arrived in with Brooks. "I'll drive slow. Will that make you feel better?" she called over her shoulder.

As he slipped into the passenger's seat, he heard the sirens of the firetruck approaching behind them.

Valance saw it too and grunted. "Look who finally decided to drop their ping-pong match and join the clusterfuck."

The firetruck pulled up slowly, parking at a conspicuous and entitled angle that blocked off an additional lane of traffic.

Valance started the engine. "At least by clearing out, we'll be spared their arrogant—"

The motorcyclist came out of nowhere, easily going over eighty, no doubt in an attempt to outsmart the traffic jam. Despite the projectile that he was, he hardly made a dent in the side of the firetruck as both he and his bike were instantly obliterated upon impact.

Green felt a strange sucking sound trying to crawl up his throat as his mouth hung open. He found he couldn't blink his eyes. Emergency lights continued to drench the stretch of highway in a frenzied, flashing chaos. He thought he saw a scrap of the cyclist's tire land not far from where

Bannockburn administered CPR to the unconscious were-bison.

Valance cleared her throat. "I'm *not* taking credit for that." She killed the engine. "But maybe it's best if we walk."

————

The two unlucky officers cut through an overgrown field occupied by a half dozen homeless settling in for the night, heating water and other substances in small pots over improvised stoves that were as likely to explode and set the field alight as they were to boil anything.

The fact that there were no explosions as they drew near confirmed what Green had already suspected: this wave of misfortune had passed.

"We ain't doing nothing wrong, officers!" hollered a man with, hopefully, more sense than teeth.

Valance waved at him without taking her eyes off the ground. "We're not here for any of you." She paused. "Hey, there aren't, you know, any booby traps out here, right?"

"No, ma'am," the same man replied.

"Great, have a good night." She walked more casually then, though Green wasn't as ready to trust the word of the man cooking up crack cocaine.

The murmur of the homeless camp faded behind them as she said, "Spinner will never be your ally, let alone your friend."

"I figured as much."

"He's not a friend or ally to anyone in this department."

"So I hear."

She glanced at him. "Bannockburn already told you this?"

"This, and more."

"Did he tell you about how Spinner nabbed himself that job?"

Green shook his head, and the opportunity to explain seemed to please her. A small part of him rejoiced, knowing he could still please a woman, even if only in this small way.

"He'd weaseled his way up to assistant chief over the years. No one really liked him, but the department makes a certain kind of concession for ambitious ass kissers who don't get into any real trouble. They make them an assistant chief to keep them happy because *nobody* trusts a cop who doesn't get into any trouble. It means he's a lazy cop. But that makes him useful for political reasons.

"Anyway, Chief Masters was a good chief. A cop's cop, you know? I have no fucking clue how a man like that ended up in the top position. It was a fluke, gross oversight on the city council's part, really. We all knew it couldn't last. But I think we all hoped it would anyway.

"Then there was this shooting down in Claw sector. It was a good shoot. We all knew it was a good shoot. A human was holding his wife and five kids hostage. That's as much as the officers knew, at least. Turns out, he'd already executed his teenage daughter. And that wasn't even the worst thing he'd done to the girl. The first cops on scene were shot at through the window, so they took cover and waited for the Telekinetics. But before Team Psycho could make it over, the husband stepped out the front door with a gun to his wife's head." She paused. "You know Corporal Lindquist over on the Claw 800s?"

Green had run into him on a few cross-sector calls, and he nodded.

"He was on scene. He was also a sniper in South America. He's not a sharpshooter, he's the *sharpest* shooter. I'd even heard of him during the war, and we were never in the same country.

"So, Lindquist had this bastard in his sights, and when that pistol lowered for a split second, Lindquist took his shot. Straight through the head. The stuff dreams are made of, really. The rat bastard dropped like a bag of fresh dog shit. I watched the video of it—it's fantastic. Good riddance."

They walked in silence for a few paces before Valance picked up the story again.

"Lindquist saved four children and their mother from an absolute monster. We all knew as much, and Chief Masters said as much in the press conference afterward. Lindquist was showered with awards, as he should have been. He did exactly what any of us would have done if we'd had his skills.

"Spinner waited until everyone in town had learned about the situation before he started spreading inconsequential details, things Chief Masters knew were irrelevant and had intentionally kept away from the media so that, just once, we could have a fucking unadulterated victory."

"What details?"

"First of all, the man who raped then murdered his daughter and would have done the same to the rest of his family, he was *mentally ill*. I mean, no shit. But there's a big fucking difference between someone who struggles with depression or has a few hallucinations here and there and a murderous pedophile with a gun. I mean, what the hell were they supposed to do? 'Uh, excuse me, sir? Are you mentally ill? If so, we'd just like to talk to you until you feel better.' Give me a fucking break. It all amounts to the same when someone's holding their family hostage: do what you gotta do to keep the hostages safe."

Green had been on enough calls with Valance to know she took it seriously when the subject was known to have a mental illness. He's also witnessed her risk her own ass to deescalate such a situation when, in all reality, she could have at least used her Taser. He couldn't begrudge her the anger here. He would have done the same thing as Lindquist. He already knew he could pull the trigger when he needed to.

"And then," she went on, "it leaked that Lindquist was taking a specific medication to manage a few conditions he took home with him from the war. Some of the side effects included violent ideation, paranoia, and blurred vision."

"Let me guess," said Green, "he didn't have any of those side effects."

"Hell no, he didn't. But that didn't stop Spinner from feeding that angle to the press. Chief Masters had had to give special approval for Lindquist to keep working while on that medication, and he'd signed off on it. The two of them went way back, though. They'd been in the academy together, so Masters knew Lindquist would sooner eat a bullet than go out on a shift if he were experiencing any of the negative side effects. And then *that* was spun into a case of favoritism." She stomped an empty beer can under her boot, then kicked it away. "If all the bleeding hearts in this town had any fucking idea about the litter their poor, precious homeless leave around…"

"So Spinner helped get Masters fired?"

"Not only that, but his 'brave' act of exposing Masters' negligence and nepotism and disregard for the mentally ill in the city got Spinner the job he has now. The City Council was eating out of all eight of his hands. They almost never promote from within the department for chief, but they made an exception for this noble crusader." They reached the edge of the field and stepped into a mostly vacant parking lot of a strip mall.

"Spinner hates your guts," Green said.

"Feeling's mutual."

"What'd you do to him?"

She chuckled dryly. "You assume it's my fault?" She shrugged a single shoulder, "Yeah, it is, I guess."

"What happened?" A car slipped soundlessly into the parking lot and made its way toward them.

"The rat bastard wanted to promote me."

"He... what?"

"Yeah. I took the corporal's exam seven years ago, just to see how I could do on it. I didn't even study. I did okay, but there were plenty of officers ahead of me. Male officers. Spinner called me into his office and said he believed this department could benefit from more diversity in the leadership. He wanted to promote me ahead of the others who outscored me."

"I assume you told him no?"

"I told him *hell* no. Then I told him I wouldn't accept a favor from him if my career depended on it, and that I knew what tricks he pulled to get the position he had, and that everyone else in the department knew, too. I said I'd rather spend the rest of my career on patrol than promote with his help. So that's what I've done."

"Do you regret it?"

Her head snapped around. "Regret it? Are you joking? I could get off to the memory of that conversation night after night if I ever had enough energy left after a shift to spare for that sort of thing."

The car pulled up and stopped in front of them, and Valance hurried around to the passenger's door as Officer Tara Marrow hollered her hello.

"You're welcome to jump in if you're not too good for the backseat," Valance called.

Green glanced around, realized he had no one who would pick him up if he put out an SOS, and let himself into the uncomfortable back seat.

Marrow looked at him through the rearview mirror. "Don't look so glum, Green. Some folks pay money for roleplaying this authentic."

Valance chuckled. "Oh, he's been a bad boy, all right."

"Maybe we ought to cuff him."

As the women laughed among themselves, Green turned his attention to the window. Out in the middle of the field, a plume of flame shot up then disappeared into the open night sky. He leaned his head back and let his eyes slip shut.

CHAPTER ELEVEN_

The swelling around Bannockburn's eyes the next day told Green all he needed to know about how the rest of the previous night's clusterfuck had gone. The Corporal likely hadn't managed more than a couple hours of sleep between when he made it home and when he had to head back out again.

But the werewolf still made it into show-up five minutes early, which was more than could be said for most of the shift.

Green was actively avoiding the eye of his corporal and cradling a Styrofoam coffee mug in his hand when Valance slid into the chair next to his. She cradled in her hands a metal thermos that steamed angrily from the small opening at the top. "Just got word from Sarge. It's you and me from here on out, Green."

He jerked his head around to look at her, found himself uncomfortable with eye contact while this close, and leaned back. "Huh?"

"Don't get all nostalgic on me, Rookie. This will never be a buddy cop movie, you and me."

"No, but what are you talking—"

"After last night's hat trick of a clusterfuck, Bannockburn and Brooks have officially had enough of us. Montoya was set on sticking us behind desks until a judge could be bothered to court order the curse reversal, but I talked him out of it. You're welcome."

Green's mind raced. Their bad luck seemed to be amplified when they were together. And now they would be together all shift?

"Can't we ride solo?" he said.

"If you're not careful, I'm gonna start thinking you have a crush on me. And no, we can't ride solo. You think I didn't already ask that?"

"I can't believe the department has enough insurance."

She shrugged and took a slip of her scalding coffee without flinching. Green was sure if he'd asked her whether it was too hot, he would hear something along the lines of "I haven't had sensation in my tongue since I had to lick my way through iron bars in Ecuador," so he kept his mouth shut.

"It's not like they can pin any of the events of last night on us," she added. "All the drivers were drunk. Well, they're not sure about the motorcyclist, because I don't know that they've scraped enough of his blood off the pavement to test it. But if he wasn't drunk, he was damn stupid for going that fast to get around the bottleneck, and stupidity is no more admirable than drunkenness. Not our fault, is all I'm saying, and if it was, good luck to any lawyer trying to prove it."

While that didn't necessarily soothe his conscience, it

covered his ass, and that was sometimes all one could hope for in this line of work.

The rest of the shift trickled in, milling around, casting bitter glares at Valance and Green, both of whom had managed to avoid OT in the middle of Highway 7. Valance made a show of tipping her thermos and spewing motivational phrases at everyone who gave her a sharp glance: "New day, new opportunity to serve and protect, Harmon!" and "The brotherhood of law enforcement is a real blessing, huh, Lawrence?"

No one much seemed to like this post-vacation Valance that kept making appearances at show-up. This version presented as much more unencumbered, slightly more nihilistic, and vastly more dangerous.

Montoya stomped in with a thick manila file of papers under his arm. He tossed them onto a table at the front, sending the topmost sheets skidding free. He didn't give it a second look. "Officer Green, you're doubled up with Officer Valance now. We have a special car for you. You're only to handle routine calls—noise disturbances, rowdy children in front lawns, and so on."

Valance raised two fingers then didn't wait to be called upon. "You talk to the chief about our hearing?"

Montoya glowered. "Yes, I did. He said he's very busy but will try to expedite it when he gets the chance."

Valance puffed amusedly, and when Montoya jumped to the daily BOLOs, she leaned close and whispered, "You really didn't rat on me, did you?"

"I already told you I didn't."

"Excuse me if I didn't believe you. Rats aren't always truthful. But clearly, you pissed off the chief, so congrats and also RIP."

God, was he really going to have to spend all shift with her when she was feeling like such a lighthearted terror?

"And last announcement," Montoya said. "It looks like Williamson won't be joining us again anytime soon. His shattered knee is healing nicely, and they wrapped up the initial investigation of the recent misconduct charges from his bar fight, but now there's a secondary investigation pending. So, we'll remain without him for the foreseeable future." The grumbling threatened to drown him out as he added, "I know, we've been short-staffed for a long time on this shift, and we have one of the hardest gigs in town. But until the City Council approves the new budget, the hiring freeze will remain in effect. If you have a problem with it, vote for new people in the next election. Anyway, I managed to pull some strings, and I got us someone else to help out for a while." The room was silent now. The electricity of anticipation caused Green's arm hair to stand on end. Though he'd never experienced it personally, he knew from overheard conversations that a new member onto a shift could either be like a life-saving blood infusion, or it could be like injecting toxin straight into a major vein.

"I'd like everyone to welcome Detective Felps from Homicide to the Fang 900s." The sergeant nodded toward the back of the room, and Green followed his gaze to see a fit figure leaning against the door frame, his arms folded across his chest as he nodded his appreciation for the lackluster applause. Detective Felps looked to be pushing six-four, but he couldn't have been a pound over 190. He was lean, wearing plainclothes—dark-wash jeans, a deep red T-shirt and a brown leather jacket—and had his badge on a chain around his neck. But the thing Green noticed above all else wasn't the detective's clothes or his dark, unreadable eyes. What stood out was his corpselike skin.

The already wan applause died out. Valance had never bothered to *begin* clapping herself, and he had the feeling she, at least, knew who Felps was—and *what* he was—before turning to look at him.

"He'll be using the call sign Fang 9-20 while he's with us. Detective?" Montoya prompted. "Want to say a few words?"

The vampire's voice was smooth and surprisingly deep for such a lithe and otherwise effeminate man. He didn't bother pushing off of the door frame as he spoke. "I thank everyone in advance for the warm welcome. I'm sure you're wondering why a homicide detective is going out on the streets with you now. I assure you it's solely because if I sit behind a desk for another second, I'm going to lose my mind. I know homicide serves an important role, but I miss being out on the street. So, when my detective sergeant asked for volunteers, I was the first to raise my hand." He nodded succinctly. "Looking forward to getting to work alongside each of you."

Was it Green's imagination, or had the detective's eyes latched onto him and lingered for just a moment too long...?

———

"Does this thing even drive?" Green asked, taking in the sorry sight of the car they'd been assigned. The sun was almost completely down below the horizon, and still, in this murky light, Green could tell their new ride was a death trap.

"Stop complaining. It makes you sound weak," Valance snapped, tossing her gear into the trunk after her third attempt to disengage the lock was successful.

Her lighthearted mood had dissipated the moment Sarge had introduced Felps, and Green was anxious to find out exactly why.

But not so anxious that he was willing to jump in this junker without any questions. And he had a lot of them. For instance, why had no one bothered to fix the metal over the rear wheel well where it was clear another vehicle had smashed into it at high speed? And why was the passenger's side mirror bent at that strange angle? And was it actually legal for them to pull someone over when the O in Police was missing entirely from the side? Could the "P lice" legally make an arrest, or would a wily lawyer manage to use that as an excuse for why his client had refused to pull over?

Then he remembered that they weren't supposed to do anything that a Boy Scout couldn't legally do, and he settled into the idea that his job was going to be incredibly boring so long as this curse remained.

Probably for the best anyway.

He shoved his tack back into the trunk and slammed it shut. On the fourth attempt, it stayed that way.

Valance tested the siren just as his hand reached for the door handle, causing him to jump and wince against the assault on his ears.

"You can't be this jumpy to start the shift," she chided as he slid into the cramped front seat and adjusted his duty belt.

He knew better than to say anything to that. "So, what's the deal with Detective Felps?"

Valance shrugged and started the car, which came to life

with a reluctant sputter. "Not sure what you mean. He seems like just a typical detective with zero political baggage who's ready to hit the streets again."

Green shut his eyes to let the sarcasm move all the way through him. "He's a vampire."

She whipped around to him, her eyes wide, her mouth a little O. It might have been a cute expression if he hadn't known anything about her. "Oh, *is* he?"

"This is about the missing children, isn't it?"

Valance was already disconnecting his body mic before he'd finished the sentence. She did hers next, and since he knew the drill, he leaned forward and disabled the dash cam. This was going to be one of *those* talks, wasn't it?

"Yes," she said finally. "This is obviously about the missing children."

"Who is he?" Green asked. "I could tell you knew his name already."

"It's a well-known name around here. You don't recognize it?"

"No. Should I?"

"Only if you give two shits about civic engagement. Detective Felps is the grandson of Senator Igor Felps."

"Is that… is that our senator?"

"Yes, it's our senator. And he's held the office for roughly a hundred and twenty years."

Green was silent. Felps was the first vampire he would work beside. It made him uncomfortable, despite the obvious parallel to how many others must feel working alongside a human like him. But humans, at least, didn't hold within their ranks the most powerful positions in the country. Not only were vampires dangerous, they essentially ran everything—government, industry, entertainment. But what was more…

"How does he even do this job? We have to respond to schools and daycares and stuff."

"Special permission," she said. "Felps had to get state approval before he could sign on. All vampires have to do that. Extensive background checks. Of course, all the background anyone needs is that he's a bloodsucker, and they should know he isn't fit to wear a badge. His daddy got him the job, no doubt."

"And what does that mean for us?"

"It means we have a babysitter. I don't know how, but someone must have found out that the Fang 900s aren't sharing all we know about the disappearing children."

"You think he knows about the swamp?" A memory of the turned Caitlin Holloway, her bloodless skin, fangs gleaming in the narrow beams of moonlight penetrating the thick tree boughs overhead, her charging, then the stake bursting through her.

The mental image of an alligator eating her corpse was just a little somethin' his guilty imagination had thrown in for fun.

They'd been so careful, though, changing into their spare uniforms afterward. No one could know about what had happened besides Valance, Bannockburn, and himself. Well, and Brooks, who he'd told with almost no prompting. She wouldn't say anything, though, would she?

"I don't think he knows," Valance said, "but he wouldn't be joining us if he didn't suspect something."

"You don't think he just missed being on the street?"

"A detective can be on the street as much as he wants to be. No, I don't buy his story." She turned to him. "This"—

she motioned to the death cage around them—"is the best thing that could happen to us right now. We need to keep our head down, stay out of trouble, and, if we're lucky, he'll believe we're just a couple of bumbling, incapable fuckups."

"I can't imagine we'll be lucky," Green said.

Valance conceded a muffled chuckle. "True. I guess we'll just have to rely on your actual incompetence to fool him."

———

After two false alarms, two suspicious persons calls that were little more than racism, and a ten-minute chase to corral a loose dog and drop it off at the shelter, Green felt like his soul was being crushed under a heavy boulder. So, when Valance said, "Fuck this. Let's get some grub," he couldn't have agreed more. The bogus report in the call cue of two clowns defecating in a woman's front yard could wait.

He let his mind wander as she drove. The bad luck had only hit once so far, and that had been while they were driving. Valance had pulled over, let the wave pass, and ignored the heavy coating of bird shit that they'd amassed after, apparently, parking under a favorite roosting spot for grackles.

But when she pulled into the parking lot, and he realized where they were eating, he groaned. It wasn't that he didn't like the food of Roman's Ramen. It was more that he had difficulty digesting his meal when he was surrounded by a bunch of werewolves who were not super thrilled that there was a human in their midst.

When they entered, Valance first, Bannockburn gave a

little finger wave to them from a booth in the back. So, this was preplanned.

He'd only ever been brought here when Valance or Bannockburn had needed to speak candidly without fear of being overheard. The place was busy, but his basic scent training indicated that he was the only anomaly here, and werewolves simply didn't snitch on each other to outsiders. It was a familiar dynamic from the job, when a werewolf victim would protect their werewolf abuser out of breed loyalty. The only solution he'd found to this sort of thing was to call in Valance or Bannockburn to speak to the vic. Not ideal, but it usually got the job done.

But that same blind creaturist loyalty worked to their advantage here.

Valance made Green squeeze into the booth ahead of her.

Bannockburn said, "They have that rosemary beef stew on special today."

"Almost good enough news to counteract what you're about to tell us?"

His face grew dark. "Yeah, almost."

He waited until the server had already taken their orders, no doubt to minimize interruptions, before launching into it. "I was chatting with Sergeant Ross from the Fang 300s a couple days ago, and he mentioned that one of his guys had found a body part out in the swamp behind Shady Grove."

Green had his hands clasped on the table, and he hoped neither of the others noticed his knuckles going white.

"Which body part?" Valance asked casually.

"Arm. From the elbow to the shoulder. Not that it really matters."

"And I assume from your spooky tone that you purport to know whose body part this is."

"It was described as pale and childlike."

Valance made a dismissive chuffing sound. "Of course it's pale. It's dead meat."

"Heather." The single word was, shockingly, enough to make her back down. It was obvious she didn't want to admit whose body part had been discovered—none of them wanted to. But there wasn't much getting around it.

Green decided to try, anyway. "We're talking about Shady Grove Trailer Park, here. I would be shocked if someone *hadn't* dumped a child's body back there."

Bannockburn nodded somberly. "I know it's not ideal to consider the possibility here, but I'm guessing that once the M.E. gets his hands on it, we're going to find out that it's vampire."

Valance said, "If this happened a couple days ago, how come you're just now mentioning it?"

"I didn't want to worry you two unnecessarily. I thought there was a good chance it would be filed away and forgotten about. After all, the detectives on Caitlin's case don't have the pieces to connect her with vampires yet. They're not going to hear about a missing human girl and discovered vampire body parts and assume they're looking at the same thing."

"We don't know she was human," Valance said. "She hadn't hit puberty yet. She could have been werewolf."

Bannockburn rolled his eyes and leaned back to allow the server room to set the fresh rolls down. Then he said, "Except if she was a werewolf, she couldn't also have been a vampire. So that only leaves us with one option. Anyway, I thought it might blow over, but then Felps shows up today."

"Yeah," Valance said, tearing open a roll and jabbing a pat of butter in the middle. "What the fuck is that?"

"You know what the fuck that is," the corporal replied. "We're being watched. Or rather, *you're* being watched. As far as I know, they think I'm just one of the boys." He shot a sharp look at Green that made the rookie pause with a roll halfway shoved in his mouth. "You need to watch your ass, though. They think she's gotten to you."

Valance chuckled. "If I could build a cult, I'd be doing that, not this. Way more lucrative. I could afford a nicer apartment."

"All the same," Bannockburn added, "we all need to watch our ass. I know you two are staying off tricky calls, and I think that's best. Just lie low for a while. The M.E. is unlikely to figure out the cause of death from a single upper arm, but from what I understand, there are already units searching for more pieces. If we're lucky, the gators already took care of the torso."

Around his roll, Green managed, "Did you just say, 'If we're lucky'?"

A slight tic of Bannockburn's left eyebrow indicated when he finally got it. "God dammit."

CHAPTER TWELVE_

"You sure this counts as an easy call?" Green asked, finishing up the last bits of his ham-and-cheese kolache from the passenger's seat.

"Nothing will be happening there. It's not like the boy can be any more missing."

Green didn't push it. Yes, she had a point, but a part of him knew exactly why she'd assigned them to this call out in Crown Tree. And it had nothing to do with them lying low.

But at the same time, they'd been lying low for nearly a week, and he suspected librarians regularly had more exciting days than he'd been having. He was ready for a little trouble, as it were.

There was already another police cruiser at the curb outside the impressively sized house, but they'd expected that. Detective Felps had assigned to the call, not five seconds after it'd appeared on the screen. Almost as if he'd been expecting it.

Valance squinted at him beneath the dull interior light of

their car. "You got something on your face." She dusted at her own chin. "Doubt these parents are going to feel like we're taking them seriously if it looks like you just went down on a pastry."

Green wiped his face thoroughly then followed her up the walkway to the address of a mister and missus Owiti. Before knocking, they listened silently on the doorstep as the sounds of young children, one of whom seemed to be having a full-on meltdown, vibrated through the front door.

It was just past midnight, so no wonder about the bad behavior. And if the teenage son was missing, that would no doubt put a kink in the Owitis' normal schedule.

They knocked, and the father appeared at the door, stepping aside and welcoming them in with a nod of his head.

"Officer Valance, and this is Officer Green."

"Thank you for coming," Mr. Owiti said. He motioned them toward a sitting room where Detective Felps was parked in a wingback chair across from Mrs. Owiti, a mug of something warm in his hands. On the floor between them were two small Owitis, one a toddler and the other no more than four years old. Green thought of the other families he'd encountered through his work with this sort of age gap. The oldest spent most of his or her life as an only child, then suddenly that was all over. Usually, when he responded to calls for families with this set up, it was because of something the oldest had done. Some act of rebellion, whether small or big.

He understood on a personal level. He'd been the youngest for most of his childhood, only having to vie for attention with his older brother Keller. And then, when he was already in high school, Kim came along and stole his place in the birth order.

The fact that it was a missing teen in the Crown Tree neighborhood raised his hackles, so to speak. It did seem to fall within the emerging pattern of abductions. But once he realized that both the parents were werewolves, his hypothesis for the missing teen changed from something sinister to merely the case of a teenage boy staying out too late to upset the parents who'd betrayed him by tacking on two younger siblings. Part of Green wanted to give the kid props for having the balls to do it. And assuming he showed up before they had to send out a search party, no harm no foul, really. There were worse ways for a teenager to rebel. Presumably, this wouldn't lead to car windows smashed out or dangerous vehicle pursuits or toy guns painted to look real aimed at police officers who carried the genuine article.

Mrs. Owiti took in the two new arrivals and seemed to approve. She sat rigidly in her seat across from the vampire. The fact that she'd even allowed him in was to the credit of Felps' people skills—but Green reckoned she was relieved to have a fellow werewolf as the backup. And the fact that Green out melanin-ed Felps by a mile might have also helped put this dark-skinned family at ease, though he doubted this couple found that as relevant as Valance's species.

Mrs. Owiti stood. "Tea?"

"No thanks," Valance replied, holding out a hand to help assure the woman it was okay to relax. "We just had some coffee. There's no need to play host, Mrs. Owiti. We're here to help. I'm Officer Heather Valance. You can just call me Heather, though." She managed an admirable balance between speaking loud enough to be heard over the crying toddler and not shouting. "It's probably best if we talk somewhere separate from the children."

Mr. Owiti rushed forward and took a child under each arm, carting them out of the room and up a set of stairs.

"Mrs. Owiti—"

"Ursula, please. And won't you two have a seat?"

They did, but the only ones remaining in the sitting room were both found on a small love seat. They squeezed in, and Green tried not to think about the butt of Valance's gun digging so fiercely into the side of his glute. "When was the last time you saw your son, Ursula?"

Felps jumped in. "I've already been through all this with her, Valance."

She shot him a look that said, quite plainly, that she didn't care what he'd already done. Then she turned back to the mother. "If you don't mind going through it with me again..."

"Of course not. Jordan went to school this morning, and he should have been back on the bus by four twenty."

Valance nodded. "Four twenty. So Jordan is still in middle school?"

"Yes. Eighth grade."

"Fourteen?"

"Almost."

"I assume you've called around to places he might have gone?"

Ursula nodded, sharing down at her clasped hands in her lap. "Yes. I called the homes of all his friends I know about. I just..." She looked up. "This isn't like him. He doesn't act out. He comes home, does his homework, then watches the little ones while I make dinner."

Green thought that might make any teen want to take a mini-vacation from home, but he stayed quiet.

"I understand."

Valance opened her mouth to ask her next question, but before she could, Ursula blurted, "Do you think this could be connected to the other missing children? They lived in this neighborhood. They were about his age. I was worried, but I thought... I thought whoever was behind it only wanted girls." She covered her shame with two hands over her face, and Green took the opportunity to sneak a glance over at Felps. The vampire had his eyes locked onto Valance as if willing her to keep her big mouth shut.

"We can't say anything for sure, Ursula. We're still gathering the facts of the case. But statistically speaking, there's a high probability that Jordan will come home on his own. Thirteen-year-olds can be flighty, even the responsible ones. Maybe he thought he told you he was staying the night with someone but forgot. I know it's hard to avoid, but it won't help anyone if you jump to a worst-case scenario."

"But the girls were his age! They went to the same school! They were werewolves, too!" She yanked a tissue from the side table and shoved it against her leaky nose.

Felps leaned forward. "I already told you, Mrs. Owiti. I don't believe Jordan fits any of the victim profiles the department has put together for those cases."

Green could feel Valance bursting to say something, but she remained quiet, no doubt for the sake of the concerned mother.

After a few more of the standard questions, Valance was the first to stand. "Thank you, Ursula. Here's my card. If Jordan comes home, would you just give me a call?"

"And mine as well," Felps said, jabbing his toward the mother. "Just ask for *Detective* Jason Felps."

It was intended as a simple one-up, but when Ursula took his card and looked down at the inscription, her tired face tightened. "Homicide?" She jerked her head up. "Why… but why is homicide here if you don't think—" Her gaze jumped between Valance and Felps.

"He's just on patrol right now," Valance said, scrambling. "He's not here in *that* capacity."

But the damage had already been done, and the three of them left the Owiti home with the sound of Ursula's sobs following behind.

Valance said nothing as she made a bee-line down the long walkway to the car. Felps pushed past Green, knocking him a step onto the lush, green lawn. "Officer Valance."

She turned, and Green didn't miss her deadly smile before she managed to school it. "Yes, Homicide Detective Felps?"

They met by the street, well out of earshot of the house, and Green gave them a respectable distance as he listened in.

"I had that handled," the vampire said.

"And what exactly do you think 'handling' a call like that looks like?"

"It's just a missing person call. The kid will come back home tomorrow."

She took a step closer. "We both know that's horseshit. Even his mother can see what was going on here."

To Felps' credit, he didn't back away. "She's just scared, thinking of worst-case scenarios. Your job, might I remind you, is to gather the information. Then you pass it along to detectives. Like me. You're not here to make judgments about what's happening."

"You think I didn't see you assign to that call a split-second after it popped up? Who tipped you off to it, Detective? Who gave you a heads up that you'd better haul ass over there and downplay it before anyone else on the Fang 900s could arrive?"

"You're paranoid."

"Hasn't failed me yet. And if you think for one second that we don't all know why you joined up with this shift, the real reason you're creeping around, you're even more chock full of shit than whatever higher up assigned you here."

"This call isn't connected. Both the parents are werewolves."

She tilted her head to the side. "What does that have to do with anything? You think one of the parents being a human in the other cases was significant?" Her brows pinched together. "Wait, but that would imply that you think someone's hunting *humans*. And what kind of a monster would be interested in stealing humans from their werewolf parents?"

The question hung like a noose in the air until Felps smartly took a step back from it. He turned to Green. "You need to be careful, Rookie. She's poison. I've heard tales, but now I've seen it with my own eyes. As soon as you get that curse lifted, you'd best go solo."

He loaded up into his car while Valance stood her ground and watched him. Then she checked her watch. "If we hurry, we can get some coffee at the V Mart before it closes."

Green nodded and followed her into their car, but after

the hostilities he'd just witnessed, which carried an air of deep historical significance on their shoulders, he was more in the mood for chamomile than caffeine.

One thing was for certain, though. So long as Felps was on the Fang 900s, the docile version of Green's former FTO wouldn't be. Scary-ass Valance was back.

CHAPTER THIRTEEN

Another week had passed, and Valance hadn't heard any good news from Ursula Owiti. Jordan was officially a missing person.

Green tried not to think about what might have happened to the kid, whose youthful, spirited face had made it onto the front page of the *Kilhaven Tribune* three days in a row.

His only consolation was that both the boy's parents were werewolves. So, barring any rogue recessive genes, Jordan stood almost zero chance of being a human. And by all standards, it indicated that vampires would have no interest in him. They couldn't turn weres, not even those yet to have their first shift.

That didn't mean the teen *wasn't* in serious trouble; it meant that he wasn't in the specific kind of serious trouble Green knew about.

And if the teen was still alive, he had a huge survival advantage: press coverage. That was due, in no small part, to the fact that he was a Crown Tree boy. Omar Owiti, his father, had made it big in real estate and ran a high-profile charity for wayward teen weres and shifters whose parents had kicked them out of the house upon learning of their adult forms—a practice not uncommon for human parents to do when two unknown and undesirable recessive genes got together in their offspring. Ursula Owiti was on Moon Cathedral's board of directors and had enjoyed a successful career as a personal injury attorney before she'd retired four years ago to spend time with her young kids. All this Green had learned from the news, which he'd followed closely on this particular story.

Of course, every second or third reported fact could be wrong, and he wouldn't be surprised. As someone who had been on the wrong end of the news himself, he knew reporters could get away with roughly the same batting average as mediocre baseball players and keep their jobs.

The coverage had done a good job of distracting him from the less desirable aspects of his life lately, namely the fact that the curse still lingered, there was no hearing date set for reversing it, and he'd come to dread his shifts for the sheer dullness of them.

"Can I ask you something without you getting mad?" Green said from his post riding shotgun while they were stopped at a light. The red glow of it filled the dark cab. He'd spent the last ten minutes eating a large order of french fries, one by one, as a means of entertaining himself. It was a Friday night, and all the calls that had appeared on the HAM were already on the verge of disaster without Valance and him dragging bad luck into it.

"You can try," she said idly, watching a homeless man push a shopping cart full of trash past them on the crosswalk. The man looked straight into one of their headlights as he passed, jerked back, shielding his eyes, then began yelling incoherently at their hood.

"Is there a particular reason we've stayed within this particular neighborhood for the last week?"

The light changed, and she turned left. "I have no idea what you're talking about."

"We've done nothing but take calls in Underwood Heights all week. Now, if we were prowling Crown Tree, that would make sense. But Underwood Heights?"

"I repeat," she said, "I have no idea what you're talking about."

"You know something I don't," he said. "And I—"

She sighed, and even her sighs carried a finality that could cut him off mid-sentence. "I know a lot you don't, Rookie. No point pouting."

"I mean *specifically*. You know something, and I think it's got to do with the Owiti case, and I think I deserve to know. We both know that if you go down, I'm going down too. You owe me the full truth here. I think I earned that much when I went all kamikaze in Spinner's office for you."

She spared him a glance. "You're right."

A chill ran down his spine.

"I owe you," she said. "And slinking around here like a couple of lazy veterans counting down the hours until retirement isn't doing you any favors." She flicked through the mile-long cue of holding calls on the HAM and tapped one, assigning them to it. "Let's go get into some trouble."

"That's not what I meant," he said, but he wasn't going to argue. Yes, Valance would drag him down with her, but he could blame her for this if it went south. *She was driving. I didn't have a choice.* And boy, was he ready for a little action.

But when he reviewed the call text transcribed from the telepaths at dispatch, he felt his high hopes sink. "Clown sighting?" he said incredulously. "You know there haven't been clowns on this continent since—" The rest of his words were drowned out by the siren. He sat back and bathed in the blue and red as Valance ran code all the way across the sector to the address listed while he finished the last of his fries.

When Green was little, and he'd heard police sirens in the distance, he'd imagined a cruiser accelerating through traffic, weaving and maneuvering at incredible speeds while civilian vehicles hurried out of the way, nearly colliding with each other to allow a mighty hero through.

But so much of that was wrong. At some point between then and now, people had unlearned how to get out of the way for an emergency vehicle. They cruised along, just as high or drunk as could be as if to say, "Yeah, get in line. We're all in the middle of an emergency. Life is a crisis."

Which meant, of course, that his imagining of the police cruiser speeding, or carrying on at any particularly urgent speed, was actually a rarity. At certain times of night, and if the emergency took place on a highway or desolate side-streets, sure. But mostly, running lights and sirens was an excruciating event wherein one's sense of urgency wasn't acknowledged, let alone respected, by a single living being in your vicinity.

To be fair, young Green also hadn't imagined that one of the valiant cops in an emergency vehicle would be suckling the grease from his fingers then subtly wiping them on his pants because the fast-food chain forgot—or maliciously neglected—to pack napkins in the bag.

Valance turned off the sirens but kept the lights as they

pulled into a quiet side street and approached the complex where the call had come from. He'd been to calls at Fortune Falls Apartments before, but it wasn't a place cops frequented. Not that there wasn't crime in the area, just that the types of crime—property theft, vandalism, and suspicious persons—tended to take a back seat to the gang fights, shillelagh assaults, and full-on family brawls taking place in other parts of Fang.

As he tried to puzzle out why Valance had assigned to this specific call, she pulled into the lot and parked in a spot outside Building 11.

A tall elf who appeared to be in her early twenties, but who the fuck even knew with their kind, was smoking a cigarette on her patio as they approached. When she spotted them, she stomped out the butt and flagged them down. "Hey," she said as if they were old friends. Her eyes were bloodshot, and Green tried to guess if she had allergies or was high. The casual tone indicated she might have smoked a joint before the cigarette. Then again, most of the elves he'd encountered maintained that nice, superior air, speaking to the cops like they were the long-overdue clean-up crew.

"Officer Heather Valance, and this is Officer Norman Green. You're the one who called in the clowns?"

"Yeah."

One of these, then. Wants help but doesn't want to lift a finger or even say more than a few words.

"And your name?"

"Aisling Corrigan."

"Can you tell us what happened, Ms. Corrigan?"

The elf folded her arms across her chest, kicked out her right foot, and sighed like this whole interaction was the cops' fault. "Sure. I was sitting on my patio, right here, and I heard something in the dark over there." She pointed, and Green followed her line of sight over to a small copse of trees that had been left in the middle of the parking lot and built around. There were four or five giant trees, one stone bench, and lots of shadows from various light sources that could trick the eye.

"They were on the bench when I saw them," she continued.

"And what were they doing?"

And now Aisling Corrigan didn't look so sure of herself. She mumbled something.

"Say that again?" Valance prompted. "Didn't catch it."

The elf ground her teeth before giving it another shot. "They were… engaged in an intimate encounter."

To Valance's credit, she just nodded and scribbled that down on her notepad. Green covertly snuck a peek and saw that she had written, "banging clowns." He shut his eyes to keep from making a face.

Valance looked up from her notes and tilted her head to the side as she asked, "Can you describe a little bit more of what you saw? I mean, were they lying on the bench, or sitting?"

"They were lying down, um, head to foot."

"Ah, okay." She scratched out "banging" and drew a two-digit number instead.

"I'm sure you know this is coming, Ms. Corrigan, so I hope you'll excuse me for going through our standard procedure. As you know, the government officially declared clowns extinct about fifty years ago, so when we do get reports of sightings, we take them very seriously."

"You want to know why I think they were clowns and not just pale humans or someone in costume."

"We also have frequent reports of clowns that turn out to be vampires, yes. You know how if a vampire goes too long without feeding, he can get those dark circles around his eyes. People often confuse those for the facial markings of clowns."

"It wasn't the faces," Aisling said. "I couldn't see those anyway. It was…" She rolled her eyes. "It was the feet. They were huge. Like, freakishly big. I only know one thing with feet that big."

Valance nodded. "Well, if they had been some kind of shifter, they could have been partially shifted. That's been known to happen during intercourse."

Aisling was clearly tired of her memory being questioned. She shifted her weight in a way that reminded him of a child stomping her foot. "What the hell kind of animal has large human-like feet?"

Valance remained calm as usual. "Could have been a dolphin-shifter. We're not that far from the gulf. The fins could easily look like large feet in this light." Just as the elf was about to snap back, Valance tucked her notepad away and said, "We'll go search the area. If it was really clowns, it might be better for you to wait inside. I'm sure you've heard the horror stories."

Aisling hugged herself tighter, lost some of the attitude, and stepped inside. As she closed the door behind her, Green's suspicions about the pot were confirmed with a thick whiff of it puffing out to meet his nose.

Only once they were crossing the lot toward the trees and well out of earshot of the building did Green speak. "What do you think it really is?"

Valance shook her head. "Anyone's guess. I have my doubts about the credibility of the witness."

"But she's an elf. They have great vision."

"They have great vision in the day. Their night vision is just as poor as yours. Maybe worse."

She paused at the bench, crouching by it before taking a few quick sniffs of the air. "Shit. Whoever she saw, really *was* doing what she described by the smell of it. And they were incredibly unwashed."

Green grimaced. "Homeless?"

"Sure, I'd go with that." She looked up. "Those woods across the street. Mind having a look while I sniff around here a little more? Whoever it is probably took off there once they knew they were spotted."

If clowns were even on the table as a possibility, which they *weren't*, he would've already had his gun out and by his side. While there hadn't been a slide on clowns in the academy, he'd heard the stories growing up just like everyone else.

Clowns were psychopaths, all of them. It was a miracle they hadn't wiped themselves out just through sheer demented evilness. They had multiple rows of teeth like sharks, and putrid green blood dripped from their eyes when they were preparing to attack. Their large feet slowed them down, but they proved useful in water. Clowns had been the only known bipedal amphibians before the government announced open season on them, and the War on Clowns announced official victory.

It had been a genocide, but not one the history books ever spoke of with any regret.

A shiver ran down his spine at the mere notion that two of those things could be creeping around in the overgrown woods ahead of him. But of course, it was impossible. He might as well have been worried about aliens. Clowns were such a part of the collective memory that they still existed in people's minds, but that was the only place they existed. The occasional reports of sightings all amounted to nothing, even if they did leave the officers who'd responded a little shaken up. That was just how scary the specter of the clown was.

So if it wasn't a pair of horny clowns that Aisling Corrigan had seen, what was it?

Valance had suggested vampires. If that was the case, maybe he *should* get his gun out. Maybe go grab a stake from the car, even.

Or perhaps there was a homeless camp out here that hadn't yet been inventoried. It could be a large one—some got that way, with generators and small tent shops for canned goods and, of course, brothels and opium dens—and if that were the case and he stumbled onto it, he might also want to have his gun in hand.

He stopped at the edge of the woods, his flashlight beam held in front of him, and freed his gun from his holster.

Tonight is not a night I shoot anyone.

A few deep breaths to ensure he wasn't feeling jumpy, then he stepped into the shadows of the trees.

A rabbit hopped across his path, and he was pleased to discover it didn't give him a start. Good. That was good. He crept on.

"Police. Just want to see if anyone's out here. You're not in trouble."

His voice didn't shake. Fantastic. Things were going exceptionally well so far. And if only he could stay in here for a few more minutes with nothing happening, then he could leave, claim he'd searched, and move on to something that wasn't taking place in a dark forest. And all before a wave of bad luck hit.

But then he heard the laughter. High, unbalanced, jackal-like. Not one, but two sources. And both close to him.

Green's light strobed across the trunks of the oak trees around him toward the source, but he saw nothing.

That laugh, though. It was unlike anything he'd ever heard. Did clowns laugh like that?

It's not clowns, you idiot. Get that out of your mind.

If that was off the table, then what in the hell *was* he dealing with?

He took control of his breathing again. "Police. My name's Officer Green. I'm just looking to see who's out here. There hasn't been a crime reported, so you're not in trouble." He decided not to mention that performing oral sex in public was illegal.

But there was silence now. No laugh. How long had he been out here? Was it long enough that he could say he'd tried?

You're a fucking police officer. Stop being a coward. Your duty is to neutralize threats. If there's something out here, you need to take care of it.

What was the threat, though, really? If it wasn't clowns, which of course it wasn't, then very likely a couple of hobos had been having a good time, realized they'd been spotted and taken off. Was that really a threat to anyone?

Yeah, this was pointless. Even if it *was* vampires having sex, what did he think he would do about it? Arrest them? A judge would have them out of jail before morning, and then he'd just have two vampires with a grudge against him. He *could* ticket them, maybe give them a warning.

He almost chuckled at the thought. If someone had told him ten years ago that he would be in a position to tell a vampire to not do as it pleased, he would have thought that person was a nutcase. He was just a human. Sure, he had a leg up on vampires in that he was allowed around schools, and telepaths couldn't read his mind, but outside of that, vampires won every other match-up.

It just showed how much perceived authority went for these days. Green put on a uniform, and suddenly he went from hunted to hunter. Just a flimsy few bits of fabric, a bullet-proof vest, and an occupational tool belt, and suddenly fewer things wanted to eat him.

Why more humans didn't become police officers, he didn't know. This wasn't why he'd signed up, but boy, was it a perk.

Yes, he'd been out in the woods long enough. The laugh had unnerved him, but he hadn't heard it again. Perhaps his theory about a homeless camp was correct, and he'd simply heard some opioid-induced laughter echoing from it.

He washed his light over the trees ahead of him a few more times, paying lip service to a search he was now convinced would be fruitless. Still nothing. And no sounds of movement, either.

But when he turned to walk back, the thing was waiting for him. It blocked his route to safety, and even before his flashlight lit it up, his instincts knew it was there. Almost as soon as the light found it, it slipped away quickly and quietly. His reflexes couldn't keep up, and he lost it in the darkness. "The fuck?"

Every hair stood up on his arms, and his heart seemed determined to escape his rib cage. He'd seen it clearly so briefly, but in that split second, there had been zero doubt in his mind of what he was looking at. But almost immediately after it'd disappeared, his rationality kicked down the door and shouted, "It couldn't have been a clown, you stupid motherfucker! Clowns aren't real!"

But… but…

The eyes. Red diamonds around flesh so pale it would have made corpses look alive by comparison. The bulbous ruby nose… the spindly fingers—had there been six on each hand? Something told him there had—and the large feet, like fleshy ivory flippers.

It had wanted to be seen, he was sure of it. Because the silent way it moved would have allowed it to stay out of sight if it'd wished, and he hadn't exactly been quiet about where he was.

The thing had *wanted* to be seen. By a police officer.

And now that he'd seen it…

He stumbled out of the woods.

No one will ever believe me.

Do I believe me?

It was a clown. I just saw it.

It couldn't have been a clown. People see the wrong thing every day.

If it *was* a clown, they really were psychopaths. Gaslighting psychopaths. They must know their mere appearance could make people question their sanity. And they delighted in it.

"Homeless camp?" Valance asked, striding over across the lot.

He looked up at her. "Huh?"

"I figure there was a homeless camp out— Whoa. You okay?"

He blinked and willed his expression to clear up. "Yeah, nothing out there."

"You hear that laughter?" she said, as they turned and headed back toward the apartment to update Aisling.

"You heard it too?" he said, a little too loudly.

"Yep. Sounded like a typical lunatic party around an unsafe bonfire," she said. "Reckon Kilhaven's brave firefighters might have their work cut out for them later. Don't mix open fires and meth, kids."

Should he even say it?

He debated the merits of telling her what he saw—no, what he *thought* he saw—during her interaction with the elf, wherein she assured the woman that no clowns had been spotted, but to always keep her door locked at night. Hollow reassurances.

Once they were back in the car, Valance shot Green another look. "You're not okay. What happened in the woods? Did you see something?"

He studied her face. Did she already know what he'd seen? Was she prodding him to say it?

A new thought occurred to him. If anyone was likely to believe he'd seen a clown, something the government had spent billions of dollars to convince the public that it had officially eliminated, wouldn't it be her? Valance loved a good conspiracy and claiming to see a clown was about as big of one as he could think of. It was a claim of the insane or the soon-to-be-declared insane. Clowns were supposed to be nothing but an epigenetic fear, an evil archetype through which other nebulous desires could take shape and present themselves in a physical form to the mentally unwell.

Maybe she would believe him if he said it. Maybe she'd taken this call because she knew there was truth to the sighting, and she wanted him to see the truth for himself. Maybe this was all just another test, and he would have to be the first one to speak of it.

"I did see something," he said. And as much as his heart had raced in the woods, it was now thrumming faster.

"What did you see?"

Her eyes narrowed on him now, and he was sure she knew what he was about to say. Perhaps she was even hoping he'd say it.

"I think you know what I saw."

"I have no clue what you saw. Just tell me, Green. Spit it out."

"A clown. I saw a clown."

A slight upward tick of her lips at the edges and he thought it was satisfaction before her mouth broke into a full smirk, and she leaned back in her seat. "Cute. But as we all know, the Commander in Chief of our beloved armed forces declared victory in the War on Clowns ages ago." She scrolled through the holding calls on the HAM and selected one with the call text *Mother says son refuses to leave bedroom. Holding car keys hostage.* "You didn't see a clown, Green. You might as well put it out of your mind. Those kinds of ideas will do you no good."

CHAPTER FOURTEEN_

Over the weekend, Green succeeded in battering his impossible memory of the clown with enough self-doubt to almost entirely eradicate it from his mind. He hadn't seen what he'd thought he had, plain and simple. Instead, he saw a homeless man, possibly dolphin-shifter, sneaking around the woods after having engaged in indecent behavior with a female in public. It's what he'd put in his report at Valance's gentle prompting, and what he would now consider his reality.

When he presented it in those terms, the call wasn't all that remarkable.

The only thing that made it stand out from any other call they'd responded to in the last week or so was that it *hadn't* taken place in the Underwood Heights neighborhood.

...Where they were prowling once again tonight. Green snuck a glance at Valance as she licked her thumb then used it to scrub at something white on the steering wheel. She had something planned, and he had no idea what. Which was probably just as well since he couldn't have stopped her anyway. So long as he kept himself from ruminating over it and becoming neurotic, his ignorance might save him some suffering.

Underwood Heights was a wholly forgettable neighborhood. It had an established look with green front yards containing thick elms and ancient oaks towering over small one-story homes, and a quarter of the houses appeared in danger of being condemned. But Green had learned that the cause of a house in such disrepair could vary widely. These ramshackle homes weren't heroin dens. And they weren't even unoccupied. The owners were still there, albeit generally in spirit form.

There was a high concentration of elderly in the neighborhood, many of whom had lived beside the same neighbors for generations, making it tempting to stick around even after they passed. Such presences were allowed to remain under a few strongly worded legislative bills. As a result, Underwood Heights was sleepy, benignly haunted as hell, and low on violent crime. Even the punk kids with too many changing hormones and not enough parental supervision knew that when you walked down the streets of this neighborhood, someone was always watching. And spirits of the newly deceased made surprisingly good witnesses once you could get them to stop talking through all of the grudges that kept them earthbound.

Taking the entirety of Fang into consideration, and excluding the anomalous Crown Tree neighborhood, Underwood Heights was one of the best places to live in the sector, and one of the most expensive. The joke around town was that the high concentration of ghosts meant the area was always a few degrees cooler in the summer, but

Green supposed that was a legend started by savvy real estate agents.

He didn't buy Valance's claim that they were prowling it like predators because it kept them out of trouble while the curse was in full swing. It was a convenient enough lie to sell Sergeant Montoya, sure, but the were-bison wasn't exposed to the presence of Officer Valance day in and day out in the emotional pressure cooker of their car; the sarge was oblivious to the waves of aggression radiating from her without her even needing to speak a single word.

And when those thoughts swirling in her mind did manifest verbally, she sounded calm and collected, not boiling below the surface. Which was, of course, an extra terrifying experience. They said still waters ran deep, but Green knew that Valance's still waters not only ran deep, but there was a murderous kraken and an endless whirlpool waiting just below the surface.

While he'd succeeded in blocking out thoughts of the clown (*it wasn't a clown!*), he hadn't forgotten the confrontation between her and Detective Felps outside the home of Jordan Owiti. He hadn't forgotten that she was a loaded gun, even if she was temporarily holstered in this dull neighborhood.

"This looks promising," she said, poking at the HAM. Green read off the text. Sure enough, the address was in Underwood Heights, just a few streets over, and the call text said *Man run over by car. Likely deceased.*

So, it may have been a sleepy neighborhood, but nowhere was truly safe from stupid.

"Promising?" Green said. "Promising for who? Doesn't look very promising for him."

"Promising for us to have something to keep us occupied so I don't lose my fucking mind in this cruiser."

"Fair point. Let's go."

"Already am, Rookie."

She pulled a U-turn and put on her lights. It was nearly 3 a.m., and the streets were empty; the siren wouldn't be necessary now except for a few little bleeps at intersections. That she didn't turn it on anyway hinted that she was in a relatively good mood and didn't need to passive-aggressively wake up every single person in a mile radius just to cheer herself up. He took it as a good omen.

When they pulled onto the street, it was immediately obvious where the incident had taken place. A group was gathered in the front yard in a tableau of shock and grief. One woman was on her knees, held tightly by a burly man in a sleeveless tee. Two more men looked seconds from going to blows were it not for a tiny woman with the biggest hair Green had ever seen on someone so white doing her best to stay between them.

Valance gave them a *blip-blip* to announce the cops' presence, and the two amped-up men backed off.

Green was the first one out of the car and hurried over to the small group. "Everyone step back from the bo-OO"—his eyes found the decapitated corpse. "From the body." He refrained from adding, "and the head, too," even though it was so clearly separated from the body that a smart lawyer could make a strong argument that it hadn't been included in Green's orders.

Valance was there, barking at the muscular man comforting the women, "Sir. Get her away from here. She doesn't need to keep looking at this."

The scene was confusingly ugly. Something awful had led

to the victim's beheading, and the mountain of questions they'd be required to summit before getting into any useful investigative work was daunting.

Among the group, Green thought he could pick out shifter and human, but he couldn't tell who was who, and the deceased was emitting a variety of other smells that masked his natural odor.

He put his flashlight on the body. Shapeshifters and weres were known to partially shift immediately postmortem, but all the hair on the limbs looked human. No signs of animal parts.

The petite woman with big hair was the first one to step up and start talking. "We just found him this way."

That proclamation usually hauled on its back a knapsack of guilt and bullshit, but this time it rang true.

"Tell me what happened." Valance took out her notepad while Green took another look at the victim. The man was pale. Not like dead guys usually were, but like another corpse he'd seen so long ago in a disgusting, blood-covered trailer in Shady Grove.

There was a set of tire tracks that seemed to hop the curb, cut through the grassy lawn, and pass right over the victim's neck before tracking dirt and grass across the driveway and back into the road.

Now, how in the hell was *that* supposed to work? Had the vic been sleeping on his lawn? Had a drunk driver simply picked the very worst time to veer off the street and into a yard?

Of course not. Perhaps it was a crime of opportunity. The driver of the vehicle was just your standard psychopath, and he or she noticed a man passed out on a lawn and thought, *I bet I could get away with murder.*

But also... no. Not that that sort of thing never happened, but there was one main problem with both of those scenarios. Something important was missing from this scene...

He called in backup and then went to join Valance for the interview. The men who had almost gone to blows were now civilly coexisting, both leaning against a white truck on lifts that gleamed in the street light on the other opposite side of the road. Valance must have told them to back the hell away from the scene if they didn't want to be implicated. Both appeared humbled as they folded their arms across their chest, and only now did Green see the obvious resemblance. No doubt cousins, if not brothers.

"It was the headlights that woke me up," the woman said.

Valance nodded. "And did by any chance see what kind of vehicle it was, Ms. Obst?"

"No, ma'am. It was gone by the time I got dressed and came out."

"And you said he lives in which house?"

Ms. Obst turned and pointed across the street and one over. "That was his wife out here wailing. I didn't want her to come out, but I screamed when I saw it and..."

"I don't blame you. This isn't a pleasant thing to find on your lawn in the middle of the night."

A grim laugh escaped the interviewee.

Once the initial interview was wrapped, and Valance had requested that everyone stick around the scene, she walked with Green over to the body.

"Vic is human?" he asked.

"Yep." She leaned over it. "What's your take?"

"I don't think he's gonna make it."

She shot him a surprised look of approval. "Tire marks on the neck." She pointed with her pen. "Whoever did this was at least thorough." She sighed and straightened up again. "My biggest question is, what kind of idiots does the murderer take us for?"

"I wondered the same thing when I realized what was missing from this scene."

"Blood," she said without missing a beat. "The corpse was bloodless before it was run over. For fuck's sake." She clicked her pen and stuck it in her breast pocket. "Although it could be entertaining to see how the department explains *this* one away. Take pictures, Green. Lots of them. And do it before the others show up, and don't delete them from your camera, even once you've uploaded them to evidence. I have a sneaking suspicion that a lot of the visual evidence from this one might mysteriously go missing when it comes time for the medical examiner to rule on the cause of death."

He did so without another word because he'd had that same feeling, too.

There was no way around it. The cause of death hadn't been the tire that had separated the man's head from his body. Because the vic was already bloodless when he'd been laid in the lawn. It was staged to dispose of a body, and there was only one way for all the blood to be removed from a human. It had to be sucked out.

"That's it for today's BOLOs," Sergeant Montoya said from his spot by the projector screen at show-up the following morning. "But I do want to mention one more thing..."

Green leaned against the back wall with Valance and

Bannockburn, all of whom were cradling coffee like it was life-saving ambrosia after a late morning on scene of the so-called hit-and-run.

While Green hadn't yet spoken with Bannockburn about the blindingly obvious cause of death, he'd seen Valance and Bannockburn speaking in low tones while Crime Scene cordoned off the yard. Bannockburn was aware of their theory.

Green perked up at Montoya's announcement. The sarge never just mentioned one more thing. He either had a commendation to bestow or a reprimand to slap on someone.

"I don't know if any of you have read the *Kilhaven Tribune* this morning, but it included coverage on last night's unsolved murder."

Valance muttered, "Not *that* unsolved," but Montoya didn't seem to notice.

"I understand that the elves have a way of finding out details, or simply guessing at them when it comes to police activities. No one is a bigger proponent of police accountability than I am." He paused to let the rich aroma of that bullshit waft through the room. "But there is a line in this particular article that disturbs me." He grabbed the paper from the top of his stack. It was already turned and folded so the article in question was ready to go. "And it reads, 'This is but one instance in a growing string of vampire attacks and abductions in Kilhaven in recent months.'" He flapped the newspaper back onto the table and looked up at his shift. "Now, there's a chance that the reporter who wrote this is just talking out of his ass. Anyone who's been unfortunate enough to have a call make the news knows that's standard procedure for these guys.

But if I find out that anyone on my shift is talking to the press, feeding them theories and conspiracies—"

For a startling moment, Green thought the sergeant was staring directly at him. Then he realized the piercing gaze was directed just to his right.

"No clue why you're looking at me, Sarge," Valance said. "I assume that if you really thought I was doing something that egregious, you'd come to speak to me in private. That seems like the courageous thing a leader would do."

"I'm not singling you out, Officer Valance. But now that you mention it, you do seem a little on the defensive."

She pushed off the wall so she was fully on her feet, and as a survival instinct, Green did the same.

"Oh, fuck off. You know I hate the media elves more than anyone on this shift. I wouldn't cozy up to those feckless weasels if it was the only way to save my life."

While Montoya didn't appear especially pleased with her telling him to fuck off, he did seem to accept her explanation. He looked about to move on, but Valance wasn't done.

"If you want to look for a leak, go talk to the M.E. We all know he's been paid off for years to proclaim whatever the mayor wants for suspicious deaths. And if someone can be paid off, then they're fair game for everyone. Now, if you don't have plans to turn IA loose on the Fang 900s, I'd love to get out on the street to do my thankless job of serving and protecting, sir."

The sergeant appeared to be suffering from a sudden onset of lockjaw. And from his post by the door, Detective Felps observed the interaction with keen interest.

Before Montoya could properly address her response, Valance was already making for the hall.

The rest of them watched her go before the corporal addressed his sergeant. "That was completely out of line. I'll handle her, sir. You shouldn't have to explain to her why she doesn't get to talk to you that way."

Montoya nodded and waved for the rest of the shift to take off. They complied quickly, quietly, and gratefully.

But when Green found Valance and Bannockburn in the lot, there didn't seem to be much reprimanding going on. At least not directed at Valance.

Instead, the two were leaning against the hood of an SUV, arms crossed, staring at Green as he approached. He paused. Wait, was *he* in trouble?

Relax. You haven't done anything wrong. Just don't accidentally call them Mom and Dad, and you'll be fine.

Felps was loading up an SUV one spot over when Green reached the two unhappy officers. "A word, Green?" Bannockburn said, though the question was entirely unnecessary. It was clear they'd be having a word with him whether he wanted it or not. In fact, just by asking it, the corporal was having a word with him…

"Yes, sir."

They waited until he was close and then stepped even closer. "Was it you?" Valance asked.

He took a quick half-step back. "What?"

"Are you the leak, Rookie? Are you talking to the press?"

With great restraint, he kept from looking over his shoulder to see if Felps had overheard that damning accusation. "Of course I'm not," he hissed. "What the hell?"

Bannockburn's dark eyes bored into him. "Montoya wouldn't have mentioned it if he didn't have good reason to believe someone on this shift is the one feeding conspiracies to the elves."

"I didn't do it! I *wouldn't* do it! Why would I even want to?"

Valance and Bannockburn exchanged a look, and then each stepped back. "Yeah, okay," the corporal said on a deep exhale.

"I told you it wasn't him," Valance said. "He's loyal if nothing else."

Green glared at her for the backhanded compliment.

"Well, it was *someone* on this shift," Bannockburn added. "For what it's worth, I'm glad it's not you."

"Yeah," Green said, "me too. Jesus."

"But now we got another problem," murmured Bannockburn. "We have a mole in the shift, and we don't know who it is."

CHAPTER FIFTEEN

Brooks' voice crackled loudly over the radio. "Fang 9-02 to Fang 9-01. Requesting backup on a domestic. Aggressor is a vet, and I could use another one over here to mediate."

Valance grinned. "That's my cue."

Green would have protested, after all, this was already a volatile situation without adding in the curse to the mix, but the waves of it rarely occurred less than a few hours apart. They'd just passed through one half an hour before. Valance had pulled into a big-box store parking lot to wait it out in a dark corner. A flock of grackles had, once again, painted the car with their shit to the point where a good defense attorney could have argued that it no longer had the proper markings to function in a law enforcement capacity.

At the very least, they likely had another hour and a half until the first inklings of bad luck started to kick in, and that might be enough time to help out at this call.

The front door of the small midcentury home was already wide open when they arrived only a few minutes later, so Green and Valance hurried in toward the source of the shouting and sobbing.

A male werewolf was in cuffs, sitting cross-legged on the living room floor, shouting his head off. Green couldn't make out any particular words coming from the man. He knew there was no point in trying; there was a certain tone or pitch that always accompanied an incoherent rant, and Green's ears had become attuned to it already.

The sobbing, meanwhile, was coming from a room on the far end of the house.

Aliyah Brooks and Tara Marrow were the two officers already on scene. Since Brooks was standing over the aggressor, Marrow must be in with the scared and hysterical victim.

The relief on Brooks' face when she spotted Valance was unmistakable. "Look, Mr. Herrera, this if Officer Valance. She served in South America, too."

But whatever positive effect Brooks had expected this to have on his nerves was misguided. Because while the mustached Herrera did stop his shouting, something eerier happened instead. He stared across the living room at Valance, his eyes wide. "La Tunda," he breathed.

All Valance got out was, "Oh shit," before things took a turn for the chaotic.

Seizing upon a moment of neglect by his attending officer, Herrera slipped free. Brooks reached for him and came up empty-handed. He lunged across the room and managed to grasp in his cuffed hands a single unremarkable red brick on a small display stand near his television. He spun and shot-put the brick straight at Green and Valance. Both managed to duck, leaving the projectile free to shatter the full-length mirror hung directly behind them.

Green flinched and whirled toward the source of the crackle, and before his very eyes, the place on the wall where the mirror had been gained dimension.

And a second after that, it started *sucking*.

In the confusion, Mr. Herrera made a break for it, sprinting toward the newly opened inter-dimensional portal. Though Green knew he risked his own ass if this interception carried him too far in the wrong direction, he really didn't have a choice. The suspect would get away, and it was explicitly against protocol for officers to follow *anyone* for *any reason* into another dimension.

One-two-three steps, and then Green lowered and leaped, smashing into the fleeing abuser. As the two of them went to the ground, Green felt something sharp slice his cheek on its soaring path across the dining room and into the newly opened vacuum.

"I won't let her take me!" Mr. Herrera shouted as he squirmed underneath Green.

"Stop resisting!"

"I know what she does to them!"

"Stop! Resisting!"

A table lamp made a beeline past them and into the yawning chasm, disappearing from sight into the swirling vortex.

Finally managing to pin the suspect to the dirty shag carpeting with his body, Green whipped his head around to get his bearings.

Brooks scrambled around, trying to hold things in place, while also calling for backup. Valance shouted down the hall for Marrow to get the victim out of the house and as far away as possible.

Wait. Hadn't he heard a case study about this in the academy?

"Was that a scrying mirror?" he demanded.

Herrera tried to respond, but his words were muffled by the carpet and overpowered by the rushing wind of the giant suck.

"Speak up! Is that a scrying mirror?" A glass bong soared out of nowhere, clipping Green on the shoulder as it passed and leaving him with a sudden and nauseating whiff of charred bud.

"Of course it is!"

"And that brick?"

"Aztec."

Just as he'd expected.

He hollered to Brooks to come to take over for him. She was glad to oblige, giving Herrera an unnecessary elbow between the shoulder blades as she lowered herself onto him and out of the winds.

Green crawled toward the portal, worried that going bipedal might make him lose his balance.

The edges of the mirror's frame now wobbled as if warped by intense heat, but there wasn't any coming off it. Would this work? If it was what he thought it was, it should be a simple fix. He set one palm against the outside of the frame, but as he reached across the sucking hole, hoping to get ahold of the other edge to pinch them together in the middle, the force of the winds proved too strong, and his left hand up to the mid-forearm was sucked into the chasm. It disappeared from his view, though he could still feel it connected to the rest, could still move his fingers.

But when he did, his fingers touched something. It was warm, hairy, possibly wet, though he couldn't be sure about that bit. He *was* certain, though, that whatever he was touching was trying to pull his fingers farther inside it.

He suppressed a retch, tried not to let his imagination run away with him, and with a single great effort, tugged his arm loose from the portal. A dark brown liquid that looked and smelled like both motor oil and feces coated his hand, but at least he still had a hand.

It was clear now that he would need help.

He hollered to Valance as books from the shelf finally shook loose and started a steady flow into the portal. On his third attempt, she actually heard him. He waved her over and told her to stop before crossing in front of the danger. Miming as best he could, he put his hands on the outside of the frame and indicated pushing it inward toward the center. She narrowed her eyes at him like he was insane before she finally nodded.

There was almost no resistance, as if Nature herself was relieved to shut off the ungodly chasm forever. They pushed the sides of the frame together, and the doorway between dimensions narrowed, narrowed, narrowed, and then blinked out.

The house became oppressively quiet until Herrera wailed again. "Don't let her take me!"

"Trust me," Valance said, "I have no desire to spend the next three hours taking you down to jail and booking you. We don't usually take requests, but I think Officer Brooks would be happy to accompany an abuser like you downtown."

"My pleasure," Brooks said, stiffly getting to her feet and dragging the cuffed suspect up along with her.

Once he was clear of the house, it was just Valance and

Green remaining, and he looked around at the mess. "We're not responsible for—"

"Fuck no. Let's get out of here."

As they entered into the open air, backup was just arriving.

"What the hell happened?" Detective Felps shut the SUV's door and blinked stupidly. His mouth hung open as he stared at the front of the house. Green followed his gaze and found that the portal must have sucked in more than one direction. The facade had a huge hole in it, no doubt directly opposite where the scrying mirror had hung, with missing bricks, dented pipes, and exposed and broken wires. He wondered if enough structural damage had occurred that the house would collapse before sunrise.

Valance followed the detective's gaze, too, and shrugged. "I think it was like that when we got here." She strolled right past him as he approached and hopped into their vehicle without another word.

Green's adrenaline was crashing fast. "Suspect tried to escape."

Felps stopped a yard shy of the rookie, his fists on his hips as he continued to inspect the damage with a curious expression. "He... tried to escape through the wall?"

"No. Well, yes, but also no. Inter-dimensional portal."

The vampire's eyes shot open. "An inter-dimensional portal was open? *Here?*"

"Yeah."

"But... what happened? How are any of you alive?"

"What happened was he threw an ancient Aztec brick through scrying mirror. The thing popped open, and he tried to escape." His mind returned to the warm, hairy mass he felt waiting on the other side of the portal. "Thankfully, he didn't make it through."

The reality of the situation appeared to be settling in on Felps like a fine mist. "How did you all manage to shut it? I've only ever seen magicians pull off that feat."

"We just pushed it shut from the sides."

"You... pushed it shut from the sides?"

That's what I said, didn't I? "Yes."

"Did Officer Valance tell you to do that?"

"He told me." Valance had reappeared. While Green suspected it was because she didn't trust him to handle a one-on-one with the detective without spilling something incriminating, he didn't mind her interruption. "I didn't have the first fucking clue how to close something like that. My first thought was to let Fire handle it. Green was the one who told me what to do."

"Huh." Felps narrowed his eyes at the rookie, but his lips remained slightly parted. "How'd you know how to do that?"

"I just read about it, sir."

Felps looked to Valance and said, "I'll be damned. He read about it." He clapped Green on the shoulder. "Great work. You might've saved a lot of lives. I'll be sure to let the commander know."

The detective excused himself and called for the city to come and handle some of the loose, dangling wires.

The firm contact of the pat in his shoulder remained fresh and tingling.

"He'll tell the commander about it," Valance grumbled. "As if all anyone wants is to get on the good side of leadership."

But as they walked back to their vehicle to type up the

report, Green couldn't help but feel like it might be a nice change to be on the right side of the people in power.

———

No commendation came for Green's timely tackle of the suspect or his quick thinking to close the inter-dimensional portal. However, a department-wide memo circulated the day after the situation with an official procedure for any scenario in which a scrying mirror is shattered by a powerful ancient artifact, and a big sucking hole into a frightening parallel reality splits open. Green let the knowledge that he had helped raise awareness be his reward.

Still, he wouldn't have minded an official commendation. There remained a chance he might get one—word could move slowly through the proper channels for anything that sounded relatively like "good news"—and a slim, albeit delicious, chance that he could end up on the list of officers invited to the end-of-year awards banquet. A metal for bravery would definitely get him laid, and he would take whatever he could to claw his way out of this dry spell.

But that was months and months away. For now, Green would continue his boring, cursed nighttime patrol rounds.

As he scrolled through the waiting calls, the occasional radio chatter the only thing helping him demarcate time on another slow and unproductive night alongside Heather Valance, his eyes spotted a line of call text that triggered a raw memory.

Suspect fled after ejecting bunnies from pants.

"It's him!"

Valance turned the steering wheel lazily as they took a right on red. "Who?"

"Trombolo the Tremendous. The magician that got away at the shipyard. You were on leave, but—"

"Say no more, I love a grudge arrest. What's the address?"

He read it off to her. "Looks like this guy was violating the gas station's trespass notice. When the clerk confronted him, he released the bunnies and got away."

"Typical magician bullshit. Why we haven't been given the go-ahead to send them the way of the clowns, I'll never know."

Green decided not to believe that she was genuinely calling for another genocide, and he also decided not to let thoughts of clowns take up residence in his adrenal glands.

That bastard had humiliated him out on the shipping docks, and it was time to clean up his mistake. He needed a clear mind if he stood a chance of making things better rather than substantially worse.

"Fang 9-01 calling all units. Anyone have eyes on the magician over near East Pineal?"

Valance slowed and whooped her siren in warning before running a red light.

Please don't let the bad luck hit, please don't let the bad luck hit...

Was there bad luck for the timing of the bad luck, or was that part random? He couldn't tell, mostly because bad luck always seemed to hit at the worst times. But then again, it was always a bad time when bad luck hit.

The engine hummed disapprovingly when Valance found an empty straightaway and stomped the accelerator.

"*Fang 9-13 to 01,*" came Officer Lawrence's voice. "*I just saw him vanish into a phone booth on 32nd Street.*"

"Confirm, 13," Valance replied, "you no longer have eyes on him?"

"He vanished on m— Nope, there he is. He just reappeared on top of the Western Bank building at 32nd and Broadstone."

They were almost in the neighborhood when Corporal Bannockburn's voice came in over the radio. *"Fang 9-80. Suspect is walking an invisible tightrope from the top of the bank across 32nd street to the roof of Luxe Nails. I have eyes on him, and he does appear to be armed with a wand."*

Valance turned onto 32nd Street, five blocks down from the intersection where the nail salon was located.

"I see him," Green said, pointing at a tiny figure suspended in midair. At this late hour, all the stores were already closed with the exception of a dingy pub that their vehicle blew right past. It was a commercial district, but unlike most of those in Fang, people actually shopped at this one.

Despite the red and blue lights hacking through the darkness, a man stepped into the road from behind a street-parked vehicle, and Valance had to swerve to keep from hitting him. A string of expletives followed, but Green hardly noticed. He was too engrossed in the magical walk taking place, now just a few hundred feet from him in midair.

Did the suspect have a tightrope somehow hidden up there, or was this truly magic? That was always the question in one's mind, wasn't it?

They pulled up below him just as one of the suspect's feet didn't land right. Valance slammed on the brakes as the magician wobbled thirty feet above them. Green had his door open in a second and was on his feet and ready.

Arms flailing, Trombolo the Tremendous emitted a

strange unsteady moan of fear. Then something shook loose from the cuff of his pants.

The white of the fur stood out starkly against the dark sky, and Green rushed forward the catch it. He lunged and felt the fluffy thing land safely in his hands. While he was relieved, he knew better than to relax. Because where there was one pantsbunny, there would be more. He tossed the little puffball into the grass by the sidewalk and looked up just in time to catch the second one tumbling toward the asphalt.

"Valance! I'm gonna need more hands."

She tossed into her shoulder radio, "9-01. Need more backup beneath the suspect. He's raining bunnies." Then she ran forward to help.

Green was so focused on catching one bunny after another that he didn't even notice Bannockburn and Lawrence until they were right next to him, also fully occupied catching bunnies.

Meanwhile, the suspect had regained his balance overhead but seemed to enjoy shaking animals loose from his breeches as a means of distraction or perhaps simple entertainment.

"Shit," Valance muttered as she tried to empty her arms of the wiggling bunnies. "It's misdirection! He's misdirecting us! Forget the bunnies."

"Ha-*ha!*" the magician declared.

Green caught a few more, but now that the suspect knew they were onto his tricks, he shut off the bunny faucet and finished his perilous crossing. Green remained behind with Lawrence to catch the last few and set them on the sidewalk before hurrying after the others.

But this wouldn't do. They were pursuing him on foot? That would never work with a magician.

Green paused, lagging behind while Valance kicked open the door to the nail salon and proceeded inside. Bannockburn and Lawrence split up, each hustling around the outside of the building to the back, no doubt looking for a fire escape onto the roof. *Think, Norman. Think! If he disappears, where will he reappear?*

The answer came to him in a flash-bang.

The suspect would appear somewhere dazzling. Ta-dah!

Green looked around. When the magician had disappeared from the phone booth just a few minutes prior, he'd reappeared on top of the tallest building on this street. Magicians may be obnoxious creatures, but they had a flare for the dramatic. They were entertainers at heart.

He scanned the darkened block for the showiest place to appear. It would be a gamble, and if he was wrong, he would be making himself completely useless. But if he was right…

His eyes landed on a small park at the end of 32nd street. It was poorly lit aside from the fountain, which glittered in the lights from below and the moon above. At the center of the fountain was a tribute to a local war legend, Harver the Hairy. The werewolf was reported to have killed three of his own pack to defend an innocent female vampire from their unsavory clutches. Valance would call that being a traitor, but Kilhaven thought it was admirable.

Green really didn't give a shit either way. Both vampires and werewolves had murdered untold numbers of humans in the war, and no one bothered to total all *those* deaths for public consumption.

But if the suspect was going to appear anywhere along

this street, that would be a great place to do it. The largest bronze statue in the center depicted Harver the Hairy pulling the vampiress close against his body in an erotic embrace—legend had it that she'd been so grateful for the rescue that she'd seduced Harver immediately following the encounter. This strange detail that had always made Green question if Harver hadn't simply murdered his kin to be able to rape her all by himself. And to the side of that statue, a saddled stallion reared up in a victorious whinny. (Green had recently learned that the stallion's intimidating penis pointed east to welcome each new dawn, though he failed to grasp why that was a significant part of the scene.)

That was it. The stallion. The perfect place for a big reveal.

But as soon as he was hidden behind the hedges surrounding the fountain, his brain began pummeling him with how stupid this was and how much everyone would make fun of him if this didn't pan out.

But if it did…

That thought kept him crouched, his Taser aimed right at the air above the horny stallion's saddle.

Minutes passed with the sounds of an active foot pursuit piping through the radio on his belt at irregular intervals. From what he could tell, the suspect wasn't looking to disappear; he was looking to outrun.

A loose bunny hopped up to him, and he petted it on the head for a moment, letting it sniff and nibble on some unidentified substance caked around the edge of his boot.

Then:

"Suspect vanished! I repeat!"

He silenced his radio, and a second later, a figure in a black satin cape appeared astride the stallion. The magician clearly thought he had a moment to get himself sorted out before the big reveal. As he tugged the corner of his cape free from underneath him so it could properly billow behind him, Green pulled the trigger.

The Taser struck beautifully, one barb planting itself in the side of the Trombolo the Tremendous's left glute while the other managed to miss the loose fabric and lodge itself in the flexing muscles just below the magician's left shoulder blade.

"GNUH!"

He went down and landed with a splash, and Green rushed forward. "Fang 9-07, subject subdued. I have him at the Harver the Hairy statue at the end of 32nd street."

After lugging the suspect free of the dirty water, Green slapped on the steel cuffs. Then, he went for the silvers and his spare pair of irons, unable to remember which of the three materials kept this sort from vanishing.

A small trail of curious white bunnies hopped after Lawrence and Valance as they emerged from between two brick shops and jogged over, their flashlights bobbing along the ground ahead of them.

Valance chuckled when she saw the soggy suspect, his clothes sticking to him so that there was nowhere left to hide any more surprises.

And yet two more hopped free from the left leg of his trousers to join their friends.

"How in the hell did you catch him?" Lawrence demanded, breathing heavily, a splash of the amorous pink of exertion highlighting his defined jawlines in the moonlight.

"I was waiting for him."

"Great work," Valance said, shocking both of her male

shift mates. "I guess when you have no physical advantages, you gotta get smart." Then she added, "Did you get his wand?"

"Oh shit."

"Jesus," she said, lunging forward and smack-frisking the suspect until she found it in his coat pocket and wrenched it free. "I take back everything positive I just said."

She inspected the wand in her hand for a moment, then addressed the magician. "I need you to empty out your shirt."

"I have nothing up my sleeves!"

"Sure." She tapped the end of the wand to the magician's midsection. Bags upon bags of chips and candy poured from his coat sleeves, forcing their way out despite the three sets of cuffs he wore.

As much as Green wanted to be the one to book him, he felt something start to wake up inside him. "Valance?"

"Yeah, I feel it, too. Lawrence, you're on. We gotta split before our curse attracts hawks, and this bunny party turns into a bloodbath."

Green shivered. "Can you imagine the car after hawks got done with it?"

She shook her head. "I'd rather not."

They passed Bannockburn on their way out. He was winded and trying not to be, sucking in air through fully flared nostrils.

"Green caught the guy, but our luck's about to run out."

"Green... caught him? How?"

Valance laughed. "I'm starting to suspect the rookie might have a brain in that skull of his."

CHAPTER SIXTEEN

Norman Green wasn't sure if this was the first time his shift had held this kind of get-together or if it was a somewhat regular occurrence, and he'd simply never been invited before.

He pushed open the heavy door of the Bear & Wolf and looked around for a face he recognized.

The pub was one of those places that looked much bigger inside than it did outside, and the wooden tables and booths were arranged in a horseshoe shape around the bar, which was clearly the main event.

It was crowded, which was no surprise on a Thursday night, but he managed to pinpoint his shift mates based on noise alone. They occupied a booth and spilled over into the neighboring table by the dartboard, where Jeremy Lawrence was yelling in frustration as Aliyah Brooks did a victory dance.

They do look awfully comfortable. I guess they do this all the time. Did they just invite me out of pity?

The voice inside him that insisted he didn't belong, and never would, spoke in the affirmative.

He mentally swatted it away, though. Not these people. Not the men and women he worked beside every day. Sure, he and Jeremy might never become best friends, but they'd been through a shooting together. Jeremy, along with Aliyah, had saved his ass from experiencing a horrifying IA investigation all by his lonesome when they fired their weapons after the suspect was clearly down. Both had made that decision independently, and he couldn't forget it.

Petty stuff, he thought, as he went ahead and ordered himself a pint. None of that mattered when stronger bonds were tying them all together.

"Uh-oh, fun's over," Jeremy announced dramatically when he spotted Green approaching.

It's just an overused joke. You're not really spoiling the party.

Brooks swatted Lawrence on the chest. "You kidding me? This is the man of the fucking hour! He's saved each of our asses this week." She met him halfway and slung an arm around his shoulders. "I saved you a seat."

"That's my seat, asshole," Lawrence said.

Green didn't take a seat but said hello to his other shift mates.

Valance was on the far end of the round booth, dressed casually with her dark hair flowing down past her shoulders —always terribly unsettling—and sipping a dark beer. Corporal Bannockburn was next to her, helping himself to a basket of fried pickles and ranch. On his other side was the righteous Patrick Harmon, who looked as if he was already regretting coming to a place like this. He'd have to drink extra blood at his Draculan service on Sunday to repent.

Space in the booth on the other side of Valance was

empty, but Tara Marrow appeared and filled it in. "Oh, good, I thought you might bail," she said.

"Detective Felps not gonna make it?" Green asked.

Valance huffed into her beer.

"Yeah, no," Marrow said quickly. "Mostly because he wasn't invited."

So they're okay with not inviting one person from the shift. Was that me before? Have I been that person?

Valance made a waving motion with her hand to Marrow. "Scoot. I gotta use the ladies' room."

Two hands wrapped around Green's upper arm, and he turned to find the smooth face of Brooks staring at him. "You like darts?"

"Don't let her trick you," Lawrence groused from his seat. "She's a shark. She'll destroy you."

"I won't put any money on it, then," Green said.

Brooks winked at him. "I knew you'd be up for it."

It occurred to him then that she might be flirting, and he remembered the one chance they almost had. Could tonight be the night? It *would* make working alongside her tricky afterward, but that was why it was called a "bad decision." Green had made and survived plenty of those, most of which hadn't held so much promise of a good time.

He decided to check back in on that in a few beers.

As Brooks set up the chalk scoreboard, Green's eyes fell on something across the room that jolted him before he knew why.

Valance was talking to someone. Another woman. And he recognized that woman.

Corporal Knox.

Well, former Corporal Knox. She'd been fired for reporting the vampire attack in Shady Grove.

Green looked over to Bannockburn and saw that he, too, was looking at the interaction, and he appeared equally as thrilled by it.

It wasn't a secret that Valance and Knox had remained friends after the firing, but something about the woman's reappearance here tonight felt… off. Was it the timing? The circumstance? He couldn't be sure.

Maybe she just wanted to come and see her old shift. Maybe it had nothing to do with Valance's pet project that would, in all likelihood, cost Green his job someday.

The two women made for the rest of the group, and Green turned toward the dartboard quickly to pretend he hadn't seen them.

Brooks was the first to call out. "I'll be damned!"

"Huh?" Green said, turning innocently. "Oh! It's Knox!"

All those sitting got to their feet and gleefully greeted their wayward leader.

Knox went through the line of old friends, and Green wasn't sure where he stood in that lineup. He'd only worked with her for a few weeks before she'd been fired. Would she even remember his name?

But she finally made her way through and smiled at him. "Green! Great to see you again. I hear you've had quite a week."

Before he could answer, Brooks chimed in. "He has. Saved everyone's ass from an inter-dimensional portal *and* arrested a shoplifting magician."

Knox's eyebrows lifted. "You talking about Kyle Todd? *That* magician?"

Valance stepped forward. "That's the one."

Tilting her head, she said, "How'd you get him? I've

been in pursuits with him before, and those goddamn bunnies thwarted me every time."

"Fucking bunnies," Valance muttered.

"I just waited where I thought he would appear," Green answered. "And then he appeared there."

"Huh. Not a bad strategy. Glad it panned out. You would've looked like an idiot if it hadn't."

Green laughed, "Yeah, that occurred to me, don't worry."

Knox looked up at Valance, who had a steady few inches on her. "Looks like you trained him up right. Good work."

"Let the record show I did not train the rookie to hide in hedges. But I'll take credit for him arresting shitheads."

Brooks stepped forward impatiently. "Can we get back to it?"

He thought he caught her shooting a pointed look at Valance before dragging him off for darts.

As it became apparent over the next ten minutes, Lawrence wasn't kidding about Brooks being a shark. She whipped him handily, and he was obligated to get the next round of drinks because of it.

But the drink he bought her after that was completely his own choice.

The round of shots that Valance bought for the shift, which more than one person sniffed suspiciously, was entirely unnecessary and nudged the team's energy from friendly to regrettable.

Harmon, whose only alcoholic drink was the shot, was the first to call it a night, and Knox said her adieus not long after that.

The only person who hadn't grown progressively louder over the last hour and a half was Bruce Bannockburn, but the werewolf *had* seemed to grow bolder, and he stared at

Valance in a way that made Green want to reach for his weapon.

A fingertip traced up Green's thigh under the table. He followed the trail of the hand to the arm to the torso of Brooks, who was pretending to be interested in what Lawrence was saying across from them.

Her caresses grew braver, rising up a little higher on his thigh with each pass. Green tried to gauge the situation to see if he could actually get away with allowing a hand job under the table if things continued in this direction.

But in the process of that assessment, his eyes landed on something more pressing. In the booth, Valance was holding court. Or maybe she was holding hostages. Her speech was slurred and loud as she bombarded Marrow with a story that included the words "eternal banishment" and "scrotum." What really caught his eye was that the corporal's arm, which had been slung over the booth behind her, had slid down to rest around her shoulders.

The situation with Brooks was ill-advised, but if that arm around Valance's shoulders meant what he thought he did, *that* developing situation was downright explosive. Valance was drunk. Not tipsy, drunk. And if Bannockburn was intoxicated, it was only slightly.

Not to mention that if the two of them became involved when the situation at work was so precarious...

Is this really about work?

He didn't like that inner voice. Not even a little bit.

"Wanna shoot some pool?" Brooks whispered in his ear.

"Huh?"

"The pool table's finally open. Nine ball?"

"Oh, uh, no. I'm even worse at pool than I am at darts."

"Fine," she crooned, "then you wanna get out of here?"

A muscle just above his belt tensed as her words landed. He hadn't just been imagining it. Granted, the strokes on his thigh were pretty much a dead giveaway, but this was confirmation. This was the invitation to take her home and ravage her. To show her what skills a human had. To explore her delicious body and let her show off her moves. And he was sure she had all kinds of them.

He noticed Lawrence watching them closely across the table while pretending he wasn't, and that was almost the clincher right there. Lawrence thought he had a claim on Brooks because she'd been his FTO and they'd hooked up before, but Green could march out of here right now with Brooks draped over him, and then Lawrence would see who the real alpha male was…

But he couldn't leave.

Shit.

Shit, shit.

Shit, shit, shit.

He couldn't leave here with Brooks so long as Bannockburn had his eye on a prize who would, no doubt, be willing to blow up everything in the name of revenge.

"Aliyah, you know I do. I wanna leave here with you and not emerge again until next year. But…" His eyes traveled back to Valance, who was chugging her beer, seemingly oblivious to Bannockburn's machinations.

Brooks groaned. "Not you, too."

"What do you mean?"

"It's like battered woman syndrome with you men. She puts your balls in a vise, and you think it's true love. Jesus."

"Wait, *what?* What the hell are you—"

She slipped her hand from his thigh and stood, looking down at him with a mixture of pity, sadness, and disgust. "Listen, I get it. I had a thing for my FTO, too, until he was arrested for domestic violence. But you should know, she'd never going to go for you, and if she does, it'll be the worst thing that's ever happened to you and your career." She grabbed her purse from the back of the chair, then turned to Lawrence. "You wanna get out of here?"

His eyes grew wide as he looked up at his former field training officer then around to see who might have overheard. No one but Green was paying any attention, though. "Yeah, sounds good."

Lawrence clapped him on the back as he passed and muttered, "You had a nice go at it, Rookie."

Green shut his eyes and gritted his teeth to keep from shouting.

But now that he was committed, he'd better see this thing through.

He waited until Valance made another bathroom run, and then waited for her just outside the hallway. She reentered the narrow space wiping excess water from her hands onto her pants, and didn't notice him until he was right in front of her. She stared at him through unfocused eyes. "You waiting on the ladies' room? It's open now."

"God dammit, Valance, I—" *passed up on a wild night of sex for you.* "I need to know something."

"Yes?"

"Are you interested in going home with Bannockburn?"

Her face scrunched up. "Bruce?! Fuck no. Did he send you to ask? That pussy." She could hardly manage the sibilants of the last insult.

"No, he didn't send me, but I can tell he's about to offer to give you a ride home, and my guess is he would walk you to your door, and one thing would lead to another. So if you don't want that…"

"You know he's my cousin, right?"

"I do."

She was silent for a moment as she glanced over at the corporal. She returned her blurry focus to Green. "Wait! I took my own car here! I can take myself home!"

"Hell no. I know you won't like to hear it, but you're drunk."

She narrowed her already squinting eyes at him. "I've been drunker."

He sighed. He should have known she would resist. "Let me give you a ride home."

"You gonna try to fuck me, Rookie?"

He groaned. "No. No, I'm not. If I wanted to get laid tonight, I would have already left with Brooks. But I passed on that so I could make sure you get home safe without the corporal forcing something on you that you don't especially want."

"He couldn't overpower me if he tried."

"When you're like this? Yeah, I think he could. But we both know it doesn't always take overpowering."

She looked him up and down in a not-so-subtle fashion. "I guess I'm at no risk of banging you, and you *definitely* couldn't overpower me if you tried."

"So sweet of you to say, now will you let me give you a ride home?"

She sighed, flopping her arms at her sides. "Fine. You can be my chauffeur."

She stomped back to the booth and leaned clumsily over Marrow to get her things. "We're getting out of here," she announced, jabbing a thumb toward Green.

Bannockburn shot him a look of pure venom. "Not like that," Green mouthed, shaking his head. But even if it wasn't like *that*, it was this like this: Green was cock-blocking his corporal.

Valance managed to walk in a fairly straight line down the sidewalk to his car, and if he hadn't been trained in identifying the signs, he might have thought she was sober.

In fact, the gregariousness of Heather Valance drunk was about that of normal woman sober.

But he knew her too well. She would regret all of this open and vulnerable behavior in the morning. She might be able to take meds for the headache she'd have, but he knew there were other kinds of hangovers that aspirin couldn't cure.

There was silence in the car between each direction she gave, and he wondered what she was thinking about, but not enough to ask.

"This it?"

She leaned heavily against the passenger side window, staring out. "Yep. This is my little shithole."

He didn't want to say it, but indeed, the place wasn't in an especially nice part of town. Not that Valance could afford prime Kilhaven real estate on a cop's salary, but after so many years on the job, she made significantly more than he did, even while she remained on patrol. She could have done better than this, he was sure.

He helped her out of the car, then she shoved him away and insisted she could walk. With the stimulation of the bar fifteen minutes in the past, the sedative effects of the alcohol were getting their moment in the spotlight. Valance shuffled toward the front of the tall, authoritarian block of apartments, fumbling with her keys as she went.

He watched her go. *I should just wait here. This is far enough.*

Walking her up to her front door wasn't necessary. She'd killed men more times than he'd had sex. Even drunk, she would be fine.

But when her foot missed the first step, and she tumbled forward onto the concrete stairs, he knew he would be walking her all the way up. Blood trickled down her shin from a cut on her knee when they finally reached her third-floor unit.

She shoved open the door, stumbled across the threshold, and he got his very first view of the home of Heather Valance, the nightmare with a badge.

It was bleak. It reminded him a little of his own apartment—mismatched furniture, mostly bare white walls, dingy carpet, and a faint odor of mold.

Sure, it was tidier than his place, but that was about the only difference he noticed in the short moment he had to take it all in.

She tossed her wallet and keys onto the coffee table, where they skittered off and onto the floor at the foot of the couch.

The open door wasn't an invitation so much as an oversight, and he thought this was where he ought to end this perilous journey into uncharted territory.

"Want a nightcap?" she asked, hoisting up two glass tumblers and a bottle of whiskey from behind the kitchen counter.

"Uh, no, thanks. I'd better get going."

She set the bottle back on the counter, but one of the

glasses didn't quite make it and shattered on the floor. "Shit."

Green sighed, crossed the threshold, and shut the door behind him. "Don't move, you'll only track it around. Broom?"

She pointed toward a small closet, and he opened it, tried not to notice her old army uniforms folded neatly on the top shelf, and returned to clean up the mess.

"Now I really need a drink," she said, pouring herself one in the surviving tumbler.

He emptied the dustpan into the trash, tapping it against the side. "There'll be shards of glass in your shoes. Here. Take them off."

She slid up onto the counter and held out a foot to him. Was she serious? She sipped her whiskey and didn't lower her leg.

So, he untied her shoe, loosened the laces, and slipped it off.

As he worked on the second, she said, "I think we're in trouble, Green."

He tossed the second shoe to the side and straighten up to meet her gaze.

Valance clutched the drink in her hand, and her expression looked suddenly tight and pained.

"What do you mean?"

She spoke softly now. "I think we're in trouble."

"Who's we?"

She tilted her head back and stared up at the ceiling, and his eyes roamed the smooth curve of her throat before he could stop them. "You. Me." She looked down at him again. "Bruce, Aliyah, the down of Kilhaven. The world."

"Uh…"

"The vampires are preparing. I think they'll make their final move soon."

Was this the paranoid ramblings of PTSD, or was she finally going to tell him what the fuck, precisely, was going on?

"Did you learn that on vacation?"

"I learned that in the war. And I learned it on the streets. I just confirmed it on vacation." She slid off the counter so they were hardly a foot apart. "The weapons of war always find their way home, Norman. Always." She tossed back the last of the amber liquid, then walked past him toward a short hallway. "If you follow me, we'll screw, and I don't think either of us wants that, so you can show yourself out." She slammed her bedroom door behind her.

He had no desire to follow. She could pass out on her bedroom floor, and he'd have still done his job here. She was home, and she was safe.

All he had to do now was get the hell out of there.

He wouldn't be able to lock the door behind him, but the odds of a home invasion were slim, and the odds of even the most black-out drunk Valance failing to fill a home invader with lead were even slimmer.

A sole display on the wall above her couch caught his eye, and he headed over under the pretense of placing her keys and wallet somewhere she could easily find them the next day. He reached down and set them on the coffee table then treated himself to a little snooping. Inside a small glass case was a series of medals. He recognized a few. Medal of Valor, Medal of Freedom, an Iron Heart. His very first thought upon seeing them, which was likely proof that he'd spent too much time around her, was, *They gave her these to shut her up.*

He took a step back, but not before noticing something else.

Deep gashes in sets of four scored the drywall around the glass box. And sticking out of one was a small ball of dark gray fluff.

Fur, he realized with a jolt. Valance's fur. And Valance's anguished scratches.

He took another quick step back, feeling immediately like he'd seen way too much, and then hurried out of her apartment and down the stairs to his car.

CHAPTER SEVENTEEN_

Shattered glass across the asphalt. A dislocated bumper. Alcohol-thinned blood flowing in a steady stream from a gash on a cherub's head. A human woman crying after the shock.

But there was nobody to scrape off the pavement, so all in all, Green was fairly satisfied with the fallout from this totally preventable crash.

Of course, that didn't mean being on this scene wasn't dangerous. This particular intersection had already taken three lives in the last few months. Some were just like that. Wrong part of town, wrong type of people, bad visibility, not enough signage on how a green arrow was different from a solid green.

For some people, though, there could never be enough signage, as was the case with the drunk driver currently getting his head bandaged by the medics.

Nobody had died, but if he and Valance remained on this thoroughfare at two in the morning and a wave of bad luck hit again, there would be ample opportunity. Beer goggles already had a way of filtering out flashing red and blue lights, and he hadn't forgotten the clusterfuck on Highway 7 that had ended in a vaporized motorcyclist and over three hundred thousand dollars' worth of damages to city vehicles.

Green tried to listen to the sobbing woman standing before him, but he was losing patience. She wouldn't directly answer his simple questions and kept slipping into a language he couldn't identify—Hebrew? Enochian?—before deep wails took over again.

She wasn't especially injured, just shook up. And he couldn't blame her. The drunk cherub had taken an unprotected left in front of her, leaving her no time to react, if the two demolished vehicles were any indication.

The speed limit was thirty-five on this particular stretch of road. Maybe that's why he found himself lacking patience for her hysterics. No way a car going anywhere near the speed limit would have caused that severe of an impact. She must have been going close to sixty. Of *course* she didn't have any time to react and swerve. She was outpacing her headlights.

He jotted down a few more notes then checked to see if the intox cherub was done hogging the ambulance. "Ma'am," he said, interrupting her. "Ma'am, I'd feel better if you got checked out by the medics before you take off. Your arms look a little rough, and there's a good chance you'll wake up with whiplash in the morning."

Hers were the typical markings of a deployed airbag, so he wasn't especially concerned. Mostly, he was just drained.

Drained from what, though?

He knew immediately, though he didn't even let his inner monologue say it.

They passed Valance and the cherub, the latter in handcuffs, and Green took his charge over to the medic. The two officers didn't say a word as they passed. Didn't even make eye contact.

It had been like this all shift. No doubt, Valance had taken the rest of the weekend to think about her behavior at the bar. She'd have had to take a taxi back there the following day to get her car, which was never a high point. The cost of the ride was a drunk tax and the length of the ride one's penance.

But maybe Valance didn't care. Maybe it was only Green who'd obsessed about the supposedly fun night out with his shift all weekend—the missed chance with Brooks, seeing Valance unable to make it up the stairs on her own, their muddled conversation in her kitchen, the scratches in the drywall. *"The weapons of war always find their way home."*

What had she meant by that? Was she referring to herself? That shitbag Herrera had certainly looked at her like she was a weapon right before he'd smashed open the portal to escape into the unknown.

An hour later, they sat in the idling cruiser, still on scene. The cherub was passed out in the back seat but probably breathing, and both Green and Valance were busy filling out their reports before heading down to jail. Neither said a word.

A car pulled up behind them and parked, and Valance peered at it through the rearview mirror then cursed. A moment later, Detective Felps was at her window.

Green wondered if she would refuse to do the small courtesy of rolling it down and simply pretend he wasn't there. But after an unsettling delay, she pressed the button, and the window lowered.

Felps leaned down to look into their cab. "Just wanted to check in and see if you needed any help wrapping this up."

"So nice of you to join the shift tonight," Valance said. "We'd be lost without you."

"Sorry," he said. "Got called in by Detective Sergeant Packer. Had to miss show-up."

"Sounds like homicide could really use you back in the office."

"Maybe so. Looks like they found another body part of Caitlin Holloway. There were splinters from a stake lodged in it. Case has officially been moved to homicide."

"About time," Valance said. "Young girls don't go missing for this long unless they're dead. Or"—she narrowed her eyes as if in deep thought—"considering there was a stake involved, *undead*."

The pale skin around Felps' lips tightened. "A stake through the heart will kill anyone, Valance. Don't let your imagination run away with you."

"I promise not to if you promise not to let your brain waste away, Detective."

The window was already rolling up before he could get his mouth open to respond, and it was fully shut just after he said, "It's not—"

She started the car, and he got the point.

Green, who, against his best judgment, had started to warm to the vampire (the compliment after the portal call had nothing to do with it, he told himself), shot the detective an apologetic cringe behind Valance's back to show he was just a literal passenger on this ride.

Once they were on the road, Green's desire to ask a slew of frantic questions ate at him, but he knew it would have to wait until they didn't have the mics recording and a passed out drunk in the back seat. So they rode in silence, though Green swore that the grinding he heard wasn't coming from the junker's engine but from Valance's mouth.

When they entered the jail, Green spotted Lawrence across the way and felt his stomach knot up into a spring-loaded fist. He shouldn't want to punch the man who was Aliyah Brooks' second pick when he himself was the first, but he did. He wanted it very badly. Or maybe he merely wanted to punch himself.

Valance spotted Lawrence, too, and pushed the cherub over toward him. "Feel a wave coming on. Can you take him so we can get out of here before we cause a complete jailbreak?"

The handsome officer's eyes shot open. "Yeah, yeah, of course."

"Here's the paperwork." She shoved it at him, thanked him, and hustled toward the door, dragging Green, who felt perfectly fine, out with her.

He hurried down the stairs into the sally port, a step behind her as always. "I feel fine, Valance. Usually, we have bad luck around the same time. You think it might be—"

"Don't be dense. Get in the car."

Once they were in (the door was stuck, and he had to yank on it a few times before it opened), Green understood.

"Are we in trouble?"

She stared ahead through the windshield at the concrete wall. "I don't think so."

"Felps knows, doesn't he?"

"He thinks he does."

"It was a warning."

She rolled her head toward him, an eyebrow arched. "I know that. But I'm not worried."

Futility caused him to laugh. "How are you not worried?"

"I've been found out before, Rookie. Comes with doing things you're not supposed to do all the time. The trick is to keep the people who know from telling anyone else."

"You don't think Felps has mentioned his suspicion to anyone?"

She pressed her lips together and shook her head. "No. He doesn't want to seem paranoid. It would be a little cliché if he decided to blame a vampire murder on a war veteran who fought some of the most disgusting vamps around. There are reasons no one's fired me yet, Green. Ones you clearly haven't grasped yet, and that's fine. But I'm not as vulnerable as you think I am."

"Don't take this the wrong way, but I'm not worried about *your* career."

"Hey, fair enough. But I won't let them take you down." She twisted the key in the ignition, and the engine issued a dry, wheezy cough and sputter. Grunting, she pumped the gas and tried again. The car begrudgingly awoke and began its creaky purr.

Green, meanwhile, noticed almost none of the mechanical battle. He was too preoccupied with the fact that Valance had just promised to protect his career. Was he just making this up, or had the loyalty between them been entirely one-sided until this moment? Now that he considered it, that seemed to very clearly be the case.

Would she stay true to her word on this? Or was he just a pawn she would wait until the bitter end to play?

He couldn't be sure. But what he did know was that the simple morsel of information she'd just shared with him would keep him following in her dangerous footsteps for much longer than was prudent. Had he ever had a choice in it?

"Valance, I just wanted you to know that I have no plans to tell anyone about what happened after the pub the other night."

He waited for a response but got none. It was as if he hadn't spoken. She pulled out of the sally port and onto a poorly lit street.

He nudged the topic forward. "Listen, everyone has a little too much to drink sometimes. I've been there. And it doesn't change how I see you. I just want you to know that."

They approached a four-way stop, and as soon as the tires fell still below them, she gave him her full attention. "If you don't stop trying to make me feel better, Rookie, I *will* murder you and make it look like you had an accidental discharge."

His hand fell protectively to the gun on his belt, and he nodded.

She eyed him closely for a second longer before turning her eyes back to the intersection. "Good talk."

CHAPTER EIGHTEEN

Green was five minutes late to show-up the following afternoon, and he wasn't the only one. Valance looked a bit like she'd collided with a bus, and he knew the feeling. Her afternoon must have gone about as smoothly has his.

It had been a mild bout of bad luck, but that meant it lingered longer than the intense hits. The handle of his favorite coffee mug had snapped off when he grabbed it from the cabinet above his sink. His toilet had overflowed. The end of the toothpaste tube had popped open when he squeezed it, sending the paste in a jet across his countertop, wall, and hand towel. And then, to top it all off, his water heater stopped working, and he'd been forced to take a cold shower, though that might have been less a matter of his luck and more an ongoing issue with the apartment complex.

And then the luck had hung around like a fog that wouldn't lift as he sat on his couch, completely ready to walk out the door the moment he thought it was safe.

Now he was late. Would it ever end? How long could the department justify keeping them around while the curse persisted? Would they eventually get sick of the inconvenience and stick him on paid leave?

They might do that anyway if they suspected he was involved in the Caitlin Holloway staking. Keep him out of the way while they investigated. Valance, too. It was awfully convenient, and the fact that it hadn't happened yet only strengthened the case that Felps hadn't shared whatever suspicions he might have with superiors.

Valance didn't seem bothered by her own tardiness. She helped herself to some coffee in the kitchen before making her way to show-up while Green hurried past and tried to slip inconspicuously into the meeting room.

Instead of crossing to his new favorite spot in the back, he lingered by the door, which meant he was nearly shoulder to shoulder with Detective Felps. The vampire nodded at him and stepped to the side to make a little more room before returning his attention to the sergeant.

Montoya didn't seem to notice the late arrival and kept on talking about the department's new youth initiative that paired repeat juvenile offenders with a cop mentor. When the offer to sign up came, no one volunteered.

"About what I figured," Montoya said, scribbling on a sticky note that he attached to the stack of informational flyers.

He went into the BOLOs, by and large the same faces they'd seen on the projector screen for the last few weeks, and then added one final announcement. "This next bit is highly sensitive information. I have word from above that we absolutely cannot have this leaking to the press." If he thought he was subtle with his suspicious scan of the faces in the room, he was mistaken. "I told Lieutenant Fukumoto that no one on this shift leaked the previous erroneous information to the papers. I hope no one's going to make me a liar."

He pressed his clicker, and the projector brought up two new faces Green hadn't seen before. Both young, smiling. They looked like class pictures, likely from fifth or sixth grade. One boy, one girl.

His stomach dropped. He knew what Montoya was about to say, but he dreaded it all the same.

"Day shift took two calls today out in Crown Tree. This is Melvin Brown, and this is Rhiannon Ripley. Twelve and eleven, respectively. Disappeared from a birthday party this morning, but the parents aren't sure exactly when. It was one of those big ones with inflatable things and ponies and so on that rich people do. Ended at four p.m., and Brown and Ripley were nowhere to be found."

Corporal Bannockburn jumped in. "You said inflatables. Have we already checked with that company? There was a ring of human trafficking up in Pan City that used the deflated bouncy houses to hide kids away and cart them off."

"I believe we have detectives looking into that, yes."

Felps said, "We're sure the kids didn't just run off together? Twelve and eleven are old enough to get into trouble."

Montoya opened his mouth to respond, but before he could:

"For fuck's sake." Valance had snuck in when Green wasn't paying attention. "Are we really going to play this game? Covering all the angles but the obvious one? Let me guess, at least one of each of their parents is a werewolf, and neither of the missing has experienced their first shift. Am I close? Now, how in the world could I have guessed that if there wasn't already an explicit pattern here?"

"Officer Valance, I will not have you showing up late and shouting your conspiracies at me across the room."

"Conspiracies? Sarge, I don't think you want me to start on the conspiracies I have floating around my head. But five children missing from the same wealthy werewolf neighborhood, all prepubescent, final species unknown, is not a conspiracy. This is a serial kidnapper. Or serial kidnappers, as in several. And you would have to be a fucking imbecile not to guess who would target *that* demographic."

"Officer Valance, I don't know where you think you get off, but you're about to get slapped with a serious reprimand if—"

"Do you even give a shit about the victims, Sarge?" She scanned the room. "Do any of you give a shit about it anymore? Or do you all know I'm right but, you give more of a shit about your job than the lives of a bunch of innocent kids? Why the hell even work this shit job if not because you care? No one in leadership gives a fuck; we all know that, except you. I thought some of you would have the balls to stand up and call this what it is."

"Valance!"

"Save your breath, Montoya. I'm done."

The door closed behind her a moment later to a flammably silent room.

Montoya pinched the bridge of his nose, his head down, while the rest of the room focused intensely on their steaming coffee or their boots. Green risked a look around and found Bannockburn staring at him. The corporal nodded for Green to go after her.

Was he insane?

But Bannockburn remained insistent with his wide eyes as he raised his fists and mimed turning a steering wheel. Finally, Green got it.

Presuming they were free to leave, he slipped out of the room and ran into the parking lot after Valance. "Hey, how about I drive today?"

———

They took a coffee break when that evening's luck ran thin. Green, exercising an uncharacteristic amount of forethought, ordered an iced coffee at the drive-thru, which he promptly spilled all over his lap. It felt a little like a virgin sacrifice, a tribute to the gods of piss-poor luck, so that maybe later he could be spared a worse mishap.

Valance didn't order a thing, and he suspected it was because the tension in her jaw was so tight, she couldn't have opened it wide enough to slip even a straw inside.

After the accompanying nausea faded, his lap dried, and his manhood could peek its head out of hiding, he risked it, pulled back around, and ordered a hot coffee. He was rewarded for his earlier sacrifice by being able to enjoy the drink without randomly losing his grip and scalding his balls off.

They sat in the parked car outside the MacDougall's while he sipped, and Valance continued to brood. Now that his nervous system had adjusted to the heightened baseline of being stuck in a metal coffin with the ticking brunette bomb, he found the silence quite enjoyable.

Getting to be in the driver's seat for once was also a nice change.

The oversized pickup truck in the parking space next to theirs backed out, scraping the side of the cruiser the entire way. Green rolled down the window, peered over at the other driver, who looked about as frightened as she could while also appearing stoned, and he waved that it was fine and she should proceed on with her night's plans. Initiating contact on a minor drug charge that he might not be able to prove anyway, while under the hold of the curse, was one rookie mistake he would not be making tonight. Officer discretion existed for a reason.

Only once she decided this wasn't a trap, she did as he instructed and drove off.

He turned and jotted down this particular incident in the log before coaxing the suicidal engine to life. The afterglow of the last wave faded away, and he pulled out of the parking lot.

As he browsed the call list on the HAM for something stimulating but not ripe for a complete clusterfuck, the sound of Valance's voice jolted him.

But all she said was, "Hey, it's me."

He whipped his head around because of course, he knew it was her, and then his brain caught up with him when he spotted the cell phone in her hand.

Who did Valance even know? Was this a personal call while she was on the job? Was this her way of acting out after her show-down with Montoya?

"Yeah, there are two more. Out in Crown Tree like the others. Rhiannon Ripley, age eleven, and Melvin Brown, age twelve. Disappeared from a rich-kid birthday party this afternoon. That's all I have, but you know how those kinds of things attract them like ants to a picnic. No, no, you're right. I don't think it was spontaneous, either. Definitely. Yep, I'll let you know when I do." She disconnected the call. Green managed to drive for another quarter of a mile in stunned silence before the buzzing in his skull reached a fever pitch, and he pulled over into a small construction inlet.

With silent determination, he disconnected his body mic, the DMAV, and his radio, and shot her a look that said she'd better do the same. She rolled her eyes but complied.

"What?" she said. "You gonna lecture me?"

"It was *you!*" He couldn't find more words than those for this betrayal. "You accused me! And right in front of Felps!"

"Of course I did. It's called deflecting suspicion. What's your deal here?"

"What's my—What's my *deal*? You're leaking to the press!"

"Wrong as usual, Rookie. I'm not leaking to the press."

Green felt his next attack retreat into his throat. "You're not?"

"No. I'm leaking to Diane Knox, and *she's* leaking to the press."

"God dammit, Valance!" He smacked the steering wheel, but she didn't even flinch. "Enough of the games. I'm on your side, okay? I don't even know how I ended up like this, but I'm on your fucking side whether I like it or not." The tiny space of the cab wobbled around the edges of his vision. "You... you did something to my head, and now I'm stuck with you. So is it too much to ask that you're honest with me? Just once? Just fucking once?"

She studied him impassively. "I am honest with you. I

just told you I was leaking to Knox, who's leaking to the press."

"But I had to catch you doing it for you to even mention it."

She scoffed. "You're quite the sleuth, *catching* me talking on the phone when I was right next to you in the car."

"Why!" he shouted, losing his temper completely. "*Why* are you doing this to me?"

"What are you talking about?"

What *was* he talking about? He couldn't even be sure. Forcing himself to take a deep breath, but allowing himself the continued luxury of strangling the life out of the steering wheel, he said, "You hate the press. You know they always get the stories wrong. They stick their nose into things they shouldn't be in, and they turn the city against us every chance they get."

"You're not wrong about any of that."

"So *why* are you working with them?"

"I already explained that. I'm not. I'm working with Knox, and she's—"

He shot her a scorching look, and she paused and sighed. "Because I alone don't have the power to make the leadership admit what's going on here. None of us at the bottom do, but we all see it. Hell, even Felps sees it. But we can't do anything. The press is the only entity that can challenge this, that can crack it open even the smallest bit. I don't like it, but I don't like hardly anything about this under-appreciated job as society's janitorial services. The only reason I do this is to help people, and I can't help people without the press this time."

"They'll get all the facts wrong."

"Of course they will. When they get the facts wrong, the

department has to come out and correct those facts. And what they'll come out with will be such transparent bullshit in itself that people will start asking the right questions. It's the only way to get the truth out."

"No," he said. "It can't be." He dug his fingernails into the wheel. "Dammit, Valance, this is reckless, even for you."

She shook her head. "You have no idea how reckless it really is, Rookie. You have no idea the full extent of what's going on here. If you did—"

"Just tell me, then! Stop teasing me and just tell me! I'm sticking my neck out for you even when I don't mean to. Chief Spinner knows my name! I'm in a tight spot here, and it's all your doing, but when I ask you for the truth, you just play these stupid games!"

"They're not stupid games. I'll tell you everything once I can confirm it."

"No. No, Valance. I'm done with this. You tell me now, or I'm out."

"You're *out*? Jesus, this isn't the cherubim mafia."

"You know what I mean. I'm done helping you and Bannockburn do your stupid little stings. I wouldn't have this curse if it weren't for following you into that warehouse with all those goddamn leprechauns. And Spinner never would've called me into his office, and I wouldn't have felt like I had to take care of you the other night so everything didn't fucking blow up, and I could have gotten *laid!*"

She stared at him through an unreadably bland expression, and he wondered if she was going to make a crack about him losing his virginity finally, but instead, she said, "I'm sorry, Norman. I can't tell you. Not yet. I need you to keep trusting me."

"Oh, fuck off. That's not happening." He turned on the

recording devices and pulled back onto the road without another word.

He was done with this shit. Whatever it took to go solo from here on out, he would do it. He was done with Valance's games and her head trips and, above all, this goddamn Stockholm Syndrome that meant he wasn't done with her games and head trips at all. Not even close.

Fuck!

CHAPTER NINETEEN_

"You lasted a lot longer than I'd thought you would before making this request."

Sergeant Montoya folded his arms across his bulky chest and stared at Green with something akin to pride as the two of them stood in the main hallway of the substation the next evening before show-up.

The rookie waited for an official response.

"No," Montoya said. "Sorry. Can't happen. Not enough vehicles to spare. But if you were okay going on desk duty, then..."

"No, sir. I'll stay doubled up."

"Suit yourself."

"And, uh, could you maybe not mention it to her that I asked?"

Montoya let out an amused snort. "Can do. I'm not looking to be reported for creating a hostile work environment."

Green forced a smile, thanked his commanding officer,

and the two men parted ways, Montoya toward his office, and Green toward the car depot.

So, they were really stuck together, him and Valance. He'd just reached out his hand for the sarge to pull him free of her vortex of recklessness, and save him from the downward spiral he couldn't seem to halt on his own. And the sarge had slapped his hand away without a second thought. Did Montoya know that's what had just happened? He couldn't have. He wasn't a heartless man, and Green never got the sense that the sergeant had it out for him specifically. During those weeks when Valance was on vacation, Green had even come to believe that the were-bison genuinely love his shift... with one exception.

Montoya had been Green's last viable lifeline. Corporal was of no use. The rest of the shift had picked a side—Valance's or that of intentional obliviousness—and none could throw him a life preserver now.

As his boots found the asphalt of the lot, he looked up and saw her standing by their car in the street light. He couldn't escape her. Maybe a peaceful calm would wash over him eventually, but it hadn't shown its face yet.

This wasn't usually how people picked sides in high stakes situations, was it? Whoever they were stuck with?

He understood and, to some extent, supported her crusade to expose the truth of what had happened to the missing Crown Tree children, but... couldn't he have found someone saner to team up with? Someone who would fill him in, so he actually knew what the hell he was getting himself into? It seemed like he'd earned the right to that, at least, after sticking his neck out for her with Spinner.

His course of action now was to ignore her as much as possible. So, when she spoke to him in the car fifteen minutes later, he didn't answer. Unless it was absolutely related to the call they were on, he was locking her out. It was the only way he could think of to protect himself from more of her mind games.

I'll just detach myself emotionally from my words. Nothing she says is about me anyway. Never has been. I'll give her nothing to work with, no way into my head.

Of course, Valance picked up on the tactic right away and didn't seem bothered, which only pissed him off more.

Why couldn't he hurt her? He was adept at hurting every other woman in his life without meaning to, but when it came to Heather Valance, he couldn't do it if he tried. He couldn't get to her. Maybe no one could.

"This looks fun," she said, tapping on the HAM screen and assigning them to their next call.

Once her arm was clear of the dash monitor so he didn't accidentally have to glimpse any part of her, he checked to see what she'd selected.

He almost erupted in anger but caught himself before he spoke.

But seriously? Another fucking clown call?

This was her way of payback for him not talking. He was sure of it. He thought he'd be clever and not speak to her, and that would accomplish a single goddamn thing?

You really are a rookie, Norman.

He could never beat her with the cold shoulder. Valance could stare someone to death in silence. She could weaponize it.

And now, with a simple tap on the monitor, she'd selected a call that at once reminded him that he thought he'd seen a clown and also that he couldn't have possibly seen a clown because they had been exterminated by the federal government decades before he was born. She'd initiated yet another mindfuck.

And she's done it in silence—his chosen battlefield—and with only one finger.

Fine, she'd won another round. But Green wouldn't let his disappointment show. He would march out there, prove to himself that clowns didn't exist, and show her that he didn't scare so easily. He'd beat her at her own game.

Unless…

What if this *was* her game? What if she was still nobly training him, and this was her way of helping him confront his fear? What if she was giving him a chance to redeem himself in her eyes? Was this an olive branch rather than a jab in the ribs with her nightstick?

A pinprick of icy cold blossomed between his eyes, and he shut them against it. She wasn't even saying anything, and she was screwing with his mind. How the *fuck* did she do it?

When they pulled up to the address, something clicked, and he snapped out of his circular self-criticism. For no reason he was willing to name, the hair stood up on his arms. "This is the same stretch of greenbelt as the last clown call."

"Good eye, Rookie."

The compliment sounded light and genuine, and he loathed her for it.

He read the call text all the way through. Another couple of fornicating clowns. "Looks like the same homeless couple. Maybe they dress up as clowns to get off."

"That's some sick shit, Green, but I won't say it's unlikely."

This complex seemed older than the previous one by a

few decades. It also housed fewer units, and the layout made less sense. But Valance knew the way, taking a sharp left down a steep incline to a row of buildings that backed right up to the woods, hardly ten yards between where the open patios ended and the tree line began.

They knocked on H4 and announced themselves, and a frightened woman stuck her head through the crack of the door, peering up at the uniformed officers. She undid a chain, and the door swung open further. "Please come inside. I don't want to keep the door open." And as they stepped in, she added, "The children are in the other room. I don't want them to know you're here. They were already asleep when I saw... them."

Toddlers' toys littered the cramped living room floor, and the low ceilings and exposed stone wall gave the space a cavelike feel. Green wouldn't mind living in a place like this over his sterile and personality-free apartment, even though the odds of a mold problem seemed high. There was a musty smell to the whole thing, despite the faint lemony scent of an attempted cover-up.

On the far side of the living room was the back door. Ms. Lafferty had the long, slatted blinds closed over the sliding glass, and Green wondered how any apartments could've ever considered a large, impossible-to-cover window that was also an entrance to be a good idea.

Fear pulsed off the woman, who introduced herself as Gloria Lafferty. He smelled shifter all over this place, but he couldn't tell quite what kind. But as she lifted her arm to pull back the hanging blinds, he got enough of a fresh whiff to narrow it down to deer or raccoon. He couldn't explain why the two smelled so similar to him, but they did. And the lemon cleaner wasn't exactly helping him differentiate.

Valance led Mrs. Lafferty through the paces, and the shifter hugged herself as she spoke. "It was… well, I saw two people back there."

Patiently, with her notepad open and pen at the ready, Valance said, "Can you describe what they were doing?"

Mrs. Lafferty's face flushed. "They were, um"—her attention flickered to Green as if it was his male presence that actually made the whole thing perverse—"engaged in an adult act."

"I'm afraid I need you to be more specific. Are you saying they were engaged in a sexual act?"

Gloria Lafferty swallowed and nodded.

"And where were they when you saw them?"

"Right there." She pointed through the glass door.

Valance's left eyebrow arched. "Right there? On your patio furniture?"

"Yes. The loveseat. They were—"

"Lying in opposite directions?" Valance supplied.

Mrs. Lafferty covered her mouth and nodded again.

Green felt suddenly tired. It *was* a strange coincidence. And yet there were no clowns. Period. That was the truth of the matter, and he was downright tired of straddling the question in his head. How many false reports of sixty-nine-ing clowns could he take before he cracked? Was this a set-up? A practical joke Valance was playing on him? Would there be another similar call in a week from someone who owed Valance a favor? Was she trying to drive him into the nuthouse?

"Any idea what kind of creature we're dealing with here, Mrs. Lafferty?"

She looked like she was about to speak, but then she paused. "I can't be sure."

Valance closed her notepad and tucked it into her breast pocket. "It's okay. You can tell us what you think you saw."

"I just... it's impossible."

Green realized he was clenching his jaw and tried to relax it. No dice.

"The call text we received," Valance continued, "said it was clowns. When you called, did you think you saw clowns engaging in mutual oral sex out on your back patio?"

The shifter paused. Then, "Yes. That's what I thought I saw. I'm sorry, I know it couldn't have been that. I don't know why I said it."

Valance laid a soft hand on the woman's shoulder. "You said it because that's what it looked like to you. And that's okay. That's an important detail for us to know."

"You don't think it was clowns, though, right?"

"I don't see how it could be. But impersonating a clown is considered an act of domestic terrorism, so if someone is going around doing that, we need to know about it."

It was small comfort to the distraught and concerned mother, but she accepted the reassurance anyway, and a moment later, Green and Valance stepped out onto the back patio and heard the door lock behind them.

Green stooped down to inspect the love seat, though he was sure anything he might find wouldn't be something he especially wanted to touch or smell.

Valance's voice broke the quiet silence. "Fang 9-01, requesting backup from Fang 9-20. We could use his expertise."

Green stood and narrowed his eyes at her. "You think this is a matter of *homicide*?"

"Of course not. But I think Felps ought to be here."

A deep pulsing in his temples kicked up, and he stepped

toward her and hissed, "You're seriously not gonna tell me what this is about?"

"No, I'm not." She paused. "But I'm gonna show you something you'll never forget. How's that?"

Not as good if he was honest. In fact, it was terrible. He didn't like it at all. No thanks.

What he wanted was nothing short of a freaking heads up. But he wasn't going to start that argument here. Not when the homeless clown imposters could be listening in the woods. Would the one who spooked him the first time recognize him as the same cop?

They checked around the side of the building but found nothing, and a few minutes later, Detective Felps pulled up in front of the building. Valance hurried over to meet him.

He was hardly out of his SUV as he said, "I spent the whole drive over here wondering why in the hell you would need a homicide detective as backup on a false alarm clown sighting."

"If it isn't my favorite vampire," she replied. "Grab the shotgun, and I'll show you why you're here."

He rolled his eyes and slammed his door, leaving the shotgun right where it was mounted.

"Suit yourself," she said.

They followed her back around the building and onto the patio. "Resident says she saw two clowns head to foot here, engaged in mutual sexual gratification."

Felps stood with his arms across his lean chest, and while his upper lip curled almost imperceptibly at the mention, he remained silent and impassive.

"Once they were done, or bored or whatever, she says they headed off in the direction of the woods."

Felps waved toward the trees. "There's a homeless camp out there. They just went to join their people."

"I'd bet you your next month's detective's pay," she said, "that there *isn't* a camp out there. Not anymore." He didn't reply, but she had his attention now. And then she led them to the edge of the cement slab and pointed her flashlight down at something on the ground. All three knelt down to get a closer look.

The print was unmistakable. It was large and humanlike, but longer, larger than any human foot would ever be.

She dragged her light over the ground to reveal other prints of the same variety. Two sets.

Felps was the first to address the unspoken question. "I've heard that they sell clown shoes like this on the black market. They're designed solely to inspire fear by leaving these prints."

"Makes sense," said Valance with a restrained sort of buoyancy. "After all, clowns were exterminated years ago. This couldn't *possibly* be two of them."

Green shot her a quick sideways glance as a seed of suspicion sprouted inside him.

"I guess we ought to follow the tracks," she said. "Whoever is planting this false evidence is committing an act of terrorism."

Felps straightened from his crouch. "You don't need me for that, do you?"

"You scared to go in the woods? Spent a little too much time behind the desk, and you've lost your nerve? I thought the whole reason you were gracing the 900s was that you wanted to see a little more action. Well, here it is. You could arrest a domestic terrorist. Two, even! Not bad as far as bragging rights back at the office."

He grunted curtly. "Fine. Let's go."

Valance led the way, but not before switching her flashlight out with her gun and tack light. Felps eyed her suspiciously, but Green understood. Or at least he was starting to. Perhaps he'd finally spent enough time immersed in her conspiracies to know how seemingly disparate things could string together into a clear picture.

And he had a clear picture now. He knew exactly what she was doing.

Fuck, she might be a genius.

And close on the heels of that: *I can't believe this is happening.*

Green followed her lead and drew his firearm before entering the woods, but he kept hold of his flashlight in his left hand and held the gun with his right.

Felps, meanwhile, stomped noisily along in the middle of the pack and Green really, *really* wished the vampire would take it down a notch.

After a drawn-out minute of creeping deeper, Valance stopped. Felps, whose eyes had been glued to the tracks on the ground, nearly ran into her. "Look," she whispered, and she pointed toward something in front of them.

Felps aimed his flashlight at it and paused.

The footprints, which had led in a straight line until that point, now veered into a large circle. Layers and layers of them, one footprint stomping over another, as if the pair of suspects had just lost their minds and started running in a loop.

On the far side, the footprints finally left the circle, heading deeper into the darkness.

The hair on Green's arms stood on end, and he flooded the space between trees with his light.

Felps stepped forward, moved into the center of the circle, and turned slowly to examine the evidence. "Huh." He braced his hands on his hips. *"Huh."*

And then it happened. The manic, hyena-like laughter. Not in the distance, but just a few yards off.

And before the echoes of it had faded, the nightmares struck, one on each side, both charging straight for the unsuspecting detective.

Before Green's brain could catch up, Valance's gun had let off half a dozen cracks, and both the creatures were down.

The report echoed through the silent woods. Green's ears pounded. The terrifying image of a human lying dead on the asphalt in the middle of a residential street flashed across his mind's eye so rapidly that he forgot about it the instant it was gone.

He stared at what was really in front of him. That was bad enough.

Valance had just shot two people. No, not people. Not really.

But his training told him that the only thing that mattered now was trying to keep them alive. Shoot to kill, then render aid. The most perverse dichotomy of police work.

But he hardly made it one urgent step forward before Valance lunged for him and grabbed his arm. "Don't get near them."

Felps' eyes were giant saucers, and his feet appeared glued to the ground where he remained in the circle of footprints. He, too, stared wordlessly at the two *things* laid out around him.

There was no point denying it now. The two attackers weren't domestic terrorists. They were clowns.

Green kept his light on one of them, feeling lightheaded.

His conspiracy, the one he'd started weaving the moment Valance had shown them the tracks, was right. And he hated it.

Finally, Felps spoke. "Are you *kidding* me?"

"Not a joke," Valance said. Not for the first time, Green wondered if she had a telepath somewhere in her lineage with the way she seemed able to stare at someone hard enough to read their thoughts.

Felps' incredulity quickly gave way to his training. "We need to render aid."

Valance continued to stare at the detective like she might microwave his brain with her eyes alone. "Be my guest if you want to get that close to it."

He shook his head. "But they can't be real."

"And yet, here they are."

A wheezing breath from one of them broke the time warp. Green couldn't have known which was the male and which the female of this breeding pair, but one of them snapped its shark teeth in a futile attempt as intimidation then issued another maniacal laugh.

Felps stared at it in disgust. "It's still alive."

"They both are," Valance said. "I made sure of it."

The blood oozing from the thigh of the wheezing one was the color of old limes and glistened in Green's flashlight beam.

"You have a choice, Detective. You bring them in alive and cause a public panic, or you finish them out here, and we bury the bodies together."

"We can't bury them out *here*. We have to report them to

—" He drew up short. "To… someone. The department. The local government. *Someone.*"

Valance just shook her head minutely. Reporting it to anyone would be the death knell for their careers. Even Green could see that. Exposing a cover-up was generally frowned upon by those doing the covering up. They'd be given paid leave just long enough for a city-appointed psychologist to declare them unfit for duty.

And nothing would change, nothing would be done. It would be utterly pointless career suicide.

Felps looked at her with new eyes now, and after a silence that could have lasted an hour, he drew his firearm from his holster, stalked over to the wheezing clown, and put two bullets in its head.

"That's what I thought," Valance said, and she went to handle the other one herself.

When it was done, she kicked the body, murmured, "Fucking psycho," and then turned back to the two men.

He saw it in the moonlight, that twinkle in her eye that she only got when she'd won. Just a hint of glee, even as the corners of her lips curved downward in unmistakable displeasure.

They'd just crossed another line together, he and Valance. And this time they'd brought Felps with them. It was the line of complicity. They were all in it now.

"There's a whole world of evil and danger that's being kept secret from the public," she said, closing in on Felps. "You know it. I know it. But the average civilian doesn't have a fucking clue. And they're not any safer for their ignorance. We're just calling it a mercy that they'll never see their death coming. But is that mercy? Or do people deserve to know?"

"Not about clowns," Felps said.

"I agree with you there. Not about the clowns. But you know there's more at play here. If you didn't, you wouldn't have jumped onto the 900s."

He nodded but kept his mouth shut.

"I think you want answers for the same reason as I do. But if you're still set on finding out why Caitlin Holloway had splinters from a wooden stake in her, you've missed the whole goddamn point."

"That's not what I'm after." His eyes jumped to one of the oozing bodies on the ground. "Not anymore, at least. I think I just solved that mystery."

"And?"

He met her gaze again. "And I was asking the wrong question."

After another tense pause, she holstered her firearm. "I never thought I'd see the day, but you and me, we're on the same team here."

"I know."

She turned to Green. "People are going to be wondering about the shots fired. I trust you can go handle it while we dig some unmarked graves."

"Yeah, I think I can do that."

He kept his gun in hand as he made his way out of the woods.

Just as Valance had predicted, residents were congregating in the parking lot. He found Mrs. Lafferty first to assure her it was just some firecrackers that went off. Big homeless camp out there, you see. They sometimes set up booby traps to alert them of anyone approaching and scare them off. One was triggered. That's all it was.

Next, he radioed the corporal. There would be multiple

shots fired reports flooding the call takers, and he asked Bannockburn to pass along the word that it was just fireworks. He, Valance, and Felps were present when the damn things went off.

And then began the crowd control. Panic quickly dissolved into indignation that the city was allowing the homeless to camp so close to where children played. They could have their indignation, that was fine with him. It kept them occupied.

But now he knew the truth, and he couldn't unlearn it.

Valance had been right; there would be no homeless in the woods now. The clowns would've claimed the territory for themselves, maybe even with a slaying or two.

The public could never know about any of that. It would cause chaos.

And yet, who was he, really, to keep it from them?

It was an hour later, the crowd of concerned citizens long dispersed, before Valance and Felps emerged from the woods, neither speaking a word as they trudged side by side. They made straight for a tap poking from the building's bricks, both keeping quiet in the shadows, and washed as best they could. Then Felps got into his vehicle and left, not another word out of his mouth.

Green offered to drive, but Valance refused. "Your nerves are shot. I don't want you behind the wheel." She pushed past him to open the driver's side door.

"Your nerves *aren't* shot?"

"They are. But they've been shot for over a decade, so I'm used to it. Get in."

He was out of fight for the shift, so he did as he was told.

As soon as he shut his door behind him, she said, "How about a coffee?"

"I figured it out."

"What, coffee? I'm glad to hear it."

"No. Your plot. I figured it out as soon as I saw the tracks."

She grinned. "Good. I'm glad you're still learning." After a brief pause. "Felps won't be a problem for us anymore."

"You knew what he would do with the clowns."

"Of course I did. The executive order allowing the cold-blooded murder of clowns remains on the books. So Felps technically had the law on his side. And who doesn't dream of killing a clown?"

He didn't. Although he was sure clowns *would* take up residence in his dreams for the foreseeable future. "So when I saw it on that last call…"

"Yeah, sorry about that. You shouldn't let people gaslight you so easily, though. Learn to trust what you see with your own two eyes." She sighed. "Every clown call I've ever been to has proven legit, Rookie. Every single one."

CHAPTER TWENTY_

Green couldn't imagine making it a week in this job without encountering someone else's excrement. But cow paddies were far less repulsive than the usual dried and crusted stuff he found in the pant legs of the homeless, so if this checked the box for him for the week, he'd take it.

As far as total volume, it was the most excitement they'd seen in Underwood Heights in weeks. Even Valance had been forced to repress a grin when the suspect, male cow-shifter, 43, had looked them dead in the eyes across the dining room of the MacDougall's Burgers, lowered his pants, and grunted out another paddy. "No mooooo-re slaughter!"

They hadn't waited for him to pull up his pants before they'd cuffed him.

It seemed like a small victory for everyone: Valance and Green had gotten their man with very little resistance, and the suspect had succeeded in making every person enjoying their dinner put their food down and leave. His stunt might not have made them vegetarians, but Green suspected it would be a while before they could eat MacDougalls without thinking of the suspect's flaccid penis, angry grunts, and cow pies.

He stuck the man into the back of the car in the standard steel cuffs—even if he shifted his arms, he wouldn't have been able to slip the cuffs over the hooves—and closed the door. Was the smell of cow dung sticking to the hairs of Green's nostrils, or was he simply smelling the decomposition of the pitch-black swamp fifty yards off?

This was the dark side of scent training. It meant you could smell so much more of the world, and the vast majority of the world did not smell great. To say it was an eighty-twenty split would be generous. More like ninety-ten.

Valance spoke with the manager to iron out the details of issuing the suspect a no-trespass order for the future, while Green's mind wandered as he leaned against the side of their car. It was early in the shift, not yet midnight, and there was a long time to go. He did his best not to think about clowns, but the last twenty-something hours since the encounter had been a losing battle in the regard.

He'd mostly stuck to not speaking to Valance, but admittedly his resolve had begun to deteriorate with time. What was the point, anyway? They were paired up indefinitely. When would a judge hear their case with the leprechaun? How long could Chief Spinner delay it?

The curse, which had at first felt like a simple flu that required rest and lots of fluids, now felt more like a chronic illness. He was learning to manage it, sure, but everything was a little worse now. He'd never realized how much he expected to be in charge of his body's movements and functions until some of that control was taken from him.

He vowed never to take average luck for granted, but even as he vowed it, he knew he'd fall back into its pattern.

A muffled grunt from inside the lemon of a cruiser pulled him from his haze, and he banged on the window beside the suspect's head. "You take a dump in there, and I'm slapping on another charge." What charge, he wasn't sure. Valance was usually pretty good at coming up with them, though.

The suspect stopped grunting. "So, should I just pinch it off where it is, or...?"

Green bowed his head. "Just pinch it off. I'll crack a window."

After he'd done that, he leaned against the car again, staring through the restaurant's large windows where Valance was now chumming it up with the manager and two of the cashiers. Even her charisma was a weapon. She only took it out and used it when she really needed to cut to the heart of a situation. Or cut *out* the heart of it.

He turned his attention away from her and toward the swamp. The moon was nearly full, casting an eerie glow over the thick cypress trees. Under a different moon, he wouldn't have been able to see a thing with the blinding parking lot lights overhead.

Could Caitlin Holloway have been saved in the swamp that night? Could she have been taken in and rehabilitated until she could control her urges as well as Detective Felps? Yes, the baby vampire had come straight for him, but could she really have turned him? Killed him?

You're a human. Of course she could have. Humans were the only ones the vampires *could* turn. The Draculan church had based its entire theology on that fact, claiming that humans were created solely as food for the great vampires.

He had to admit that were he not himself a human, he might've bought that logic. What else were humans good for, really?

Something stirred by the trees, and he blinked. A trick of the light?

He stared not where he'd just seen the movement but nearby to allow his peripheral vision to take over and capture any further activity.

There it was again. Slow, but there. Humanlike, but something told him it was far from human.

Wait, what was he getting worked up about? It was perfectly legal for people to walk around the edges of the swamp, even creep around them. Suspicious, sure, but legal nonetheless.

He was officially paranoid. Too much time around Valance had finally done it. Could he be reconditioned? He'd heard about former cult members going through that. Did they offer it specifically for those who'd fallen under the spell of their FTO?

The sound of boots on pavement pulled his attention back toward the fast-food establishment, where Valance was strutting over, a to-go bag held up in each hand. "They insisted we leave with something."

Green's stomach tightened, and he willed the bile to stay where it was. "Not sure we're going to want to eat in the car."

"Huh?" She set the bags on the top of the cruiser and reached for her key.

"He laid another egg in there."

"Oh, for fuck's... Fine, we'll eat out here, then take him downtown."

Green wasn't sure he could handle any food until she

opened the first bag and he got a whiff, then he was sure he could. At least some fries.

They used the trunk as their table, and Valance divvied out the burgers and fries. He only got a single bite in before loose gravel crunching under thick tires announced the arrival of someone new.

The SUV pulled up behind them, and Detective Felps peered down. "Everything under control?"

"Yes, Dad," Valance replied.

The vibe between them wasn't as icy as before they murdered and buried two clowns together in the woods, but it wasn't exactly congenial. At least not on Valance's part. Green thought it wouldn't hurt her to kiss the vampire's ass a little, or at least endear herself to him if they wanted another ally, but he suspected that was about as likely as her offering up her wrist for Felps to wet his whistle.

Felps held up his hands in surrender. "Just checking."

"I'd offer you something to eat, but I think it might be too dead for you."

Green shot Valance a glare, but she didn't seem to notice.

"I eat cooked meat," Felps said flatly. "Granted, it's not as good as fresh, but laws are laws."

"Fine. You want a burger?"

"Not a MacDougall's one. That's not even meat."

She turned to Green. "Oh, so now he's a snob." She waved off the detective, and he rolled his window back up and drove on through the parking lot.

Green waited until he was out of sight then said, "Why are you antagonizing him? We need him on our side."

Her mouth was full when she paused in her chewing and looked up at him. "Just because he's not gonna turn us in and *might* share our interests doesn't mean he'll ever truly be on our side. I neutralized him last night. That's all that was." She took a sip of her soda. "And it's not our side. It's just the side of people who want to live. And I don't know that the undead will ever pick that side in the long run."

"Have you ever considered that—"

"Probably."

"—he might not be bad *solely* because he's a vampire?"

"Oh, no. I haven't considered that." She crammed a few splayed fries into her mouth.

"Murderers!" the suspect shouted at them, and she slammed a flat palm on the rear window, motioning for him to shut the hell up.

"You didn't think much of me when I started," Green persisted, not entirely sure why he was pushing this point. "You just thought I was a useless human."

"I didn't think that. Okay, the first few days I did, but you proved you were useful pretty quick." She beat on her sternum with a fist until a small belch resulted. "Why are you stuck on this?"

"I don't actually know."

She tilted her head, squinting. "Did he get to you? Did someone speak with you and tell you to get me to lay off?"

"Jesus, Valance. No. No one got to me. It just stands to reason that—"

But now he was certain he'd seen something move by the swamp. The same thing as before, no less. And it was watching him.

He returned to his burger like nothing had happened, but said, "There's someone over there. I think they're watching us."

"Over where?"

"By the swamp."

"Size? Appearance? Movement?"

"I… I can't tell with the lighting. Seemed to move like a human, but a short one."

To herself, she murmured, "Leprechauns don't usually come out here, and they wouldn't go anywhere near the swamps." She set down her food and wiped her hands clean in a stiff napkin. "You think it could just be a homeless person drugged out of their mind and wondering what the cops are doing at their favorite semipublic restrooms?"

"I think it's as likely a homeless person as those clowns were."

"What makes you say that?"

"Just a feeling."

She surprised him by saying, "That'll do." Then she chanced a look in the direction of the figure. "Let's go have a word."

Green nodded to the suspect in their custody. "And leave him here?"

"What's he going to do, poop himself into a coma? He'll empty out soon enough, and you already have the window cracked. Let's go."

But they'd hardly made it out from under the most direct light in the parking lot before the shape disappeared into the trees. "Maybe we should leave it," Green suggested. "No point in forcing a confrontation."

"Good point," she said, but she didn't slow her pace.

He hurried to catch up with her again. "Any chance you remember the last time we followed something into the woods?"

She ignored him.

Dammit.

Not a full day had passed since the clowns, and here he was, pursuing another strange thing into deep woods. Only this time, it was worse. This time it was the swamp.

He pushed thoughts of Caitlin Holloway's staked body from his mind, drew his gun, and entered the murky darkness of the trees.

———

Green cursed his clumsy steps. They weren't yet in the deeper water of the swamp, but the sudden transition from deep mud to a shallow pool of water meant more splashing and squelching sounds than he would have preferred. In comparison with Valance's lethally quiet movements, he felt like a complete buffoon.

She paused and turned toward him. "Tack light off. Let your eyes adjust."

It would be a long few seconds in the transition, at least for him. The night vision of werewolves was much stronger, and he would have to trust her to cover for him temporarily. Thankfully, she was more than capable.

He flicked off his light and shut his eyes to hurry the transition and awaken his other senses.

Confusion unsteadied him as he opened his eyes right as one of the low ferns behind him shook. "Don't shoot," came the whisper. "Valance, it's me."

Detective Felps emerged into a thick beam of moonlight, his hands raised.

Valance looked murderous. "Why are you following us?"

"Why are you wandering off into the swamp?"

"Because we're fucking cops and we saw something suspicious. Why else?"

"That's why I'm following you," he said. "I'm a detective, and I saw something suspicious: two cops on thin ice wandering off into the swamp and leaving the suspect in their custody alone with one of the windows rolled down."

"He shit in the backseat," she hissed. "We don't need your supervision. You can leave."

He took a risk and lowered his hands. "Not a chance. I'm coming with you."

"So I can save your ass again?"

"I think it's more likely I'll have to return the favor."

A cutting screech put a quick end to the conversation, and all eyes turned in the direction of it. High pitched and full-on anguish, it sets Green's nerves on end.

"Rodent," Valance whispered. "Probably a big one. Nutria, maybe."

But that did little to calm his nerves. Nutrias were huge. Which reminded him that there were even larger things out there hunting.

The mud sucked at his boots as they walked deeper, and he hoped to whatever deity might listen that he didn't lose a leg to a gator or step in a water moccasin nest. Those were the real dangers out here, not whatever his imagination could conjure.

"Shit," whispered Valance just ahead of him, and he strained to think of a time when a whispered word had felt so foreboding. She pointed at something on the ground.

It was a footprint. But it lacked the long, stretched-out look of a clown's. Instead, it was small. They were tracking a child.

Green's stomach dropped, and he looked up to meet Valance's eyes. She nodded minutely before proceeding forward.

Had she known it was this from the moment he'd mentioned it? He'd known it too, even if he had refused to so much as say the words in his mind.

Which one was it, though? And could it end a different way from the first they'd found? They were smarter now, knew what they were dealing with. Maybe it could be avoided.

Detective Felps was a variable Green could have done without, though.

A sickening smacking sound caught his attention ahead, and Valance motioned for them to stop just before a small clearing. The MacDougall's roiled in his stomach the second his eyes landed on the small boy and the giant rat.

Melvin Brown was naked from head to toe, caked in mud, and fresh blood covered his light skin in splotches like camouflage as he crouched over his meal.

The boy in the missing person picture had had deep brown skin, perhaps a few shades darker than Green's own. But this boy... there was a hint of the original coloration, but as it turned out, all vampires looked mostly the same.

Felps stepped up on Green's other side, and wore an expression of deep disgust, but not necessarily surprise.

They said nothing, only watched, and Green suspected that two very different plans were being formulated in the minds of those on either side of him.

That suspicion was confirmed the moment Melvin had sated himself on the rat and tossed it aside to scent the air.

The boy's head whipped around, and he was on his feet in a blink.

"Let me handle it," said Felps as Valance drew the extendable stake from her belt.

He stepped forward, drawing the full attention of the

fledgling. The boy's lips were blue, his eyes large, dark saucers.

"Melvin, right?"

The boy's head cocked to the side like a confused Labrador.

"Melvin, I'm like you. I know you're scared and confused, but I can help you."

"I don't think you *are* like him," Valance warned.

But Felps ignored it, inching closer to the boy.

Then Green felt it. The first tingle. *No, not now!*

He looked at Valance, whose attention was locked onto the scene in front of them, though a slight crinkle of her nose told him all he needed to know. She felt it too. Like the water being drawn away from the beach before a tsunami.

"You can sense it, can't you?" Felps continued. "I'm like you. I'm not prey. I'm the predator. Maybe no one's explained this to you, but I outrank you. You must do as I command. Refusing could hurt you. But I won't command you to do anything that could cause you harm, Melvin. I need you to trust me. I know you're scared…"

Something slithered against Green's calf, and he yanked his foot up from it on impulse. Only, the mud had locked his boot in, and he couldn't get free.

His jerk caught Valance's attention, and she shot him a look, but he only pointed toward the ground. A second later, she also tried to jerk away, and found herself similarly stuck.

Mustering the necessary courage, Green cast his attention at the ground. Not one, but two snakes were slithering around them, scenting the air by their lower appendages. The actual pattern of their markings was lost to his crappy night vision, though it would be just his luck right now for them to both be highly venomous. Valance leaned down slowly and used the tip of her stake to scoop one up and move it gently away. It slithered off, and its friend followed. If she'd tried that a few moments later, he was sure the results wouldn't have been as positive.

"There you go," Felps said softly. "Just relax. It's okay. I can take you somewhere safe where you'll be fed properly. You probably miss your parents, too. I can take you to them, once we get you cleaned up."

Melvin's pupils shrank, and his posture morphed slowly into that of a scared child. Whatever alpha vamp shit Felps was doing seemed to be working.

And then there was the low growl behind them.

It was a specific kind of sound, one Green had encountered only a few times before but would never forget. There was a gurgling to it that made it clear it was not mammalian. Green struggled to free his feet from the sucking sludge, but the more he fought, the deeper he sank. Valance twisted toward the sound, too, and extended her gun futilely.

They were between a rock and a hard place now. A baby vampire and a full-blooded ancient alligator. Both officers would have to unload their entire magazine into the scaly beast to slow it down. The sound of that would trigger whatever baser instincts were simmering under the pale skin of Melvin Brown...

The tidal wave touched land.

The gator opened its mouth and charged.

Green's gun misfired, but perhaps through sheer force of will, Valance's worked. She emptied it into the open mouth of the predator, hitting her mark even while her feet were stuck facing the opposite direction. It was over in a flash, and both officers whirled back toward the original threat.

Melvin had gone into another crouch, and Felps had his hands out, talking the boy down urgently. "It was just an alligator. They're not here to hurt you." Then he muttered, "Oh, forget it," and raised his voice. "I command you adhere to my will, Melvin."

If that was supposed to do something useful, Green didn't see it.

But it did make *something* happen in the child.

Dark gray fur shot from the boy's every pore and the crunch of bones marked the start of a violent transformation.

Felps stumbled back. "The hell?"

"Like I said,"—Valance holstered her gun and took out the stake again—"I don't think you're the same as this one, Felps."

She grunted, and her legs changed to their lupine form just long enough to allow her to slip free of the mud-logged boots.

She stood barefoot in the swamp, the stake held out in front of her, watching as Melvin threw back his head and let out a long howl.

Green couldn't believe what he was seeing. It made no sense, broke so many laws of nature. But if he was going to get out of this alive, he needed to believe his own eyes.

But still, motherfucking *werevampires*?

Valance shouted to Felps then tossed him the stake. "Bad luck. I can't do it. It'll go sideways."

He looked down at the stake in his hands then back to the transforming child in front of him. "Will this even work?"

"You said it yourself. A stake through the heart will kill anything."

There was a low creak then a crunch, and the old tree nearest to him began to topple. "Look out!" Valance yelled, leaping for him.

Her belt snapped.

She grasped at it.

A nutria ran in front of her.

She tripped over it.

Green ducked and covered his head with his arms.

Valance fell face first in the mud next to him.

The tree landed on him.

He got a mouthful of decomposing earth.

Lifting his head out of the sucking ground that had cushioned his fall and possibly saved his life, he looked up just in time to see the monstrous werewolf-vampire hybrid charging for him, hairy, bloody, fangs bared.

There was no shriek when the stake erupted through Melvin's chest, only a surprised wheeze, then a devastating silence.

Valance pulled herself out of the mud with a loud squelching and got slowly to her feet. She squeegeed mud from her face and flicked it to the side as she stood over the murdered child.

Felps was breathing heavily as he took in the resulting scene of chaos—the fallen tree, the rookie pinned underneath it but alive, the gator with half its head missing, and finally, the small, pale body curled on its side in the fetal position.

"I didn't know what else to do," Felps whispered.

"Nothing else you could do," Valance replied. "These things don't belong in the world. This child was worse than dead already. And if we let them grow to adulthood—Jason, I've fought the big ones. No, scratch that. I've *run* from the big ones. There's no fighting them. Not close up. It takes big guns, and I mean big."

"South America?" Felps said. "They had these down there?"

She nodded. "These things were half the reason we went down there in the first place, and they were the entire reason it took so long for us to win."

"But how? How can a vampire change into a wolf?"

She reached down and helped Green wiggle free of the tree that pinned him. His back ached right around his kidneys where he'd taken the brunt of the impact, but merely peeing blood would be considered a win, given the events of the last thirty seconds.

"There'll be time for all those impossible questions later," she finished. "But I think we'd better bury this body."

Felps looked up at her finally. "Who else was it with Caitlin? Was it just you two?"

"I'll tell you after you help me dispose of this body."

He looked almost ready to, but then he spluttered, "This —This isn't like the clowns, Valance! This is... We need to report this. We have to bring this in and show—"

She swung her next words at him like a machete. "What ranking officer do you think we can show this to who doesn't already know?" She glared at him. "You're in homicide, for chrissakes. You can't tell me the case of the Holloway girl isn't blindingly obvious. Hell, you seemed to figure it out without much help. Your detective sergeant knows, too. And I'd bet the commander and assistant chiefs and Spinner himself have an idea about it. A string of missing children from a wealthy werewolf neighborhood, none of whom have experienced their first shift? Remains of one turn up in the swamp with a stake in her? Come on.

Doesn't take a genius to figure it out. But it *does* take a department-wide cover up to play this stupid."

"I can't just dump him. Think of his family, Valance. Don't they deserve some closure?"

She lowered her head. "You're right. You want to save them pain, and I respect that. Do you have any children, Felps?"

"You know I can't."

"Right, right. I don't have any, either. Neither does Green. But we don't need to, to understand that telling a woman that her abducted child was drained to the brink of death, kept in a coma for a week, and poked and prodded with instruments until the werewolf gene came forward. Then, they awoke in excruciating agony and confusion, the loving child they were all but gone. You don't need to have children to understand that no mother wants to hear *that*. That's not closure, that's just driving a stake through her heart as well."

"Is that really how they do it?" Green asked, horrified.

"It's how they did it in Guatemala."

Felps squinted at her. "But that takes an entire lab setup. And somewhere to keep the children before the first change."

She nodded.

"Do you know where it is?"

"Not yet. But I'm close."

"And when you find it?" he said. "Are you going to call it in?"

Green wasn't sure if she'd grinned or scowled, but it was all the same on her.

"What do *you* think?"

The detective didn't need to say. Everyone knew.

He looked down at the body. "He's just a little boy."

"He hasn't been a little boy for a while, Felps. You just put him out of his misery. Dust to dust now. He was a wolf by nature. We'll leave him somewhere the moon can find him."

Felps' top lip curled as he glared at her through the soft moonlight. "You're poison." Then he bent at the waist and scooped the body of Melvin Brown into his arms. "I'll do this myself."

CHAPTER TWENTY-ONE_

It was nearly 3 a.m. The jail had been packed full, and processing times were lagging. Green had offered to stay behind and clean the cow-shifter's shit from the back seat just so he didn't risk running into his ex, the telepath Nurse Hellstrom, at reception. His nerves were already shot.

They'd left Detective Felps behind to bury the body. What he'd done in between the completion of that and when he met up with them later for a debrief over dinner, Green didn't know and knew he would never ask.

"Oh, absolutely not," Felps said as he stepped down from his SUV in the strip mall parking lot and shut the door behind him. "*This* is the restaurant you picked? I can't go in there."

"Don't worry," Valance said. "You're with me."

Green couldn't imagine how that was supposed to reassure the vampire after what he'd just experienced *with her* in the swamp.

When Felps planted his feet, she turned sharply and said, "Wolves know how to keep our mouths shut. This is the best place we can be right now. I trust these people. Sure, they won't love you being here, but I'm not a fan of spending my dinner break with you either. And I assume like the feeling is mutual. We have things to discuss, though."

The neon lights of the sign for Roman's Ramen glowed like a beacon. Green had officially been here enough times to crave it the moment the scent hit his nostrils. Or maybe it was just another layer of his Stockholm Syndrome since he'd only ever come here when Valance or Bannockburn had something important to tell him that could potentially ruin his life.

Valance entered the restaurant first and waited until Felps had stepped up beside her before announcing to the handful of occupied tables, the servers, and the cook behind the line, "They're both with me. I'll stake him myself if he tries anything."

Felps grunted, and Green sidestepped to put a little more distance between him and the other two of his party.

Once they were seated, the owner, Roman, stomped over and shoved three menus at them. "Heather, this is a bridge too far, and you know it."

"If you had a clue what he'd just done, dinner would be on the house. Trust me on this, Roman. You know I'm always on your side."

"You're putting me in one hell of a position, bringing him in here. When it was just the human, I was happy to let it slide. After all, what's the worst he can do? But a— One of his kind?"

She narrowed her eyes at the owner and said, "Where'd you serve?"

"Southern Mexico," he replied automatically.

She grinned. "That's a strange name for Guatemala."

The owner scanned his surroundings quickly. "The US was never in Guatemala." These words, too, sounded rehearsed.

"Right, right." She waved off his clear bullshit. "And vampires can't turn young werewolves."

Roman's eyes went wide for only a moment before he swallowed and turned his attention to Detective Felps. "Were you in the war?"

"Of course."

"Where'd you serve?"

"Columbia."

The owner addressed Valance again. "Is he lying?"

"Fuck if I know."

"Why did you bring him here?"

"We need somewhere safe to talk. The three of us just got back from Guatemala, if you catch my drift."

Roman flinched almost imperceptibly. "Holy shit. You don't mean wolfen—" He caught himself and paused. "You're not playing, are you?" Valance shook her head. "Okay, fine, he can stay this one time. But I'm charging you double for everything. I'm gonna have to talk to each of these tables individually..."

"No cop discount?" she said.

"That includes the cop discount. Now, what do you wanna eat?"

Not the most assuring thing someone could say before preparing his food, but Green put in his order, and Valance ordered for both herself and Felps.

"I can't tell," she said, once Roman was gone, "if you're looking pale or this is just how you always look."

"I'm fine," Felps said firmly.

"Mm-hm. Okay, if we're all going to make it through this, we need to get our stories straight and be on the same page."

Felps exhaled and braced his elbows on the table before running both palms through his hair. "I can't believe this."

"Here's the story," Valance cut in. "We were at the MacDougall's, and Green saw something by the edge of the swamp. He and I went to check it out, Felps thought we might need backup. Our bad luck hit, we shot an alligator, and Green got his ass handed to him by a tree. That's it. We had to dig him out."

"What about the body mics?" asked Felps.

"During the ruckus, they got unclipped and lost in the mud."

"Mine's already synced with the car, though."

She raised her eyebrows. "Yours?"

He looked down at his vest and groaned. "When did you swipe it?"

"In the swamp, obviously. That shit couldn't make it out of there."

Green hadn't noticed his own missing, and his desire to check to see if it was still attached to his uniform was only outmatched by his desire to look like he'd noted the absence before she'd mentioned it.

"Any questions about the story?"

They spent the next few minutes ironing out the finer points. Then, when Green thought he might get a silent moment to steady his spinning thoughts, Valance said, "I think it's time I tell you about my vacation."

Felps's head snapped up from where he'd held it in his hands, and Green experienced a blast of foreboding that left him lightheaded.

"I don't have a picture of me in a bikini if that's what you two boys are so worked up about." Nobody laughed. "Ecuador. That's where I went. It's the only place I have contacts now. The rest were decommissioned. They knew too much." Roman passed by and chucked their appetizer on the table without slowing. Valance was the only one to dig in. "I helped bring down two facilities in Guatemala that made the hybrids. These were advanced facilities, and that was years ago. I imagine the technology has gotten more compact, but it'll still be expensive."

"How does it work?"

"I'm a soldier, not a scientist. But it has something to do with simultaneously repressing one gene while stimulating another and then switching back at just the right time. And you have to have the right subjects. I'd bet you can guess who the right subjects are."

Felps nodded. "Same pattern was happening down there?"

"Precisely. I thought maybe I was just paranoid after the first two disappearances here—two dots make a line, not a pattern—but then we found Caitlin Holloway, and I knew."

Green said, "But she didn't change into a werewolf. She never sprouted hair or any of that."

"She didn't have to. But I suspect if we hadn't been so quick with the stake, she would have. Or maybe her transformation wasn't entirely complete when she slipped away."

"But you didn't *know* then," Green countered. "She could have been a human who was turned."

"Okay, fine. Have it your way. I didn't *know*, but I knew."

"Go back to your vacation," prompted Felps.

She popped a pork dumpling into her mouth and took

her time getting started. There was little Valance liked more than being in control, and she had all the power here. "You know how war goes. No one's innocent. Not even the so-called liberators. It's war. It's messy. I know I killed my fair share of innocent people doing what had to be done. Anyway, we managed to bomb all the laboratories that created the hybrids—What? Don't look at me like that, Rookie. Didn't I *just* say war is messy?" She shook her head. "As far as I knew, and I knew pretty far, there were no more of the labs left, and the scientists who knew the process were neutralized as well. The technology should have died out."

"But?"

"But—Oh, thanks, Roman. This looks great." She grinned at the owner, who ignored her and promptly left. "Eat up. It's not any good when it's cold." She set out her napkin on her lap, and Green wanted to strangle her for abusing their attention this way.

Felps seemed to share the feeling. "The technology died out?"

"Right! Right. Obviously it didn't. There were a few days between when I returned the intel from my mission to my commander and when the bombs actually dropped. Someone extracted the process during that time."

"Another commando or a mole?"

"I'd guess mole."

"American?"

"Ding ding!"

"The weapons of war always find their way home," Green muttered. Then louder, "God dammit, Valance. Why couldn't you just tell me?"

"Like you said, I didn't *know*."

"But you knew."

"Sure. And after what we just saw in the woods, I now *know*."

Felps tasted his soup and seemed to approve of the warm liquid.

Valance waved down the owner. "You forgot the free rolls."

"They're not free for you. Five bucks."

"For shit's sake. Fine. It's coming out of your tip."

"Then, ten bucks."

She waved him off. "They're not that good anyway."

Green happened to know they were that good, but he kept his mouth shut.

Valance tore into her noodles, then wiped her mouth and said, "Aren't you going to ask me why we can't have vampire-werewolf hybrids?"

"I don't need to ask," snapped Felps. "It's obvious."

She looked to Green, who cringed apologetically. "Yeah, I'd like to know."

"We can't have wolfenvamps running around because they will flay every last citizen from mouth to anus."

Green choked on his broth and had to press the napkin to his lips to keep the food in. Finally, he choked out, "Fair enough."

"Vampires used to be human, which means that, as much as I hate to admit it, they aren't complete monsters. That human part keeps them anchored even with all the bloodlust."

"We prefer to call it intravenous appetite," Felps corrected.

Valance ignored him. "And werewolves are humanlike

most of the time. Yes, we can let loose, and it's *lots* of fun, but humanity is our baseline, and it keeps us anchored.

"But you squeeze a vampire and a werewolf into a single body, and there's no room for humanity. Its resting state is vampire, and it only gets fiercer from there. There's no reasoning with them. No controlling them. None. The only thing to do with one is to end it."

Felps put down his spoon. "Enough of the horror stories, Valance, okay? I think we're all well and truly set for nightmares as it is. The answer I really need from you is, what are you going to do about this? Now that you know, what are you going to do?"

"Nothing to damage your precious self-made career, don't worry."

"I don't give two shits about my career when this is what's at stake."

"Pun intended?"

"Tell me," he demanded. "What are you going to do?"

To Green's surprise, she simply leaned back in the booth next to him and shrugged. "I don't know yet. What do you think I should do?"

Felps just shook his head and stared out the window. "Hell if I know. But I can put my feelers out, touch base with some of the people in the department I trust."

"That sounds like a good start." She paused. "I'll get the bill. You can split if you want."

He didn't hesitate to get to his feet, but before he left, he looked down at them. "We're in this together, right?"

"Right."

"Can I have your word that you won't do anything rash until I can get a feel of things in homicide, and we can make a clear plan?"

Valance paused, seemed to consider it, then nodded. "That sounds incredibly sane. I'm actually glad to have you on our team."

The vampire didn't look reassured, per se, but he looked slightly less disgruntled than before as he stomped out to his vehicle.

"This one's on me." Valance reached in her pocket, threw a hundred dollars cash on the table, and scooted out of the booth.

Both took a moment to stretch before heading for the door, and Green said, "You know, I'm glad you agreed to Felps' plan. It sounds like a solid—"

"Oh please, Rookie. Letting him *feel it out*? Waiting around? Why would I agree to that bullshit?"

Green's stomach sank. "Because it's sane?" he countered. "Logical?"

She scoffed. "Exactly. It would never work in reality. No, I'll tell you what I'm gonna do." She grinned. "I'm gonna burn this motherfucker to the ground."

Green swiveled his head to take in the dining room. "*This* motherfucker?"

"Huh? No. Why would I burn Roman's Ramen to the ground?"

"I had no idea. That's why I asked. What are you burning to the ground then?"

Her eyes cut into him like daggers. "All of it."

She turned for the exit but didn't even make it a step before she tripped over an untied shoelace and landed on the tile floor with a loud crack. "Starting with that *son of a bitch* leprechaun."

CHAPTER TWENTY-TWO_

"Lissen, Officer. Lissen. Just lissen."

"I'm listening." Green stood with his thumbs tucked into his duty belt, staring down at the intoxicated man sitting on the curb at the side of the road not long before midnight. The john's words were slurred, but that made sense. You'd have to be trashed to think a five-dollar hand job was a good investment, and nothing short of shitfaced to see the transaction through.

"Lissen, just lissen. I know what you're thinking. But I couldn't resist! S'impossible to resist the siren's call! I swear I was just going out for a carton of cigarettes, and then she called to me, and I couldn't resist. If she'd asked for a hundred, I woulda had to give it to her."

"If she'd asked for $100, you might have gotten a real service." Green sighed. He'd listened enough. He'd have to break the bad news to this guy eventually. "So, you say you were lured in by her siren song?"

The john nodded his head in a wobbly circle. "Yes, *absolutely*. That's exactly it."

"Uh-huh. Just one problem. Your lady friend is not a siren. She's not even a lady, biologically speaking." He cast a glance over his shoulder at Valance. She was chatting casually with Juan Pablo Domingo, who had spread himself across the hood of this sucker's old sedan.

The john slipped off the curb as he hurriedly adjusted to get another look at Domingo. "Wha? No. That's not right. You have the wrong—"

"What'd the so-called siren say her name was?"

"Juanita."

"Right. That sounds awfully like Juan, doesn't it? And it's *Juan* on his ID, so…"

Eyes crossing slightly, the john threw a finger into the air, declaring, "There are male sirens, then!"

"No, there aren't. If you saw a fish tail of any kind, it's because Mr. Domingo is a tuna-shifter."

The john's mouth fell open. "D'you jussay *tuna?*"

"Yes, sir."

"I fucked a *tuna fish?*"

Green was just about to stick his notepad away, but now he paused. "Wait, you say you had sex with Mr. Domingo? Earlier, you said it was just a hand job. A five-dollar hand job." The odds of penetrative sex costing only a fiver were small, even in this part of town. So, if the money exchanged was a little higher, they might be able to stick this guy with a better charge.

But the john didn't seem to hear the question at all. "I fucked a fish… Wait." He looked up. "If there's no pussy…?"

Green schooled his expression.

"You're not gonna tell my girlfriend, are you, Officer?"

"That's not part of my job, no. Who you call from jail

and how you handle your personal affairs afterward is up to you."

"But the report... you're not actually going to write down that I—"

Green jotted down *harpooned a tuna* on his pad and then tucked it away. "The police report will include all pertinent information, including how much money was exchanged for what sex act and the species of both parties."

And now, the john began to cry in earnest.

"Great news, Rookie," Valance said, appearing next to him.

"Juan just committed his life to Jesus?"

"Please, Jesus wouldn't have that lunatic." She narrowed her eyes on the bawling mess in the gutter. "He really didn't know it was a tuna-shifter, huh?" She sighed and nodded for Green to step a few feet away with her, where they could still keep eyes on Domingo and his customer without being overheard. "Looks like it started out with a hand job, but Juan up-sold your guy on a bunch of other services. Apparently,"—she suppressed a smile—"Domingo's started some sort of monthly membership for his services. Not sure if he uses a punch card or what, but it's hard to beat that kind of entrepreneurial spirit. Anyway, the cash exchanged enhances the charge."

"Sounds like his community college business classes are paying off."

Valance glanced over her shoulder. Juan Domingo had transformed his lower half into a metallic fin that reflected the harsh light from the gas station. The shifter giggled and pretended to be a mermaid.

She turned back to Green. "I'll be sure to thank his professors once he stops hooking. That's not the great news

I had, though." She peeked at the john on the curb, then hesitated before reaching for her radio. "Fang 9-01 requesting backup." She added the address, and a moment later, a response came from Lawrence. *"Fang 9-13 to 9-01. Is that the prostitution call? Why do you need backup?"*

"Just get over here, 9-13," she snapped, making Green decide against asking her the same question.

She leaned close now, and Green swallowed against the impulse to step back. "Okay, the good news. You ready?"

He nodded.

"The judge saw our case today. Ruled that the curse had to be lifted by midnight tonight."

"Are you serious?"

She nodded conspiratorially, making him think that maybe it meant something entirely different to her than what it meant to him, namely, freedom of movement. "That's... that's *amazing* news, Valance! Wait, when did you hear about that?"

"Just now. Bannockburn's been keeping an eye on it through his contacts."

"It lifts at midnight, and no one even bothered to tell us? Not anyone from the court or the department or anything?"

She shrugged.

Indignation pumped throughout his body, filling his arms and legs with adrenaline. "But... we should be the *first* to know! It's practically ruined my life!"

"Pour yourself a glass of cab and stop being so dramatic, Norma. You're fine. You survived it. But also, you really expected the department to communicate anything of importance?"

Green shook his head and tried to heed her advice. She

was right. At least this was almost over. He just had to make it until midnight.

He looked at his watch. Just past eleven. "Valance, it's almost done."

She grinned wide, and he trusted nothing about that. "I know. You ready?"

He blinked. "Wait. Ready? You just mean to be out of the shit luck, right?"

"You know me better than that."

Green leaned his head back to stare up at the night sky. "Fuck."

"You're prettier when you smile, you know. And you forget one crucial detail. Leprechauns use earth magic. Earth magic!"

He didn't know what the hell that was. Did it involve droves of bunnies coming out of a person's pants? Because if it did, she could count him out of whatever plan she had in mind.

When he showed no outward signs of comprehension, she groaned. "You're kidding me. You don't know what earth magic is, do you?"

"Why don't you just tell me?"

"Earth magic is neutral."

"Uh, I beg to differ. If it's what that curse is, then it's very, very negative."

"But that's just it! It demands balance. So, yes, we've had only awful luck for months, but nature will step in and correct once that curse is removed." She jabbed him playfully in the kevlar. "Rookie, you and I are about to be two of the luckiest kids in the world, starting just under an hour."

He cringed without meaning to. "Are you serious?"

She nodded. "It's actually a good thing you pissed off the chief and got him to drag it out as long as he could. You bought us even better luck in the end, and let me tell you, we're going to need all of it we can get tonight."

"No," he groaned. "No, no, no. Why can't I just enjoy this? Why do you have to ruin it?"

"Ruin it? Are you that thick?" She clapped him on the shoulder. "Tonight, I'm gonna show you a better time than any trans-tuna-shifter ever could. You're gonna get lucky in the best possible way."

She started to back toward Juan, and he called after her, "Then why am I so full of dread?"

"Who am I, your court-appointed therapist?"

Lawrence pulled up alongside them a moment later but didn't do more than roll down his window and call out, "Yeah, really looks like you need backup."

Valance asked Juan Domingo, "He one of your subscribers?"

The tuna-shifter ran a hand over some of his more sensitive scales and licked his lips as he winked at Lawrence. "No, but I hope to make him one soon. I could cut him a discount."

"Good to see you too, Juan," Lawrence said, then to Valance. "Why did you call me out here, Heather?"

"I need you to take our john downtown."

He laughed. "Not a chance, and you know it."

"Lawrence," she said sternly. "I wouldn't ask if it wasn't important."

"What could be so important for you two shitshows on wheels tonight?"

She pressed her lips together like she might not tell him, then finally, she said, "Spinner wants to see us."

Lawrence's beautiful eyes lit up. "The *chief* wants to see you two?" He put his car into park. "Well, shit. You'd better go see him straight away."

"Gee, thanks. I'm gonna pretend you're not thrilled to see us get a slap on the wrist."

Lawrence left the engine running and stepped out of his vehicle. "If it's Spinner who wants to see you, you're going to get more than a slap on the wrist. But sure. I'll take it from here."

A few minutes later, Green shut the car door behind him and shared a look with his co-conspirator.

"What?" Valance said, taking in his disapproving look. "Like you care if I lie to him. Please, everyone knows you two want to see each other flattened by a garbage truck in broad daylight."

Green cringed. "Uh, no? I don't, in fact, want to see that happen to him. Jesus."

She crinkled her nose. "Ah, well, I don't know how to tell you this, then, but Lawrence wants to see that happen to you. Awkward. Anyway, let's get a move on. Because our good luck is going to be preceded by extraordinary misfortune. We don't want to be on the road when that happens."

"Where are we going?"

"You'll see."

———

With seven minutes until midnight, Valance pulled the car over in an empty warehouse parking lot in the now-familiar Underwood Heights neighborhood. She shut off the engine.

Green reached for the seatbelt release.

"Nuh-uh," she said. "I have a feeling you're going to want to keep that on for a little while longer."

Since he was still in the dark on her plan, and couldn't bail on it if he tried, he went ahead and submitted himself to her orders.

As long as they were stuck in the car together, he might as well ask the pertinent questions. "You think the laboratory is right around here, don't you? In Underwood Heights?"

"Yep."

The moon above them went dark, and Green looked up through the windshield to see what had caused it.

With five minutes left until midnight, the murder of crows dipped and flew lower to the ground, headed right for their junker.

"Here it comes," Valance breathed.

The poop barrage was like none Green had ever experienced. It sounded like they were caught in a hail storm, and it didn't let up until every millimeter of the windshield was covered.

But once the drumming of bird droppings on the roof ended, Valance activated the windshield wipers so they could see ahead again.

Four minutes till midnight.

Out of the darkness near one of the warehouses, a figure emerged. Green had a bad feeling about this.

"Just stay in the car, no matter what," Valance said. "Don't let anything tempt you out until after midnight."

"What if the car explodes?"

She turned toward him. "Well, that would be pretty bad luck for us, wouldn't it?"

He wondered how many commandos had heard a joke like that from her right before they were blown to pieces.

The figure approached, seemingly oblivious to the lone vehicle. Only when he crossed in front of the headlights did he look up.

"Is that...?"

Valance groaned. "Yes, I think that's the shifter from MacDougall's."

The man looked up, shielding his eyes, and when he saw who was in the driver's seat, he didn't hesitate.

He hurried over to the car, shouting at them, apparently under the belief that being out on bail meant he was untouchable, and crawled up onto the hood, slipping and sliding on the existing bird excrement that hadn't yet had time to dry.

He faced them directly as he dropped his drawers.

Valance stared determinedly, and Green wondered if that was how she always looked at men with their dicks out.

Then the shifter did what he did best. "Come arrest me! Come get me—uuuurg—now!"

"You sure I can't get out of the car?" Green said. "What he's doing violates at least one federal statute I can think of."

"Don't think I don't want to catch him with his pants down, too, Rookie. But neither of us would survive long enough to take him in, anyway."

It was three minutes until midnight when the shifter had finished unloading and ran off again.

"Valance, is it common knowledge that the moments leading up to a leprechaun curse reversal can be especially deadly?"

"What are you getting at?"

"Would the higher-ups in the department know it? Spinner?"

"Oh yes, they'd know."

"And still, the only way you and I found out about it was through the corporal's tip-off?"

She nodded.

"What would have happened if we hadn't known and were just out on a call right now?"

"I suspect *at least* two officers would be down tonight."

He didn't ask any more questions after that. He didn't need to.

Green's phone rang from the side door compartment, and he pulled it out and looked at the caller ID. It was his mom.

"Don't answer it," Valance warned.

"But she never calls. Someone might be in trouble." His thoughts leaped immediately to his little sister, and he answered before she could protest further.

"Hey, Mom. What's going on?"

He listened for a response, to gauge the tone of her voice so he could prepare himself for whatever tragic news might follow.

But the sounds that erupted through the speaker left little doubt as to what was happening back home.

"Hello?" he said again. "*Mom?*"

His follow-up was met with a sensual moan. Heavy breathing. Deep, masculine grunts.

His mouth fell open, and he pulled the phone away from his ear to stare down at it in horror. The sounds continued to pulse from the speaker, filling the car with a tinny and wholly unwelcome lust.

"Yes, just like that, Harold! Harder! Harder!"

Green ended the call and threw the phone onto the floorboard like it'd burned him.

"Everything okay at home?" Valance asked amusedly.

"I–I think it was a butt dial."

Valance chuckled. "Sounded like it. Oh, don't act so horrified. How do you think you came about? Good for them for keeping the fire alive, really." When he didn't say anything, she went on. "Rookie, when a man and a woman are bonded together in holy matrimony, sometimes they like to—"

"It wasn't my dad's name she was moaning."

"Oh, fuck."

Silence.

Two minutes left until midnight.

BLAM!

Green jumped and tried to duck and cover as best he could while buckled in. His ears rang, and he stuck a finger in one to make sure it wasn't bleeding. Then he checked the rest of his body because he was absolutely sure what he'd just heard was a gunshot.

He was fine.

Ears still ringing, he checked on his partner.

She was okay.

Sense returned to him slowly. The blast had come from in the car. It wasn't the sound of a pistol, though. Which meant it had to be the shotgun they kept in the compartment in front of him. Had the pellets destroyed the engine? Punctured a tire?

He reached for the compartment to check the damage of the random blast.

"Don't!"

He yanked his hand back.

"Don't check on it until after midnight," she instructed. "We're both alive, and that's all that matters."

One minute until midnight. Green's heart raced, partially from the recent blast, but mostly from anticipation.

A light in the night sky caught his attention. It grew brighter quickly. A shooting star burning up in the atmosphere? Seemed like it, but there was no tail. Or at least none he could see.

Wait. If he couldn't see the tail…

"Incoming," Valance said. "Hold on to something."

He braced on the dashboard with his right hand and covered his balls with his left.

The meteorite was a small one, but it got the job done. It smashed into the warehouse lot with such force next to them that the police car was launched into the air, flipped, and came to rest upside down in a matter of seconds that felt like an eternity.

Debris rained down on the exposed underbelly of the vehicle, but Green hardly noticed it. His window was shattered, and through the open hole, he could make out the smoldering remains of the impact.

The clock on the dash turned to midnight.

From beside him: "What'd I tell you about the seatbelt?"

His was currently cutting into him as he hung upside down, but yes, he was glad he'd worn it.

Was it over? Had they survived? His whole body ached from the last few minutes, but he was alive. There was that. "Aren't we supposed to have good luck n—"

Another massive impact on the other side of them made his teeth rattle in his skull, and the car was thrown again, flipped, and landed right side up, tires once again touching asphalt.

"Yes," said Valance. "It's time for the fun part. But let's not get ahead of ourselves. Check the gun box."

He reached forward, shocked that the mechanisms were even working after the battering of the two meteorites, and saw that the shotgun *had* discharged, but it had shot straight out the side of the car. There would be no damage to the engine or tire at that exit angle.

The sound of a phone ringing pulled his attention back to the cab, and he looked around for the source, unsure where his cell had ended up in the fray.

Valance reached down and plucked it from the space by her feet. "It's for you." She held it out.

He checked the caller ID, but he already knew who it would be. This would be humiliating at best. Now really wasn't the time. "I can call her back later."

"I think you'd better answer it now."

He winced and braced himself but continued to do as he was told. "Hello?"

"Hi, sorry to call so late. This is Donna Capri. I hate to bother you, but I found this cell phone at the supermarket this morning, and I'm trying to figure out whose it is. Yours is the most recent number listed, so."

Green lowered his head and exhaled. "Yeah. This is Norman Green. You have my mother's cell phone. I'll text you her address in the morning."

He disconnected to find Valance grinning at him. "Not your mother after all? It's lucky that good Samaritan called you when she did so you didn't have to obsess over it."

A thunderclap from the clear sky, and then clouds appeared and opened up overhead. "Almost time, Rookie."

The rain poured until all the crow and shifter shit

dripped onto the ground around them. Green didn't even mind getting wet through the shattered window.

She started the engine. "Still works. You ready for the luckiest night of your life?"

Finally, he exhaled. "About damn time, really."

CHAPTER TWENTY-THREE

Valance slowed the cruiser to a crawl as they approached a fork in the road.

"What is it?" he asked.

"I've narrowed it down to two possible locations for the main hub of the experiments. One's to the right, the other's to the left. I haven't been able to eliminate—"

A bolt of lightning struck a tree in front of them, causing it to split down the middle. The dislodged half tumbled over and blocked the fork to the right.

"Guess it's the one to the left," she said, and she sped up again.

"It's not that I don't trust you," Green said, "but how exactly are two of us going to take down an entire operation like this without backup? I don't know anything about science or tech. I wouldn't even know what to unplug first."

"You know how to use a stake, though, right?"

He groaned.

"And I know you can handle yourself in hand-to-shillelagh combat."

"God, no…" he groaned. "Not more leprechauns…"

"Take it easy, champ. We won't be going in alone."

"Who's meeting us there? Shouldn't you radio to them where we're going?"

"You really don't get it yet, do you? We don't *need* to radio. We're riding this wave all the way back to shore, Rookie. We're getting *lucky*."

They pulled into a row of upscale stores, and Valance turned off the headlights and parked. They were the only car in the split-level parking lot built around the existing geography of the land. Rather than flattening the hills, this developer had leaned into it, allowing a little copse of oaks with stone stairs between it to connect the higher and lower levels. "I got a little something for us in the back, don't worry."

When she opened the trunk and he peered inside, all he saw was a large gun case. Well, guns could kill leprechauns, at least. But he really, really didn't want to shoot anyone tonight.

But then she opened the case. The first things that caught Green's eye were the shiny gold medallions. "We're not risking it again," she said. "Don't give this to anyone, no matter what."

He slipped the leprechaun coin around his neck and tucked it under his bulletproof vest.

The rest of the case was occupied by a large collection of wooden stakes.

"Here you have your run-of-the-mill extendable one. Just press the button so it extends, then drive it through the heart. This little one"—she held it up—"is non-lethal. Keep it in your breast pocket, and if they get ahold of you, stick it in their neck. It'll incapacitate them. And this one"—she held up what looked like a compact bazooka—"is the stake launcher. You wouldn't think you can aim well with it, but check this out." She flicked a small switch, and a laser shot out from the tip. "Easy as pie. Take one of each."

"How am I supposed to hold all of them?"

"Well, this one has a strap." She threw said strap over his shoulder, and he felt the weight of the stake launcher hit his back. "This one tucks into your pocket or vest. And this one… take your Taser off your belt. You won't need that."

Once they were set, they crept toward the row of shops. A pizza parlor, something called cryotherapy, an orthodontist's office, and a clothing boutique. "Which one is it?"

"All of them," she whispered.

He scanned the signs again. "All of them?"

"What, you think vampires have figured out how to turn *werewolves*, but you don't think they can manage a few shell businesses as cover?"

"How did you discover this was the place?"

"I'm trained to gauge distances. Every single one of these businesses' interiors is only half as deep as the building itself. A lot is going on back there that we don't see."

"But this area, how did you know to look *here*?"

"For one, it backs up to the same swamp as Shady Grove. But also, Tartan Lane runs right behind this place. Starts in Crown Tree, where it's called Holy Hog Boulevard, but the name changes a few miles down. Easy transport. No stop signs, no traffic cams, almost no traffic. The perfect route to take a child you've just abducted. Every other route out of Crown Tree requires getting on the highway, and no one with half a brain would risk that with all the traffic cams and plate readers up and down there."

They watched the quiet facades of the closed shops for a moment longer, crouched behind a stone wall that separated the parking lot's two levels.

Nothing moved. The shops appeared empty.

"How are we going to get in there?" Green asked.

"Through the front door."

"But, won't they notice us?"

"No doubt. Let's go."

She got ten yards on him before he hustled after her. The air in those first few minutes after midnight had carried a special charge, but that electric feeling was quickly fading, and he wondered if it had taken his good fortune along with it.

But he needn't have feared, because the moment they reached the exterior lights of the shopping center, the air lit up around him again with the same frenetic ions.

Valance chose the orthodontist's office in the middle of the row as their point of entry, and when she tried the handle, she found it unlocked.

They strolled right in.

The walls around the waiting area were covered in posters with things like "Brace yourself for a beautiful smile!" and "Fang ten!" with an image of wolves on a surfboard.

Valance pushed open another unlocked door that led to a narrow hallway. Dim security lights glowed at the end underneath an exit sign. Only, if Valance was right, this wouldn't take them back outside.

A small sign by the door read, *Alarm will sound if door opened.*

Valance pressed against the bar, and the door opened. No alarm.

They found themselves in another dark, cramped space. There was nothing on the walls and no clear use for this area. Other than, perhaps, an *in-between place*. A sinister sally port. A buffer in case a patient couldn't read and walked out the back.

Valance whispered, "Stakes out."

She reached the door ahead, gripped the brass knob, and pushed it open.

Light streamed into the room, and they stepped quickly into it.

The back room ran the length of the building, just as Valance had predicted. It was broken into a series of cubicles, the walls of each perhaps only six feet tall, each space opening to the long hallway in which he and Valance stood. The low paneled ceiling left him claustrophobic, as if they'd stumbled into a long coffin, but the steady beeps of medical monitors and the rhythmic whooshes of ventilators told him they were in the right place.

As of yet, the two officers hadn't been seen, but he suspected that would soon change. There was no conversation to be heard, no footfalls on the cheap linoleum flooring, but the raised hair on his arms told him that they were not alone.

Green took a few cautious steps and peered into one of the cubicles. It was as he'd expected. Each of these makeshift spaces was fashioned into a hospital room. No, not that exactly. He searched his mind. *An operating room.*

And in the middle of this particular operating table lay a motionless child. Green recognized him immediately as Jordan Owiti. There was a thick tube down his throat and nearly a dozen thinner ones stuck into his veins. Beside the abducted boy, a vampiress in white silk scrubs measured liquid from a vial into a syringe. Green took a quick step back, and the sudden movement caught the vampiress's attention. She jerked her head up, and her eyes flared red. "Intruders! Police!"

Green hurried back to Valance until they were shoulder to shoulder, the wall covering their six.

"Here we go," the werewolf breathed, grinning ruthlessly. She tossed the stake from one hand to the other, waiting for the first attack.

She didn't have to wait long. The vampiress shot dark talons from the ends of her fingertips and launched herself straight at Valance.

But one of her feet snagged on a cord, and she didn't fly so much as flop.

Valance couldn't have moved the stake out of the way if she'd tried, and the vampiress felt hard on it, screeched, and then collapsed, her silken scrubs soaking up a growing splotch of dark blood.

"One down…"

The other vampires weren't far behind, and they emerged from the rows of cubicles, talons already out.

"Fifteen, no, sixteen to go," Green added.

"Whatever you do," Valance said, "don't let your useless fear of dying ruin the fun we're about to have."

But the vampires didn't strike. They waited, and Green shuddered to think of what they might be waiting for.

And then the leprechauns began pouring from a room at the far end of the long hall.

Green groaned. "Not more fucking shillelaghs."

"Don't ruin this with your negativity, Rookie."

The little guys rushed them, yelling their ululating battle cry. Green fumbled to grab his gun without dropping his stake as the leprechaun leading the charge reared back, ready to land his magical and horrifyingly dense stick right between Green's eyes. But before that could happen, the ornately carved tip of the shillelagh caught an exposed wire dangling from the paneled ceiling, and the leprechaun's little body was jolted and smoking before Green could pull the trigger.

Since when was wood a conductor?

As if reading his mind, Valance said, "There's a steel rod through the middle of them. That's why they hurt like hell. Heads up!"

Infuriated by the barbecuing of their friend, a wave of half a dozen leprechauns charged, weapons out but not so high as to make the same mistake as their brave ad toasty leader.

Don't make me shoot them, don't make me shoot them…

Fifteen feet, ten feet, five…

The ceiling above them collapsed, crushing every last one of the little enemies beneath a heavy wooden beam.

Green blinked and coughed through the cloud of disturbed insulation, and a moment later, a figure popped up from the rubble.

It wasn't a leprechaun.

"Tah-dah!" Trombolo the Tremendous stood grinning then looked around. His brow furrowed. He straightened his black satin cape. "Where the hell…?" Then he spotted his uniformed audience of two. "Slight miscalculation," he said apologetically. A leprechaun began screaming from beneath the rubble for someone to kill him, just put him out of this agony. The magician took a quick step to the side. "Hot damn." Then he disappeared again in a flash.

A door behind them smashed open, and Green whirled

around, expecting to see more leprechauns pouring out from the direction of the storefronts. But that wasn't the case.

Corporal Bannockburn slowed to a halt, apparently surprised by the bright room he now found himself in. His eyes located Valance first. "You see him?"

"The magician?"

"Yeah, I was chasing him, and..." He paused, looked back over his shoulder, and saw the waiting vampires with their talons out. "Fucking hell, Heather. You didn't."

She grinned. "You made it just in time, Bruce."

He backpedaled until he joined her and Green in the center of the hallway, just as the last few the leprechauns made their final stand, rushing toward the pile of rubble that pinned their fallen comrades.

Don't do it, Green thought. *Just go home. Forget about this. You don't have to die for this.*

The new charge had hardly made it two yards before more of the ceiling collapsed directly above them. More anguished screams from the leprechauns followed in short order as a waterfall of white bunnies rode the pink insulation to the ground, landing safely before hopping away in all directions.

"Christ," whispered Bannockburn. It seemed he was getting the gist of what they'd been experiencing since midnight.

With the leprechaun forces expended, the vampires were left with no option but to do the dirty work themselves. The three officers formed a protective triangle, and Green holstered his gun to free up both his hands for staking.

From the back of the pack on Green's side of the hall, a vampire stepped forward. He was dressed in white silk like the rest of them, but he wore a black cape to distinguish himself. "Well, if it isn't La Tunda. I'd heard you worked for the city, but I never dreamed it would be as a lowly cop. I thought you would have learned your lesson and stayed away from guns and dirty work after all the people you got killed in Guatemala."

Valance faced him, and Bannockburn moved to cover her six. "Am I supposed to know who the hell you are?"

"I am Esteban Kingsblood," he said, prowling forward, "sworn enemy of the timberweres, commander of the Colombian campaign, liberator of the—" He made to step over one of the fallen leprechauns, but the moment he straddled the body, it exploded like a water balloon, showering everything within a ten-foot radius with an oozing purple goo, including his white robes and black cape.

Valance sucked in air. "Guess we didn't get that drug off the street completely." And then she whipped the bazooka around, took aim, and pulled the trigger. The stake impaled Esteban Kingsblood straight through the heart.

But it didn't stop there. It hit with such force that it went clean through, taking a small deflection, perhaps off one of his ribs, and skewered two more vamps before hitting the back wall, ricocheting, and taking out one more.

For a moment, nobody breathed.

"Twelve to go," Green announced.

"Great," she said. "Twelve is my lucky number."

With their leader gone, the remaining vampires flew into a rage.

"Stake," Bannockburn called. "*Stake, stake, stake!*"

Valance passed him a spare from her belt just in time for the corporal to raise it and puncture the first attacker.

It devolved into chaos from there, but the air around

Green remained charged with that shimmery feeling as he spun and tripped over one of the loose bunnies, causing fangs to miss him by an inch. The stake in his flailing hand found its target effortlessly, and another vampire shrieked out the last of her unlife.

There was no time to check on his fellow officers as he felt the wind from talons brush against his cheek, and before he knew it, a vampire had him in its clutches. "Call me old school," it hissed, "but there's nothing quite like turning a human."

He slipped the tiny stake from his vest and thrust it into the vampire's jugular. The creature screamed, and Green was able to pull free just in time to avoid Bannockburn's stake coming through from the back.

With each downed vampire came a shower of blood, until all Green could see was crimson. The air filled with high-pitch agony and rage followed closely by Valance's unbridled whoops of glee.

By the time the last vampire lunged at her, misjudged, and kabobbed itself on one of the fallen wooden rafters, there wasn't a square inch of clean white silk in sight.

Green searched *himself* for a piece of fabric that wasn't soaked in blood to wipe the gore from his face but found none. Figures.

No sooner had he thought that than a string of colorful tied-together scarves floated down from the exposed rafters where the magician had previously fallen through. All Green had to do was hold out his hand, and the center of the tied scarves landed in his palm. He wiped his face then handed it off to Bannockburn, who did the same.

The blood didn't seem to bother Valance, though, and she nodded approval as she surveyed the damage.

"You enjoying yourself, Heather?" grunted Bannockburn testily.

"Yes, sir. But we're not done yet."

A side door to the room burst open, and Sergeant Montoya appeared.

Green wasn't sure who was more shocked, the bison-shifter who'd just stumbled into this bloody nightmare, or the officers glimpsing their sergeant out in the wild, away from the office, right where they needed him to be when they needed him to be there.

Montoya continued to stare wide-eyed. "Just what in the hell..."

A sudden movement behind the sergeant caught Green's attention. It was too far away, though. He'd never reach it in time to—

Then he remembered.

He whipped the launcher over his shoulder, lined up the laser sight with the lone vampire's heaving chest, and pulled the trigger.

The stake found its target, of course, and Montoya was treated to a small sampling of the bloodbath the others had just enjoyed.

"Hell with a hand grenade," breathed the sergeant.

Green took the tied handkerchiefs from Bannockburn and brought them over, offering them up. The sergeant accepted without acknowledgment and wiped the blood from around his mouth and nose. His disbelieving expression was locked onto something else entirely.

"Is that..." Montoya stepped closer, "Rhiannon Ripley?"

"It's all of them," Valance announced. "All the ones they haven't killed or cut loose, that is."

"But"—he looked down the long rows of cubicles, nearly two dozen of them—"there are so many."

"And from what I've seen, all the beds are occupied."

The reality settled in on him as he continued to gape. Perhaps the sergeant *had* been complicit in the coverup, but it was clear now that if that were the case, he hadn't understood the extent of what he was helping to obscure.

A door behind them opened, and Detective Felps stepped in and cursed loudly and repeatedly.

But the sergeant didn't seem to notice the new arrival. "What are they doing to them?"

Felps was the one to answer. "Turning them into wolfenvamps." He paused at the opening to one of the cubicles, staring at the occupant. "Damnation."

"We're going to need paramedics," Valance announced. "Lots of them. And some more cops, too, for when some of these poor little things wake up. I doubt all of them can be saved."

That woke the sergeant from his stupor. "I'm not sure I follow."

Valance's words took on a hint of impatience. "Some of them will already have turned. Felps wasn't fucking with you. They'll be wolfenvamps, and you can't save those, you can't redeem them. All they know is killing."

Montoya shook his head as if fending off her harsh reality. "We'll put them in an institution, then. Valance, you can't just kill children!"

"Suit yourself." She made for the door.

"Where are you going?" the sergeant demanded.

She paused, scanned the room, shot him a curious look. "Away from here, obviously. This place is a mess."

———

Officer Green jogged to catch up with Valance as she disappeared from the gory scene.

"Val—" The word fell dead in his throat as he emerged into the outdoor air of the split-level parking lot.

Lights and sounds filled the previously empty landscape. It must have been a slow night in Fang, as every officer from the 900s and the holdovers from earlier shifts had parked their cars scattershot around like someone had just dropped pickup sticks to determine the angle for each vehicle.

The ambulances were there, too, though they'd have light work. Maybe a few of the leprechauns had merely been knocked unconscious by the falling ceiling, but all the vampires were definitely goners, and there wasn't a cherub's chance in a hurricane the paramedics would knowingly treat something as deadly as a potential wolfenvamp.

Then he remembered the night he'd shot the human, and he realized that those ambulances were likely for him. He hadn't fired his gun, but he'd staked a whole mess of vampires. He'd need to go to the hospital to get checked out and draw blood for drug testing...

"Valance!" She wasn't heading toward the ambulances or their junker of a car. She was heading straight for the news vans... while still covered head to boot in vampire blood.

Green was fairly certain elves observed a vegetarian diet, but at that moment, they looked ready to devour her. A few who had been milling about, taking their time to set up, no doubt accustomed to the slower pace of proceedings at this sort of event, bolted to their feet and started scrambling for their recording devices.

One of them shouted, "speed!" right before Valance stopped only a few feet in front of them.

The questions came at her rapid-fire.

"What's your name?"

"Is that blood?"

"What happened here tonight?"

"Whose blood is that?"

"Are there any officers down?"

She let a few more wash over her as Green caught up, and then she said, "I can't comment on that right now. I just need you all to please give us about ten more yards to conduct this investigation. Please back up—just ten more yards—and we'll set up a clearer perimeter soon. This is a very fresh scene."

She thanked them and turned, nearing knocking right into Green. "Sweet chupacabra! I know you're hopelessly dependent, but give me a little space to breathe."

He hurried after her as she made for the paramedics. "What was that all about?"

"Securing the crime scene."

"Bullshit," he said. "You wanted them to get a good shot of you covered in blood."

"Sounds like you got me all figured out."

He risked it, reached out, and grabbed her arm to stop her. He needed a physical anchor anyhow after the bloodbath that had just ensued. "Stop."

She did, but she didn't turn to face him completely.

"What the hell just happened, Valance?" He leaned closer. "Is it over?"

She grinned. "It's over, all right. The sham of a treaty, that is."

He blinked and felt the air catch in his lungs. "Hornstooth, you mean?"

"Of course. You and I just blew it straight to shit."

You and I.

He struggled to make sense of it. "But the treaty kept everyone safe. It kept the vampires from openly killing weres and everyone else."

"Did it, though?"

"*Yes,*" he insisted, "it did!"

"Well, you might be right about the 'openly killing' part. But the way I see it, it didn't *really* slow them down. It just kept everyone else from fighting back."

Green found himself speechless, and she turned to face him dead on. The glee she'd exuded during her killing spree was nowhere to be found, replaced by raw malice that made the blood pound loudly in his ears. "It might take a while for the propaganda you've been spoon-fed your whole life to work through your system, so let me spell it out for you: fuck vampires. Fuck every one of them on the planet. Fuck those vampires experimenting on children, and fuck Felps, too. All of them. This world won't be safe until we're allowed to do to their kind what we did to the clowns. It's open season, Rookie."

"But Felps is on our—"

"*Don't* you dare say he's on our side. He's not. He never will be. We're living, and he's a perverted, bloodthirsty corpse. We don't *want* him on our side."

The vitriol in her words nearly choked him. "What are you gonna do now?"

"First," she said, "I'm going to spend the night being poked and prodded, just like you. But in the morning, I'm going to use my administrative leave and remaining luck to head out to a casino boat and rob them blind."

He let go of her arm and stood dumbly as she marched over to one of the ambulances and climbed on up.

Another bloody figure appeared next to him a moment later. "You all right?"

Corporal Bannockburn's gruff voice did little to soothe Green's frayed nerves. "She just said the Treaty of Hornstooth is off."

Bannockburn grunted. "She may be a lunatic bitch, but she's not wrong. It was a sham from the start."

"But it reduced murders."

"I didn't say it was a *bad* sham."

"But Valance…"

Bannockburn clapped him on the shoulder. "Don't worry, I didn't know what I was signing up for, either. I genuinely thought it was about the kids."

Green shook his head. "It was never about the kids."

"It might have been *a little* about the kids. That's what I'm telling myself from now on, at least."

They were silent a moment before the corporal spoke again. "We'd better get this process started. It'll be a long night."

"We'll have plenty of time to catch up on our sleep during leave."

The werewolf chuckled darkly. "You have a point. But if there's one tragedy that comes from this, it would be you wasting all that good luck."

They reached the next available ambulance and Bannockburn waved off an overzealous paramedic coming at them with a handful of tiny disinfectant wipes. "Don't waste supplies. Nothing short of a firehose of holy water will get us clean."

They sat beside each other on the bumper, and Green hiked up his sleeve for another paramedic to take his blood pressure.

He turned to the corporal again. "Will the streak last?"

"For a few days, I'd guess. So do me a favor. Once we get done processing, promise me you'll go take advantage full of that good luck. Get laid, take risks, ask for things you wouldn't normally stand a chance of getting. And don't just do it for you. Do it for everyone." Bannockburn looked out over the chaotic scene—the sergeant barking orders, the paramedics rushing from the building to unburden themselves of their most recent meal, the officers hurrying inside with their arms full of black body bags. He sighed. "And just enjoy it while you can. I have this sneaking suspicion that everyone in this department is heading into the shittiest luck of our lives."

END OF BOOK 3

Turn the page for more from Kilhaven...

HEX TRAFFICKING

Two Kilhaven Police officers pulled over a commercial semi-truck traveling north on FM 293 at 1:30pm last Monday after it was seen careening between lanes. Officers suspected the driver, Margery Roan Huffman, human, 49, of distracted driving and pulled her over to issue her a verbal warning. However, during the verbal interaction, officers report that she began acting erratic and agitated, and they asked her to step out of the truck so the cargo could be searched. At first glance the enclose cargo space appeared empty, but upon closer examination, a false bottom was found. In it were 7,000 hex bags, some of which had broken open during transit.

Huffman was arrested and Stubborn Hauntings Unit agents were called to the scene immediately. Huffman claims she was herself under a hex that could only be lifted if she completed the shipment, but she refused to provide further information as to who might have hexed her or why. She faces up to twenty years in prison for hex trafficking and two counts of hexing a law enforcement officer. Both officers suffered severe boils and unwanted erections as a result of the broken hex bags and are still undergoing testing and treatment by licensed witchcraft professionals.

———

**Don't stop now.
Grab the next Kilhaven Police.**

Vampires gone wild.
Green catches the scent of conspiracy.
Valance goes off the rails.
You will love this shit.

www.books2read.com/kilhaven4

The Jessica Christ series

What readers are saying about Jessica Christ:

"H. Claire Taylor offers gentle yet pungent humor and is a worthy successor to Garrison Keillor, Edward St Aubyn or Mark Twain."

"Sometimes random scenes pop into my head and I'll start hyperventilating from laughing so hard all over again."

"The humor in this series is somehow so dark and light-hearted at the same time. . . . H Claire's writing is amazing—the flow and tone keep you reading and wanting more, like a conversation with a dear and raunchy confidante."

Tap here for the first Jessica Christ book.

BROCK BLOODWORTH is a private person. He wishes to remain "off the grid" as much as possible. You will not find him on social media, so don't waste your time. If you wish to reach him, consider contacting H. Claire Taylor instead. She's much friendlier.

H. CLAIRE TAYLOR is the author of the Jessica Christ series and deserves a morsel of credit for co-writing the Kilhaven Police series and putting up with Brock's shit. You can learn more about her and her comedy projects atwww.hclairetaylor.com.

Find more by Brock and Claire:
www.ffs.media
contact@ffs.media

facebook.com/authorhclairetaylor
twitter.com/claireorwhatevs
bookbub.com/authors/hclairetaylor
goodreads.com/hclairetaylor
amazon.com/author/hclairetaylor